3/12

Praise for *A Little Night Magic*

"Lucy March's writing is delightful and delicious. In the vast realm of all things paranormal, *A Little Night Magic* is like rain on a scorched desert: welcome and nurturing. What a wonderful treat. Every word I devoured had me craving more. Tobias and Olivia's journey was touching, magical, and utterly romantic. I cannot recommend this book enough. Lucy March is destined to be a superstar."

—DARYNDA JONES, author of *First Grave on the Right*

"Lucy March's novels have it all; they're sexy, funny, heartfelt, and warm, full of characters you want to eat waffles with and strange little towns you want to visit, all seasoned with a dash of the supernatural. Lucy March is sublime!"

—JENNIFER CRUSIE, author of *Maybe This Time*

"Fresh and funny, warm and sexy. I can't wait for more books from Lucy March."

—SUSAN ELIZABETH PHILLIPS, author of *Call Me Irresistible*

"*A Little Night Magic* is a wholly original novel about magic and community, women and the bonds between them, and of course . . . love. Cast against the reassuringly familiar small town of Nodaway Falls, it is less a tale of magic than about the journey of a woman to herself. Don't miss it."

—BARBARA O'NEAL, author of *How to Bake a Perfect Life*

Also by Lucy March

Wish You Were Here (written as Lani Diane Rich)
Ex and the Single Girl (written as Lani Diane Rich)
Crazy in Love (written as Lani Diane Rich)
A Little Ray of Sunshine (written as Lani Diane Rich)

A Little Night Magic

Lucy March

ST. MARTIN'S GRIFFIN

NEW YORK

A LITTLE NIGHT MAGIC. Copyright © 2012 by Lani Diane Rich. All rights reserved. Printed in the United States of America. For information, address St. Martin's Press, 175 Fifth Avenue, New York, N.Y. 10010.

ISBN 978-1-61793-660-9

For Jenny, who saved my life,

thus making it possible for me to write this book

1

There's magic linoleum at Crazy Cousin Betty's Waffle House.

Okay, maybe it's not *magic,* exactly. It's this one weird sparkly blue square, in the midst of all the solid, checkerboarded blues and whites. I first noticed it when I was six, and I remember tugging on Betty's periwinkle blue skirt and pointing down at the floor. Betty, who'd seemed ancient to me even then, knelt down to level her wrinkled eyes with mine.

"Oh, that? It's a magic square," she'd said. "Step on it. Make a wish. It'll come true."

"Really?"

She winked. "You bet. But don't go just stepping on it every time you want a new doll, or a motorcycle. Magic's not to be messed with, Olivia." And then she stood up, mussed my hair, and moved on.

I didn't believe her. Even at that tender age, I could tell bullcrap when I heard it.

But then, right after I'd started working at CCB's, I desperately wanted Robbie Pecorino to ask me to prom. On a whim, I stepped on the square late one night, and boom—two days later, he asked me. So, that was cool. But then there was the time I wished my college boyfriend, Charlie, would give me a little more space, and he ended up dumping me to date his roommate, Neil. Finally, six years ago, when I was twenty-two, I used it to wish my mother didn't have cancer anymore.

Two months later, she died.

I stopped wishing after that. I mean, I didn't *really* believe that it was magic and could grant wishes, but . . . I kind of believed it was magic and could grant wishes. *And* that it was a sadistic little bastard, to be avoided at all costs. Whenever I took orders at Booth 9, I always stood either too close or too far away, just in case I absently wished for anything while standing on the square. Still, on that Friday night in June as I swished my mop over the square, I considered, just for a second, making the wish that would finally help me get my stupid act together.

"You're not done yet?"

I looked up from where I was standing in the middle of the dim and empty dining room, mop handle in my hand as one white-Kedded foot hovered over the square, and there was Tobias Shoop, CCB's night cook, his broad form clad in his standard outfit of crumpled jeans and a black T-shirt. He had a smile that was a little too big for his face, and one of his front teeth sort of overlapped the other, and his five o'clock shadow came in almost while you watched, but I loved him, goddamnit. And I had to do something about that, because loving this man was gonna kill me. I couldn't wish the love away with him standing right there looking at me, though, so I pulled my foot back and started mopping again. "Do I look like I'm done?"

His bulk nearly blocked all the light streaming from the kitchen into the dining room as he leaned against the doorjamb, simply watching me in that way he had of simply . . .

watching. He gave me one of his classic Tobias looks—a combination of total focus and mild smolder that I had been stupid enough to mistake for romantic interest—and strode toward me. "You need help?"

"Nope." I set the mop aside and looked at him, his dark hair glinting with premature strands of gray at the temples. My fingers itched to run through that hair, to indulge in the same traitorous instinct that had screwed everything up in the first place.

"I'm almost done," I said coolly. "You go. I'll lock up."

His response to this was to cross to Booth 9, haul himself up on the table, and stare at me.

I continued mopping. "You can leave, you know. Believe it or not, before you got here, I used to lock up by myself all the time."

"I don't mind."

I do, I thought. I swished my mop over the square, wishing he would just go away and leave me alone. Tragically, I wasn't standing on the square at the moment I wished it and so he remained right where he was.

"You ever going to stop being mad at me?" he asked.

"I'm not mad," I said automatically, then swished my mop over the square again. *I wish you'd break out in boils. Swish.*

"I'm not an idiot, Liv. I know you're pissed." He let out a long sigh. "Can we at least talk about it?"

"I'd be happy to, but I don't know what you're talking about." *Swish swish. I hope your ear hair grows freakishly long. Swish.*

"Bullshit."

I stopped mopping and looked at him. "If you're trying to get on my good side, you suck at it."

"I'm not trying to get on your good side," he said. "I just want us to be like we used to be. You know. Before you got all mad."

Grow a clubfoot. "I'm not mad."

He hopped off the table and grabbed my arm, and I felt the electricity rush through me, the way it always did at his touch. I pulled my arm away and forced myself to look at him, doing my best to maintain an expression of steely indifference, but likely landing somewhere between abject adoration and poorly suppressed rage.

"You're saying we're fine, then?" he asked, his tone thick with skepticism.

"Yep."

He crossed his arms over his chest, challenging me. "Then come over tonight and watch *The Holy Grail*."

I looked at him, softening for a moment, remembering all the nights we'd spent over the last year and a half watching stupid movies, talking for hours about nothing and everything. Then those memories had a head-on collision with the memory of what happened during Movie Night last Friday, and I stopped softening.

A clubfoot and a hunchback. "Can't. I have to pack."

He released my arm. "Pack? For where?"

I took a breath, feeling a little nervous but keeping what I hoped was an air of confidence in my tone. "Scotland."

He drew back in surprise. "Scotland? Why?"

"Because that's where the dart landed," I said, keeping a sharp tone of defiance in my voice. "I'm starting in Scotland, anyway. I'm going to travel all over Europe. You know, like college kids do after graduation."

"What? Backpacking?"

"Yeah. The idea just popped in my head, and at first I thought, *Wow, that's insane,* but the more I think about it the more awesome it sounds. I've got money saved up, and between that and the sale of the house—"

"You're selling your *house?*"

"—I should have a good six months before I have to settle down and get a job somewhere, but by then I figure I'll know where I want to be. I'll waitress again, maybe, but this time in Italy, or Vienna. Or, if I have to come back to the States, maybe Atlanta, or San Diego. Somewhere warm, I think."

"What the hell are you talking about?"

I stopped to look at him, taking him in. He was broadly built, and had the kind of quiet strength about him that no one ever tested. He was smart, confident, and thoughtfully quiet, until you got him talking about the things that fascinated him, like sci-fi/fantasy novels and the way conspiracy theories spread like viruses of the intellect. He was the simultaneous symbol of everything that was right with my life *and* everything that was wrong.

And it was time to let him go.

"I'm talking about leaving. Going. Good-bye."

He absorbed this for a moment. "If this is because of what happened between us last week—"

I snorted, a little too loudly. "Back it up, Superego. Not everything is about you."

"The timing seems a little conspicuous, that's all."

I shrugged. "I mean, yeah, sure, throwing myself at you after *a year and a half* of waiting for you to make the first move, only to be rejected and then completely ignored for *three days*—"

"Christ, Liv, I said I was sorry."

"—might or might not have inspired me to print out a picture of you and put it on my corkboard, and I might or might not have thrown a dart at you and missed, hitting my world map poster by mistake."

"Well," he said flatly. "At least you're not mad."

"I will neither confirm nor deny any of that, but the fact is, when I blew the plaster dust off my world map and saw that gaping hole next to Edinburgh, it hit me what a great idea it was." I sighed and looked at him. "I'm twenty-eight, Tobias. I'm tired of waiting for my life to come find me, so I'm gonna go find it."

He stared at me. "This doesn't make any sense."

And suddenly, insanely, I felt tears come to my eyes. "I have to leave first."

He shook his head. "What the hell are you talking about?"

"I'm talking about you." The terror on his face sent a jolt of pain through me, and I held up my hand to keep him from saying anything, not that he was jumping at the chance. "Don't worry. I'm not going to kiss you again. I've learned my lesson."

"Liv—"

I held out my hand to stop him from talking. "You're not a small-town guy, Tobias. Someday you're going to leave, and when you do, if I haven't left first, I'm going to spend the rest of my life pining away for you. That's what happened to my

6

mother with my father. I never even knew the son of a bitch, but whoever he was, he took part of her with him and she never got it back and that's not going to happen to me."

There was a long, horrible silence in which my heart sputtered along on the hope that he would take me in his arms, tell me that the rejection last Friday was all a misunderstanding, and wherever I went, he wanted to go with me. But all he said was, "When are you leaving?"

I curled the mop into my grip, holding it against my shoulder. "I'm giving myself some time to get the house on the market, and get all my stuff sold or into storage."

He took a step closer. "When?"

"My flight leaves on August tenth."

"You bought your ticket already?"

I shrugged. "Spontaneity without commitment is just wishful thinking."

"So . . . six weeks, then?"

"Yeah."

He nodded, then leaned back against the table at Booth 9, one foot absently resting on the square as he did. I would have worried, but Tobias wasn't the kind to make idle wishes. If he wanted something, he just went after it.

And if he didn't, he didn't.

He cleared his throat. "Every time you see a goat, I want a picture. You with the goat."

"What the hell are you talking about?" I said.

"Europe's lousy with goats. That way you won't forget."

Our eyes locked for a few moments, and I lost all reason. In a flash, a dozen scenarios rushed through my head. Him asking me to stay. Me asking him to come with me. Us together, giving the camera to a local, standing next to a goat, every scenario ending in a kiss . . .

. . . but that kind of thinking was exactly what I was trying to get away from. I swished my mop over the magic square again, and wondered if I could wish this love away through the mop, rather than through my feet.

"Liv?"

I looked up at him. "Go home. I can't do this with you standing right there."

"Do what? Mop?"

I glanced down at the square, then back at him. "No. Wish."

"Wish for what?" he said, and then the bells on the front door jingled.

"Oh, thank *god* you're open!"

I looked past Tobias's shoulder to see a short, roundish, middle-aged black woman standing in the open door, a swoosh of hot summer air ruffling the skirt of her bright orange sundress as it went into battle with our underpowered air-conditioning. "I took the first exit I could off the Thruway, but there is not a single light on down Main Street except yours. Ten o'clock at night. Y'all have some kind of power outage or something?"

"Welcome to nightlife in Nodaway Falls," I said, then looked at Tobias and whispered, "I must have forgotten to lock the door."

The woman smiled. "Nice name for a town, Nodaway Falls. I like a town with a nice name." Her voice had a tinge of Southern honey, and her face sparkled with goodwill. "I'm so glad you're open, as I just happen to have the most unnatural craving for waffles."

She took a stool at the counter and without so much as a look toward me, Tobias headed for her.

"Menu's gonna be kind of limited," he said. "We were just about to close, so most everything is put away, but I can whip up some quick waffles for you. You'll be done before Liv finishes mopping, anyway."

He gave me a lame half-smile, and I returned it. Ordinarily, a comment like that would have warranted some sort of rude gesture, but there was no *ordinary* for us now. Where we had been comfortable and rude before, now we had awkward politeness between us. The realization made me so sad that I had a sudden strong urge to curl up under Booth 9 and cry for a little while.

The woman raised a dismissive hand in the air. "Don't you worry, baby. I don't even need a menu. You just give me the sugariest, most fattening thing you've got."

"That'd be the chocolate Belgians, with hot fudge, vanilla ice cream, and whipped cream. You want the cherry on top or is fruit too healthy for you?"

The woman leaned forward. "Are they those little radioactive red ones, all soaked in sugar and artificial dye?"

"Maraschino?" he said. "Yep."

She ruminated, then said, "Give me four. And some coffee, please."

"You got it," Tobias said, and pulled out the baby coffeemaker the morning waitress, Brenda, kept under the counter for days when she had to open at the crack of dawn; our industrial cof-feemaker didn't deliver the goods fast enough for Brenda. I set the mop in the pail and hurried over.

"I got it," I said, quickly rounding the counter and taking the coffeemaker from him. "It'll go quicker if we work to-gether."

He eyed me for a moment. "Go home. I got this."

"Quit arguing and cook." I plugged in the baby coffeemaker, flipped open the filter basket, and grabbed the carafe to fill it with water. By the time I looked up, he'd already disappeared into the kitchen. I stared at the door, then was overcome by a strange tickle inside my nose. I sneezed, turning my head into my shoulder in classic waitress style.

"You feeling all right, baby?" the woman asked, watching me intently, as she set her purse, still open, on the counter next to her.

I picked up two mugs and set them on the counter, shaking my head to rid myself of the tingly sensation in my sinuses. "Yeah. Guess it's a bit of hay fever."

"I see," she said, her eyes still on me. "You get hay fever often?"

"Not typic—" and then I caught a scent of something sharp and sneezed again. I sniffed a couple of times and sneezed again. "Hell," I said once I recovered. "What is that?"

"Hmmm?" She reached for the ceramic bowl filled with sugar packets.

"That . . . smell. It's kind of tickly, like pepper but it smells more like . . . licorice, maybe?" I looked up to find the woman watching me, one eyebrow raised. She took her purse off the counter and set it on the stool next to her, then pushed the sugar packet bowl away with a sound of disgust.

"What is wrong with women these days, filling their bodies full of unnatural chemical substances until they're nothing but skin and bones? Let me tell you something, baby. Any man who can't appreciate a woman with a little meat on her doesn't like women much in the first place. You got any real sugar?"

It took me a moment to realize she'd asked me a question. "Oh. Sure." I reached under the counter and grabbed the sugar dispenser, then got some half & half from the cooler and set that in front of her as well. I pulled the carafe from the coffee-maker, poured us each a cup, and put it back. I left my coffee black, sipping it while she loaded up her mug. I don't really like black coffee, but the calories in cream and sugar weren't worth it, and it wasn't like I could dump my usual sugar-free non-dairy creamer in my cup after her little speech.

"So, what's your name, baby?" she asked as she stirred.

"Olivia." I glanced down, motioned to my name tag. "Most people call me Liv."

"Davina Granville." She held out her hand, and we shook, and then she watched me for a moment. "Pretty name, Olivia." She sipped her coffee, keeping her eyes on me. "Are you named for anyone in your family?"

"Not from my mother's side."

She stopped stirring. "What about your father's?"

"I never knew my father." Behind me, Tobias slid a plate onto the pass and dinged the bell. I went to the pass, and when I reached for the plate, he tugged it back.

"Go home," he said.

"Give me the plate or neither one of us is ever going home," I said. He hesitated a moment, then released his grip on the plate. I slid it in front of Davina and said, "So, are you staying in town or just passing through?"

She angled her head at me. "I haven't decided yet, but I think I might be staying."

"Oh, there's a great bed-and-breakfast over on Augustine Street, just two lights down that way, take a left, there's a big, yellow nineteenth-century Victorian there, you can't miss it. Grace Higgins-Hooper and Addie Hooper-Higgins run it, and they've restored it completely to the period. It's amazing." I leaned in and spoke in a hushed tone, even though we were alone. "Come here for the breakfast, though. Addie puts flax-seed in everything she cooks."

Davina laughed, took a bite of her waffles, and closed her eyes. "Mmmm."

I smiled; I loved seeing people eat Tobias's waffles for the first time. "He's pretty good, huh?"

The metal kitchen door swung open, and Tobias came out. He sidled up next to me at the counter and bumped my hip with his, nudging me toward the door.

I straightened up. "All right. That's it. Go home. You're driving me nuts."

He took me by the elbow, pulled me aside, and said, "*You* go home."

"I need to finish mopping."

"I can mop."

I gently pulled my elbow from his grip. "You want me to

not be mad at you anymore? Stop hovering. I'm not twelve. I can close by myself."

He looked at Davina, then back to me. "Fine, just . . . be careful, okay?"

"Yeah, whatever. Good night."

He let out a sigh, headed to the door, and finally left. I walked back over to the counter and leaned against the wall, then looked up to find Davina watching me in a way that made me kind of wish I hadn't sent Tobias home so quick.

She put her fork down. "Tell me something, baby. Do you believe in magic?"

I took a moment to adjust to the conversational whiplash, then said, "What? You mean like, magicians? Illusionists?"

"No." Her eyes were wide and, now that I got a good look, just a bit crazy. Not that I wasn't used to a fair amount of crazy—I'd lived in Nodaway my whole life, you wouldn't believe the bell curve we had on insanity here—but at that moment, it was making me a little uncomfortable.

"I need to mop." I headed out from behind the counter toward the mop bucket, where I figured I could finish my work and by the time I was done, she'd be done.

I finished mopping under the tables, then crossed back toward the booths and the magic square, figuring it couldn't hurt to wish this woman would finish up quickly and go. I glanced over to make sure she wasn't watching me.

She was. She had turned around on the stool, her back to the counter, her eyes sharp on me as if she was searching me for something. It was creepy. I wrapped one hand tight around

the mop handle. She had size on me, but I had a hefty industrial mop and youth on my side.

"It's getting late," I said. "Why don't you just finish up and
we can both get out of here?"

At that moment, without a word, she pulled something out
of her purse and lobbed it at me. On instinct, I moved forward,
one hand still on the mop handle, and grabbed it out of the air;
it was an old gym sock, filled with some sand-type of substance
and tied in a knot in the middle.

"Ugh." I pinched the cuff between my fingers and held it up
and away from me, then looked at her. "Okay. You just busted
the bell curve."

And then I sneezed. And I sneezed again. The weird pep-
pery smell from earlier came back stronger, overwhelming my
senses, and my eyes watered and I sneezed again.

"Yeah, I thought so," Davina said, and through my sneezing
and watery eyes I could see her advancing toward me. "Now
don't be alarmed, but you know it had to be done. It wasn't
right, them not letting you be what you are."

I stared at her through watering eyes, my sinuses screaming.
"What I am?" I sniffed and tried to blink away the discomfort
in my eyes. "What am I?"

She stopped about a foot away from me, and angled her head,
amazement in her smiling eyes as she watched me. "Why, you're
magic."

"No, I'm not. I'm a wait—*achoo!*—waitress." The sharpness
in my sinuses intensified, and I shook my head, trying to rid
myself of it all, but it only got worse.

"Oh, you're much more than that, Olivia," she said, and took the sock from me. I backed away from her, sneezing again. She tossed it toward the stool where she'd been sitting, a good ten feet away, but still, I couldn't stop sneezing, and I was starting to panic. I stepped back again, and this time, my foot landed on the wet strands of mop and I lost my balance. I pulled at the mop handle, accidentally whapping myself in the face with it as my arms flailed like a cartoon character's. Davina shouted something and ran for me, but gravity won out and I fell, cracking the back of my head against the magic square. Dazed, I blinked a few times, then saw Davina leaning over me, saying something I couldn't make out, and looking concerned.

"What did you do to me?" I asked, or at least I tried to ask, but my ears were still ringing from the impact, so I'm not sure if any actual words came out.

"Liv!"

I opened my eyes what seemed like a second later, and there was Tobias, hovering over me.

"Oh. Hey." I pushed myself up on my elbows, and he helped me the rest of the way up, pulling me up by my arms, which were all pins and needles; I must have pinched a nerve or something when I hit the floor.

"What the hell happened?" He helped me up to sit in Booth 9, where I gratefully collapsed, feeling a little dizzy.

I shook my head out and looked at the spot where Davina had been; all that was left was her half-finished meal, and some bills laying next to the plate. No sign of her.

"I . . . slipped. On the mop."

He leaned over me, put his hands on either side of my face to hold me still as his gaze flicked back and forth between my eyes, as if measuring the pupils or something. The lights felt exceptionally bright, and I squinted, then swatted his hands away.

"I'm fine. I just fell. What are you doing here, anyway?"

"Forgot something. Came back. *Found you splayed on the floor.*" He hit that last bit hard, driving his point home.

"Calm down, drama queen," I said. "I slipped. It's no big deal."

"You lost consciousness. It's a big deal." He surveyed me, looking worried. "You sure you're all right?"

I nodded, although I wasn't *entirely* sure; I felt a little dizzy, and all my limbs were tingling, but I didn't want him making a big deal out of anything. He'd have me in a hospital ER in a heartbeat if he suspected something was wrong. So I pulled on a smile, met his eye, and said, "I'm fine."

He relaxed a little and straightened up. "Okay. You sit here. I'm gonna clean up and walk you home."

"I don't need—" I began, but then his eyes narrowed and I knew the only thing standing between me and six pointless hours in a Buffalo emergency room was my compliance, so I held up my hands in surrender. "Fine."

He walked over to the counter and started bussing. For a long time, there was just silence, and then he said, "She left you a good tip."

"Yay," I said weakly, then leaned back in the booth and waited for Tobias to take me home.

2

"She threw a stinky gym sock? At your *head*?" Millie Banning diced the green peppers at my kitchen table and scrunched her nose. "Wow. That's really weird."

"Yeah, I know. She said I was magic, or something." I threw the tomatoes I'd just chopped into the bowl of pico de gallo, then shook out my hands, which were still tingling. "She left while I was knocked out. I hope she's okay. I don't think she meant me any harm or anything, but she's obviously nuts."

Millie shrugged, some of her ash-blond curls falling out of the plastic clip that seemed permanently attached to the back of her head. She pointed her knife at me. "Okay, enough talking around the Tobias thing. What happened when you told him you were leaving?"

I angled my head, staring down at the bright green herbs between my fingers. "Wait. Stacy hates cilantro, doesn't she?"

Millie nodded. "She says it tastes like soap."

"Oh. Right." I scraped the herbs off my chopping board and into the garbage, then reached for a jalapeño.

"And once again, you're avoiding my question," Millie said.

"What? Oh—Tobias? He didn't say anything, really. He was

surprised I wanted to sell the house, but aside from that . . ." I sighed. "You know. Whatever."

"You don't have to pretend with me," Millie said. "I know it's bugging you. And I'm sorry." She turned her attention back to the green peppers, and began chopping harder. "You and I, we're not like Peach and Stacy." *Chop.* "Naturally thin and beautiful and perfect." *Chop.* "It's harder for girls like us."

Girls like . . . *us*? I loved Millie, she was one of my favorite people in the world, but she was . . . well. In the twenty-odd years we'd been friends, I'd seen her wear makeup exactly twice. Her hair was one of her best features, with that lovely kind of curl that dances down her shoulders, but she always kept it swept up tight in those ugly clips. Everything in her wardrobe was a variation on beige, and her standard outfit was a turtleneck under a shapeless jumper, which made her look, well . . . kind of squat.

I glanced at my own reflection in the glass door that led out to the back hallway. I was wearing jeans, and a pretty green scoop-neck shirt, and I had hair and makeup kind of going for me, but if I had to be honest I looked, well . . . kind of squat. Peach and Stacy were the beauties in this group, and Millie and I were the quirky ones with the good personalities. That was just how it was.

I sighed, reached for my margarita, took a big gulp, and decided to change the subject.

"Do you think I should sell the house?" I asked. "It's not like I'm paying much for it, just property taxes and insurance. Maybe I should keep it? Do you think?"

"Hmmm." Millie thought for a minute, then said, "I don't know." Her face lit up, and she dropped her knife to grab a pencil and a pad out of my junk drawer. "Pros and cons." She jotted the headers for the two columns on the page. "Pros: You own it outright."

"Cons," I said. "It's too much space for one person."

She scribbled. "Pros: It's interesting and fun."

"Oh, please," I said. "It's Willy Wonka's country home."

Millie jutted her lower lip out. "I like Momelia's aesthetic."

Momelia. Millie's own mother had died when she was very young, and her grandmother had raised her in an old farmhouse on the outskirts of town, so it had been natural for my mother to become Millie's surrogate mother. Millie had never been quite comfortable enough to call her Mom, but one day, she'd accidentally morphed "Mom" and "Amelia" while talking to my mother, and the nickname had stuck.

"What aesthetic? Modern Flea Market?" I scrunched my nose. "Forget that nothing matches, and I have a guest room that is chartreuse. The exterior is *pink.*"

"I like it," Millie said, ever loyal to the memory of my mother and the legacy of her outrageous taste.

"It's like living in a box of Strawberry Nesquik."

Millie shrugged, conceding the point. "You could always paint it."

I tapped my finger on the Cons side. "Willy Wonka."

Millie dutifully jotted it down. "Pros . . ." She thought for a bit, then said, "It's right next door to Peach."

"Right," I said. "And Cons . . . it's right next door to Peach."

Our eyes met and we both laughed. Bernadette Peach was the kind of person you love, not because of any particular qualities you could name, but just . . . because. She traveled in a swarm of perfume and Aqua Net, a shameless bottle blonde with a Barbie-doll figure and a fifties' fashion sense. She was achingly gorgeous, slightly narcissistic, a little thoughtless sometimes, but fiercely loyal. She and I had become friends because we were the same age and we lived next door to each other. When we got to school, she bonded with beautiful Stacy Easter, and I bonded with the more cerebral Millie, but Peach would not allow those differences to pull us apart. I was her friend, I would *always* be her friend, and that was that, so instead of dividing along lines of beauty and social grace the way most kids do in school, we ended up uniting as a foursome.

"Speaking of Peach, on the pro side for keeping the house, she bought her parents' house when they moved to Florida specifically so we'd stay neighbors."

Millie shook her head. "You can't let other people's choices influence your decision."

"I can if she kills me," I said, "which she will."

Millie smiled and jotted "Peach will kill you dead" on the pro side.

"I am going to miss the Confessionals," Millie said. "We've been doing this every Saturday since, what? Junior high?"

"Yeah," I said. "You don't think you guys will do it without me?"

She shook her head, and stared down at her list.

I tossed the jalapeños into the bowl. "Okay. Cons. I still have to manage the upkeep of it while I'm in Europe."

"But what if you decide to come back?" Millie said. "Can you imagine living in Nodaway and not living here?"

I looked around at my kitchen. The bright yellow walls, the daisy curtains moving gently in the breeze from the open window over the sink, the chink in the plaster in the ceiling from the time the fire alarm went off while Mom was cooking bacon and she hit it with the butt of the fire extinguisher to turn it off and missed on the first whack.

"No," I said. "I can't imagine living anywhere else if I'm going to be here, but . . ."

She put the pencil down and looked at me. "But you're not coming back."

Slowly, I shook my head. "You remember my mom. Even on her best day, part of her was always missing. I don't want to be like that."

"And leaving is going to prevent that?" she asked, her voice cracking a bit.

I sighed. "Dumb as it sounds . . . I think so, yeah. If my whole life changes, if it's not just that I'm losing him, maybe I won't notice it so much. Do you understand?"

"Yeah," she said, her eyes sad. She took the pad and pencil and began scribbling, then twirled it around so I could read it. She had drawn lines through all the pros and cons, and had written, *"In bocca al lupo,"* with a little smiley face.

I laughed. "What does that mean?"

"It's an Italian idiom. Basically, it means good luck." She reached out and clasped my hand. "Promise me you'll write, and send pictures."

"Don't worry," I said. "Europe's lousy with goats."

She gave me a confused look, and I laughed.

"I'll write. I'll send pictures."

The front door opened and Peach hollered, "Party's here!" Millie grabbed the margarita tray while I balanced the bowls of chips and pico.

"Hey, do me a favor?" I said. "Pretend you're surprised when I tell Peach and Stacy about Europe. Peach will be hurt that I told you first without them."

Millie nodded, and we went out to greet Stacy and Peach.

"Liv!" Peach danced into the hallway, holding a plate in one hand as she pulled me in for a hug with the other arm. She stepped back, then peeled back the pink-tinted Saran Wrap to show me her brownies. "They have chili powder in them, to go with the Mexican theme. Hey, Millie!"

Millie and I exchanged glances of affectionate amusement as Peach hugged her.

Stacy stepped in wearing dark jeans and a black Marvin the Martian T-shirt that read, YOU. OFF MY PLANET, and stuffed a bottle of tequila in my hands.

"Hey, Liv," she said, and flashed her patented knock-you-out smile. Stacy was one of those women whose neck-throttling beauty never made it on her own radar. She had huge chocolate eyes, apparently poreless skin, and a body any other woman would kill for. She just didn't care. She'd grown up with an alcoholic father who'd left her and her older brother, Nick, in the care of their crazy mother, and after that, being preternaturally pretty didn't seem so important.

Peach tucked her arm into Millie's and dragged her into the living room, and I leaned into Stacy as we followed behind. "So, what are you confessing tonight?"

She spread her hands, the picture of innocence. "Nothing to confess."

"You have nothing to confess? That's three weeks in a row for you."

She shook her head. "I have no secrets in this town. Betty reports anything I do to the masses at CCB's within twenty-four hours."

"Well, maybe stop fooling around on the pool table at Happy Larry's, and news will stop traveling so fast. Speaking of which, I heard about Amber Dorsey catching you with Frankie Biggs."

She raised a brow at me. "Hence, why I have nothing to confess."

We took our seats in the living room—Millie on the big pink floral love seat my mother had bought at a flea market when I was seven, Peach on the leather La-Z-Boy I'd gotten a few years back, and me and Stacy together on the key lime couch that matched nothing else in the room. Or the house.

"So," I said, reaching for my margarita. "I'll start." I took a deep breath. "I'm going backpacking through Europe."

"Awesome." Stacy grabbed her margarita and took a sip.

"Europe?" Peach crumpled her nose. "Why?"

Millie gave Peach an exasperated look. "It's *travel*. She doesn't need a reason."

Stacy gave a small laugh. "Seriously. A few weeks in Europe can do a lot of good for a girl. Speaking of which, I hear Germans are particularly good in the sack. Bag one and report in, will you?"

"Actually," I said, and shot a look at Millie for moral support, who smiled encouragement. "It's going to be a little longer than a few weeks. A lot longer." I swallowed my nerves down, and wrung my hands, trying to squeeze that damn tingling away. "I'm not coming back."

I looked at Peach, waiting for the explosion lit by the shock of my betrayal. There was none. Instead, she nibbled a bit on her lower lip, her eyes locked on Stacy, who was checking out the nail on her index finger.

"It's really about making a big change, and I don't think I can make that change if I plan to come back."

Peach was still eyeing Stacy distractedly, who was eyeing her index fingernail. The only one paying attention to me at all was Millie, and she already knew everything.

"I promise, I'll write. I'll send pictures. We can Skype." I looked at Peach again, who was still focused on Stacy, and I felt a jolt of annoyance run through me.

"Peach? Are you even listening to me?"

Her eyes squinched shut, and I was sure she was going to lay into me when she spit out, "Nick and I are getting married!"

Stacy looked up casually from her fingernail. "Nick who?"

Peach blinked. "Nick Easter."

Stacy laughed. "My brother? You and my brother?" She thought about it for a moment. "Huh. Liv, you got an emery board?"

I motioned toward the end table on her side of the couch, and she stretched over to grab the emery board sitting there.

Peach let out a long breath, and began to ramble. "We've been dating for about six months. We didn't want anyone to know because . . . well, you know how people in this town are. And it's been a job of work keeping it secret, let me tell you.

Secret dates in Buffalo, weekend 'business trips' to Rochester. The whole nine, seriously." She turned to me. "I'm sorry, but you know I couldn't tell you, Liv. You can't keep a secret to save your life, and if Betty found out, the whole *town* would know, and we just weren't ready to have the whole town in bed with us, you know? Not until we knew for sure that it was forever and now . . ." Peach's face warmed with joy. "Now, we know."

"So . . ." I said carefully to Peach, "you're not upset that I'm going to Europe?"

Peach blinked at me. "Europe? Hell, no. I think that's great. It's about time you had some fun. I'll watch the house while you're gone. When are you coming back again?"

"She's not," Stacy said. "Were you even listening?"

Peach's eyes flew wide open. "What? What the hell are you talking about?"

"I just told you," I said, exasperation seeping into my tone. "I need to make a change, a big one, and if I plan on coming back—"

"You . . . you and Nick are getting married?"

Millie had been so quiet that I think we had all forgotten she was there. She stared at Peach, her eyes wide and, to my surprise, a little wet.

"Um, yeah," Peach said, looking at Millie but obviously keeping her feelers out for Stacy's reaction. "We've been together since New Year's Eve. We both got drunk at Ginny Boyle's party, and then things kind of . . . happened."

"I know," Millie said, her face hard as stone.

"You knew?" Peach said.

"She's his secretary," Stacy said. "The secretary always knows."

"I didn't think it would go anywhere," Millie said. "I thought it was a distraction. Something temporary. You're getting *married?*"

Peach turned her focus to Stacy. "You don't mind, do you? I mean, it's kind of cool, right? We're going to be sisters!"

Stacy pulled the file away from her index finger, blew on her nail, tossed the emery board on the end table, then sat back, her eyes on Millie even as she spoke to Peach. "Welcome to the family. Mazel tov."

Peach put her hand over her heart. "Oh, thank *god!* I was so worried you'd be mad." She grinned at Millie. "It's such a relief to get it out!" Then she looked at me and said, "Now, what is this crap about not coming back from Europe?"

"Excuse me," Millie said, and hopped up from the love seat, rushing out of the room. Peach and I stared after her.

"What's up with Millie?" Peach asked.

"Seriously?" Stacy looked from me to Peach, then back again. "Really, you guys don't know?"

Peach's brow furrowed. "She hasn't had a boyfriend in ages. Do you think she's jealous that I'm getting married?"

"I don't think so," I said. "That's not like Millie."

"She's in love with Nick, idiots," Stacy said, her voice low. "Has been since high school."

Peach and I went silent, and then I said, "Not possible," just as Peach said, "Oh, come *on.*"

Stacy sat forward, keeping her voice down as she spoke. "With her grades and the money her grandmother left her, Millie should have gone back to the Ivy League mother ship from whence she sprang and made it with some guy who wears corduroy and reads Foucault. Really, do you think being the secretary at Nick's landscaping business is the best she could have done?"

Stacy had a point, but I still couldn't wrap my head around the idea of Millie being in love with Nick Easter. Honestly, it was a little tough to imagine Peach with Nick. He was gruff, bald, and a little schlubby, and he used to shoot at us with his BB gun when we were kids. He'd grown up okay, was basically a good guy, but I wasn't the kind of girl who forgot welts.

"No," Peach said, shaking her head emphatically. "She would have told us."

"Oh?" Stacy said, eyeing Peach. "Just like you?"

I exchanged looks with Peach, and then Millie came back into the room. She had a hard smile etched into her face, and while her eyes were a bit red, she was obviously trying to hide it. She sat down, reached for her margarita, and took a gentle sip, then said, "Liv, these are really good."

I glanced from woman to woman, examining the faces, each more tense than the other. So, I did what needed doing—I jammed my elbow into the eight-hundred-pound gorilla sitting between us, and tried to shove it under the carpet.

"Oh my god, guys, the weirdest thing happened last night at work. This woman came in with a stinky gym sock and she threw it at me and I fell and got knocked out."

"Speaking of work," Stacy said, talking over the last part, "how did Tobias take the news about you leaving?"

I reached into the bowl for some chips, and dipped one in the pico. "Fine. He's happy for me."

Peach put her margarita glass down on the coffee table. "Wait,

Tobias knows? You told Tobias before you told us?" She turned to Millie. "Can you believe that, Mill?"

Millie shrugged, not meeting Peach's eye. Peach picked up her margarita glass and took another drink.

"Of *course* she told Tobias first," Stacy said.

I looked at her. "You say that like you mean something by it."

She raised one brow at me, and those eyes that knew everything dared me to challenge her.

I looked away. "I've told you a thousand times, there's nothing between me and Tobias."

Stacy shrugged. "Right."

Peach made a thoughtful sound and said, "Do you think he might be gay?"

I choked on the chip, and had to down half my margarita to dislodge it.

"He's not gay," Stacy said.

"Well, has he dated anyone since coming to town? A man like that doesn't come to a town like this without getting it regular, and I don't think he has since he got here." She reached out and gave the arm of the love seat a tentative touch. "What do you think, Mill?"

Millie didn't respond, just stared down at her shoes.

"He's not gay," Stacy said.

Peach pulled her attention from Millie. "No, I think I might be on to something here. I mean, he hangs out with Liv all the time. But he's never tried to sleep with her. Right, Liv?"

That one hit me in the gut, but I couldn't bear telling Peach and Stacy about Tobias and my unrequited love. Not right now. It had been hard enough admitting it to Millie.

"Nope," I said, feeling a little sick. "But . . . you know . . . just because he doesn't find me attractive doesn't mean . . ."

"It's not about being attracted to you or not," Peach said, getting into her argument. "A guy spends that much time hanging out with a woman, horniness and opportunity are going to overlap eventually. Has he ever even *tried* to get in your pants?"

"No," I said, swallowing hard. "But I may not be his type of woman. Maybe he likes them prettier, or thinner—"

"Shut up, you're gorgeous. Any man in the world would have to be gay not to want you." She grabbed a chip and pointed at me with it, accentuating her argument. "I'm telling you, I think he's gay."

"He's *not* gay," Stacy said again.

Peach threw her hands up in the air. "How do you know?"

"Because I slept with him, and I've slept with gay men before. Trust me, I know gay. He's not gay." Stacy looked at me. "Sorry, Liv."

The thing about shock is that it hits in a flash, and even as you're laughing and saying, "What are you sorry about? I think that's *great!*" you know you're full of shit and that it's gonna hurt like hell later. My hands, which had finally stopped tingling earlier, started up again, and I shook them out, then turned to Peach.

"See, I told you he wasn't gay. He's been sleeping with *Stacy!*" My laugh sounded tinny even to my own ears, and I reached for my margarita, hoping the drink would keep me from making noise of any kind.

"He hasn't *been* sleeping with me," Stacy said. "We *have slept* together. Totally different."

And then a thick blanket of awkwardness fell over us. The three of us went quiet, and Millie, who had been quiet all along, continued to stare into her empty margarita glass.

"Okay," I said, slapping my hands down on my knees a little too hard, making the tingly sensation in them even worse. "How about a game of Apples to Apples?"

Millie stood up. "I think I'm going to go home."

Peach stood up, too, her smile extra-sunny, and too tense to be real. "Let me drive you, honey."

"It's just a few blocks. I'll walk." And then Millie hurried out, without a single word to the rest of us. We sat there in silence for a while, then Peach picked up her margarita glass, downed the last of it, and refilled it.

"I'll bring this back later," Peach said, and walked out. Thirty seconds later, I heard the front door to her house slam behind her.

Stacy and I sat stiffly next to each other in silence for a while, and then finally she said, "Well, it's probably about time for me to go." She got up from the couch and headed to the door. "I have to go prepare to collect and reassemble Mom's brains once she hears that Nick's marrying a Barbie doll."

I followed her toward the door, still feeling a little numb. "Okay."

She turned to me. "It was a long time ago, Liv. He'd just gotten here, it was before I knew how you felt about him. That's why I never told you. I'm sorry."

"Oh, no, I don't . . ." I smiled at her, took a deep breath, and said, "There's nothing between me and Tobias. Really."

She gave me a dubious look, then turned and left. I shut the door behind her, leaned back against it, and stared at the ceiling, trying to stop the visuals of Stacy and Tobias, naked and writhing, from running on an endless loop in my head.

I was unsuccessful.

So I finished off the plate of Peach's chili brownies and went to bed.

"Oh, Livvy, thank god you're here!" Betty pulled her glasses down to the tip of her nose, and looked at me over the frames. "I can't read this goddamn thing."

The place was dead, as I knew it would be between the Sunday lunch and dinner shifts. I sat down at the counter and glanced at the number at the bottom of the invoice. "One thousand, two hundred seventy-nine dollars and forty-eight cents," I read. I watched as she scribbled the number down in her ledger, then said, "You know, they have computers for that sort of thing now."

"I'm seventy-three years old," she said. "You want to teach me how to use a computer?"

I handed the invoice back to her. "Game, set, match."

She smiled, shut the book, and stuck it under the counter, then leaned over the counter with a glint of glee in her eye. "You'll never guess who Frankie Biggs is screwing now."

"You know what I love about you, Betty? Your complete lack of shame." I grabbed a menu and glanced at it. I hadn't come in to eat, and even if I had, I already knew that damn thing by heart, but I was feeling nervous, and it gave me something to do with my hands.

"I don't need shame," Betty said. "I've got the goods. But if you don't want to hear it . . ."

"No, I really don't." I put the menu down and drummed on it with my fingertips, then shook out my hands, which were still feeling tingly. The sensation kept coming and going, and I figured eventually it would go altogether, but it wasn't making me feel any better. "Hey, have you ever pinched a nerve? Is it normal for your hands to tingle for a few days afterward?"

Betty slammed her hand down on the counter. "Dixie Connors!" And then she laughed maniacally.

"Dixie Connors? My high school English teacher, Dixie Connors?"

She gave me an exasperated look. "Do we have two? Isn't that just the best?"

"It's unlikely, is what it is," I said, and shook out my hands. "Who's your source?"

Betty straightened up a bit. "I don't reveal my sources."

"You reveal everything," I said. "Which means it's Addie Hooper-Higgins, who was also the one who told you Henry Dinks got abducted by aliens. Just because Addie runs a bed-and-breakfast does not make her reliable, you know." I put the menu back in the holder next to the register and pushed up from the stool, my arms and legs feeling like jelly as the nerves set in. I tried to make my voice casual as I said, "Is Tobias in?"

She shrugged. "Should be, although he might be taking a break."

"I'm gonna go talk to him." I kept my eye on the door to the kitchen, then pointed a finger at her. "And you stop spreading gossip."

"I'm going to hell anyway," she said as I passed by. "I might as well have fun on the way down."

I took a deep breath and pushed through the big metal door into the kitchen. Kenny, the stoner community college kid who did prep during the days, was hulling strawberries at the industrial metal island, his head bopping in rhythm with whatever was playing on his iPod. Tobias stood at the grill, cleaning it off meticulously as he always did during the dead zone between shifts. I stared at the back of his head for a bit, the image of Stacy's fingers running through his hair zooming through my head. I shook my hands out again as the tingling got worse, and when I looked up, Tobias was standing with his back to the grill, mild surprise on his face.

"Hey," he said. "How'd the Confessional go?"

"Great," I said, my voice sounding a little squeaky in my ears. "So, you and Stacy, then?"

I hadn't intended on bringing up Stacy. Well, okay, I *had,* but in my head on the way over, I'd imagined smoothly maneuvering it into the conversation so that it was him who brought it up, in a natural way. And then he would tell me that the sex with her wasn't any good and he was drunk when it happened, and maybe that she drooled when she slept, and then I would feel better and be able to go to Europe without that stupid hole eating away at my gut the way it had since Stacy dropped the bomb.

"Me and Stacy?" he said, wariness in his voice. "What about me and Stacy?"

I shot him a dark look, and he lowered his eyes, then nodded as if coming to some internal decision. He took me by the elbow and led me out through the back hallway to the unadorned cement patio where the deliveries came in. He grabbed the two foldable nylon chairs we kept out there for people on their break and set them out, motioning for me to sit down. I took one seat and he took the other, resting his elbows on his knees as he leaned forward.

"All right, let's have this out," he said.

I sat up straight, trying not to be mad, because I had no right to be mad, but my words came out clipped anyway. "You should have told me."

"It wasn't your business," he said, his tone simple, but the cut of it hurt too much, and I pushed up from the chair.

"Okay, then," I said. "Sorry to have wasted your time."

He shot up and grabbed my arm before I could leave. I stood where I was, lacking the energy to wrench myself away, but I didn't look at him. I couldn't.

"It's not your business any more than it's my business who you sleep with," he said.

I met his eye. "Yeah, but I haven't been sleeping with your best friend."

He lowered his eyes. "It was a long time ago. Pretty much, right after I came to town. I bumped into her at Happy Larry's one night, and we played a little pool—"

"Lalalalalala!" I said, putting my hands over my ears. "No details! There isn't enough brain bleach in the world for details!"

He gently pulled my hands down from my ears, and it took him a moment to release them entirely. I could see that there was pain on his face, and I hated it. He could either love me entirely, or not at all, but this in-between, just-as-a-friend stuff was going to kill me dead. It probably wasn't doing him much good, either.

"I figured you already knew," he said. "I thought she had told you."

"Well, she didn't." I took a step back from him; the mere proximity of him hurt. "Not until yesterday, and it's been driving me nuts ever since."

He grabbed my hand suddenly, but not in a romantic way; he quickly examined the palm, then looked up at me. "What's the matter with your hands?"

I pulled my hand back. "Nothing."

"You keep shaking them out." He eyed me. "What's going on?"

"Nothing," I said again, and crossed my arms over my stomach, tucking my hands under my elbows. "I'm just . . ." *Insanely, stupidly, unjustifiably jealous.* I sighed. "You have to understand what it's like growing up with someone like Stacy Easter. She's beautiful, she's smart, she's thin. Confident. Strong. She's got that whole sexy librarian thing going on . . ."

Tobias's mouth quirked at the edges. "Maybe you should have slept with Stacy."

I gave him an unamused look, and he dropped the smile. "Sorry."

"I'm always 'the friend' with her," I said. "She's the hot one, and I'm the one men talk to to get access to her."

He stared at me for a moment, his eyes narrowing. "That's crazy."

"Oh, please. On my best day, I'm average looking. I eat waffles all day and I look like it. I'm wishy-washy. I have freckles. No one should be almost thirty with freckles. I'm graceless and my hair is the weird kind of curly and I just thought that . . ."

He waited for a moment, then prodded. "What?"

I huffed out a sharp breath. "I thought that maybe, just once, at least with you, maybe *she* was the friend. And to find out that I'm just the consolation prize after things didn't work out with her—"

"Okay, shut up." He took a sharp step toward me, his eyes blazing. "You're nobody's consolation prize."

"Right," I said. "I'm not even that."

He put his hands on my shoulders, gripping them hard. "Listen to me. The way you see yourself is completely messed up, and I put up with it because arguing with you about this stuff is like talking to a brick wall, but I've had it. Stacy's . . . just Stacy. Yeah, she's pretty, but she's the kind of woman who makes a man want to get a blow job under the pool table at Happy Larry's. Women like that, they're a dime a dozen. You, Liv . . . you're the kind of woman that makes a man just *want,* and that's rare. And amazing. A guy finds that maybe once in a lifetime. If he's lucky."

His eyes moved over my face, and his breath was a bit ragged, and for a moment I thought he was going to kiss me, but then he took a breath and released his hold on me, blinking a couple of times.

I stared at him, dumbfounded, and then in a sudden fury put the flat of my hand against his chest and pushed as hard as I could. Taken off guard by the assault, he stumbled back a bit, and I advanced on him, poking my index finger into his solar plexus.

"See, *that's* what I'm talking about! You say stuff like that to me and then you don't kiss me. And then when I kiss you, you treat me like I'm insane. Well, you know what? I'm not insane, and I'm not making this all up in my head! Stop gaslighting me, Tobias."

"I'm not trying to gaslight you, I'm just . . ."

I stood there, tapping my foot but as usual, he went silent just as things got interesting.

"Okay, you know what?" I said, cutting into the dragging silence. "This suddenly silent thing you do was cute for the first fourteen months or so, but now, it's getting old."

I started toward the alley to make my way out to the street where I could only hope an eighteen-wheeler would come speeding out of nowhere and put me out of my misery when Tobias said, "Don't go."

I turned back to face him. "Don't go . . . *what?* Don't go from here? Don't go to Europe? What, Tobias? What do you want?"

He opened his mouth as if to say something, and then stopped, the same way he had last week when I'd kissed him and *he'd kissed me back, damnit,* but then held me at arm's length and looked at me and said *nothing.* Except now, he wasn't even looking at me.

He was looking at my hands.

I glanced down, and realized I'd been shaking them out again, absently trying to shake off the intensifying tingling. I tucked them under my elbows again and said, "What?"

"What's happening with you?"

"Nothing. I'm fine. Now, what were you going to say?"

"Liv." His voice was stern, and the tone took me a bit by surprise. "You need to tell me what's going on."

I crossed my arms over my stomach and tucked my hands under my elbows. "Nothing's going on. My hands keep falling asleep, that's all."

His brow knit. "Since when?"

"It doesn't matter. Stop changing the subject. Do you have something to say to me or not?"

His expression was dark and worried, his eyes still focused on my hands. Finally, he raised his eyes to mine and slowly shook his head.

"Liv, I don't . . ." He released a breath. "I can't right now, but—"

"Stop." I closed my eyes as it all hit me at once. The pain, the loss, the humiliation, the stark desire for something I would never have. It was too much. I felt the tears prickle at the edge of my eyes, and I knew they were going to fall, and he was going to see them, and there wasn't a damn thing I could do to stop it. I took a deep breath, and my chin quivered a bit.

Damnit.

"Liv," he started, but I held up one hand to stop him as I used the other to swipe at my face.

"Believe it or not, now's a good time to shut up, Tobias."

"I'm sorry," he said quietly.

"Don't be," I said, meeting his eye as dryly as I could. "I'm fine."

Then I turned on my heel and headed out toward the road, ignoring him as he called my name.

3

Happy Larry's is exactly the kind of windowless pit of doom you'd expect from a dive called Happy Larry's, but there are days when a girl needs to match her bar with her mood, and that day, Happy Larry's was a match.

Happy Larry, scruffy and growly in his mangy, sleeveless MANAGEMENT RESERVES THE RIGHT TO KICK YOUR ASS T-shirt, did not appear to be very happy with my appearance in his establishment. You could never tell with Larry; between the untamed beard and Coke-bottle glasses, he was a hard man to read on facial expression alone.

"What the hell are you doing here?" he growled, confirming my original suspicion.

I took a stool and leaned over the bar. "I'm here for the same reason that everyone else is here. Too miserable to be anywhere respectable, not quite ready to jump off a bridge."

Larry stared at me.

"Fine. Be that way." I reached into my front jeans pocket and slammed a twenty down on the bar. "Serve me whatever is going to get me drunk the fastest. What do I want? Vodka? Tequila? You got anything in an IV drip?"

Happy Larry's expression remained unchanged. "Go home."

I drummed my fingers on the bar for a moment while I deliberated, then made the call. "Make it tequila."

Happy Larry grunted something, but he took the twenty, then set a salt shaker, a shot glass, and a slice of lime in front of me. He pulled a bottle of tequila out, and filled the shot glass. I stared at it for a moment, then glanced up at him.

"How many calories are in this?"

Happy Larry stared at me blankly.

"I'm going on a diet," I said glumly. "Starting today. When I get on that plane, I'm going to be svelte."

Nothing from Larry. Jesus, it was tough to crack this guy.

"Okay. Maybe not svelte. But I wanna wear my skinny jeans. I figure fifteen hundred calories a day ought to do it, and you know what that is, Larry? That's two pieces of lettuce and a whiff of a chocolate-chip cookie. So, what I'm asking you, Larry, is . . . how many calories?"

Happy Larry continued to stare at me.

"So you don't . . . know? Then? The calories?"

Slowly, he shook his head.

"You know what? That's okay. No, really. Don't apologize." *I bet Stacy never asks about the calorie content.* "It's early in the day, I'll look it up and adjust for it later. Or, you know. Maybe start tomorrow. You gotta work your way up to these things."

Then I salted my hand, licked it, downed the shot, and sucked the lime.

"What?" I said as I nudged the empty shot glass back at an obviously surprised Happy Larry. "I went to college. I know how to drink tequila. Give me another one."

He shook his head as he poured. "You puke on my floor, you're cleaning it up."

"God, Happy. *One time,* I puked on your floor. I was sixteen. Let it go, man." I salted my hand, did the shot, then shook my head. I may not have gotten rid of the tingling in my hands, but now the rest of my body at least matched. The sharp edges of agitation that had been poking at me seemed to soften a bit, and I felt my spirits lift.

"You know what?" I said. "Tequila's good. Gimme another."

"You bet." He stuffed the twenty in the till, gave me two fives and three ones in return. "In twenty minutes."

"Grudge holder." I swiped my money off the counter and shoved it back in my pocket, then swiveled around on my seat to take in the place. The only other customers were Frankie Biggs and Doug Holt, playing a game of pool in the back, and some guy sitting in a booth in the dark corner opposite, scraggly hair hanging down as he leaned over his glass. I let my gaze wander back to the pool table, and Frankie Biggs. Another man who couldn't keep his hands off of Stacy Easter.

They were everywhere.

"I'm gonna go play pool," I announced.

Happy Larry motioned toward the pool tables. "I care deeply."

I got off the bar stool with a little trouble—*Wow, I'm a cheap date*—and when I looked up, my eyes locked with the guy in the corner. Or, at least I think my eyes locked with his; I couldn't see him very well, the combined effects of the dim lighting and the eighty-proof tequila in my bloodstream. In a knee-jerk response of vigilance after a thousand cautionary tales from my mother based on True Stories from *Reader's Digest,* I took in little details about him for the police report I'd probably never have to file—tallish, dirty-blond hair, midthirties, beat-up work boots, jeans, dark T-shirt, a few days' of beard growth on his face—and then I looked away and made my way over to the pool table, where Doug was chalking his cue.

"What the hell are you doing here?" Doug said.

"You know what I love about this place?" I said. "The way everyone makes a girl feel so welcome."

Doug's eyes went from me to Frankie and then back again. "Did Amber send you here to check in on Frankie?" He looked at Frankie. "I'm telling you, man, you need a restraining order."

I shook my head. "Amber didn't send me." I turned to Frankie. "But I've seen her recently in CCB's, and I think the restraining order could be sound advice. She's really pissed off."

Doug gave Frankie a told-you-so look, and Frankie shook it off. I stood there, one hip jutted in what I thought might be a sexy manner, maybe, and wondered what Stacy would do in this situation, what it was about her that made her so instantly irresistible to every man walking the planet. The truth was, even though I'd been with her in a ton of bars and watched the men come streaming over, I never noticed anything in partic-ular that she did. It was just something she *was.*

"You want something?" Frankie asked finally.

I thought about all the sassy, sexy, alluring responses I could give to that question, but as I looked at Frankie, all I could see was the ferret attached under his nose, and I just couldn't do it. Try as I might, I was no Stacy Easter, and I had to accept that.

"No." I sighed and unjutted my hip. "I just came over here to see if you would try to sleep with me."

Both guys looked up immediately from the game. Seriously, it was like dogs with a whistle.

"We'd have a shot?" Frankie asked.

"No," I said quickly. "Nothing personal. I just kind of wanted to see if you'd *try*. You know. Medicate my wounded pride. It was either you or that guy in the corner—" I motioned to the corner booth and paused. "Oh, he's gone."

"For what it's worth," Frankie said, chalking his cue, "if I thought I had half a chance, I'd try." He took his shot, missed, and Doug started casing the table.

"Really? You're not just saying that?"

Frankie examined me for a moment, then shrugged. "Sure, I'd give it a shot."

I have to say, that was much less comforting than you'd think. But still. It was nice of him.

"Thank you, Frankie." I stared at his *Magnum, P.I.* moustache for a moment. "You ever think of shaving that thing?"

Frankie ran his hand over his mouth. "Are you kidding? You wouldn't believe what this does to girls in the sack."

"Gross," I said. There was a moment of awkward silence, and I added, "Well. I'm just gonna go back over there, then."

Frankie smiled and nodded at me, and Doug grunted something and took his shot.

I stepped away from the pool table slowly, cheeks flush with embarrassment, and started back toward the bar. Before I got there, I could hear Doug saying something about, "crazy fucking chicks," and I poured myself onto a stool and rested my face against the bar.

"Let me ask you something, Happy," I said. "If I find out a guy I know has slept with one of my best friends, and it bothers me enough that I go confront him and then come here to get drunk, that means I should move up my trip to Europe, right?"

"I'm not pouring anything for another fifteen minutes," Happy said.

"Yeah, that's what I thought, too." I raised my head and gave him a grim look. "Serve me now, and I'll leave immediately."

Happy grabbed the bottle and poured.

When I stumbled sideways into the alley beside Happy Larry's, I thought at first that it was the tequila making me lose my footing. I didn't realize I'd been pulled into the alley until my elbow hurt from someone's stone grip, and my face smacked into someone's hard chest.

"Ow!" I said, touching my left cheek as I pulled back from him. "That's still sore!"

"You Olivia?" His voice was rough and scratchy, layered with deep country and, unless I was mistaken, whiskey. I stepped back and squinted up at the guy, immediately recognizing him as the guy from the booth in the corner. In addition to the details I'd taken in at the bar—*your paranoia has finally paid off, Grandma*—I noticed that his eyes were slightly red at the edges, likely the result of Happy Larry's cheap whiskey and refusal to adhere to state indoor smoking laws.

I wrenched my arm from his grip and took a step toward the

street, but he blocked me, and so I ended up stepping farther back into the shadows of the alley.

"Are you Olivia Ford?"

"No," I said.

He advanced on me, and I stepped farther back into the alley.

"Was your father Gabriel Ford?" he asked.

"Far as I know, he was Some Guy Named Dave." I stepped back and my thigh hit the metal trash bin. "I'm leaving now. Touch me again, and I'll scream."

He held up his hands, but I could see annoyance and tension on his face, and it was not comforting. "I just want to talk to you."

"Sure, because men pull women into alleys all the time just to talk." I glanced around and thought, *What would Stacy Easter do?* Puke on his shoes, probably. Not much of a help. Then I caught the trash cans in the corner of my eye, and I pulled the lid off one and held it between us like a shield. "Stay back."

The guy advanced on me another foot, which freaked me out a bit because while I was okay acting like I would hit him with the lid, I wasn't entirely sure *how* I was going to hit him with it. Straight-on in the face, I guessed. Maybe? While I had the standard waitress's upper body strength, I sadly lacked the standard waitress's thirst for blood.

"Put that damn thing down so we can talk."

"I don't want to talk to you. I've had a very bad day, and I just want to *go home!*" I waggled the lid in front of me, trying to look threatening, but I probably just looked like an insane, drunken waffle waitress who had stepped tragically out of her element.

That was when I noticed how hot the trash can lid felt in my hands. I glanced up to see if maybe there was a ray of sunlight on it or something, but we were in the complete shade of the alley. I shook my head and tried to focus. "Get out of my way!"

"Not until I get some answers," he said, shaking his head slowly, and freaking me out even more. The lid handle was getting hotter, and the tingling in my hand was getting worse, making my arm shake, which made the lid shake.

"I'm looking for a—" His expression went from irritation to slight concern. "You okay?"

Ow. The heat in my hand was beginning to hurt, and I felt a little dizzy.

"I'm fine," I said, catching my breath. "Why?"

"You look like you're going to vomit."

"It's not out of the question." I whipped the lid up, but my arms were so weak and tingly that it just kind of wobbled in my hands. The lid wavered a little in the air and I tried to steady it. "Now get out of my way."

"I just need to ask you if—"

I didn't hear anything he said after that; the tingling heat in my fingers escalated into an electric buzz running up my arms and into my shoulders that distracted me too much. I could almost feel it in my teeth. What the hell was up with this damn lid? Was it electric or something? I tried to tighten my hold on the handle as best I could, but then . . . I don't know if it was the glare of the sun bouncing off nearby windows or what, but despite the shade, something that looked like electrically charged strings of yellow light danced over my hands, and spread out to the rest of the lid, and I screamed and dropped it to the ground with a clang.

Only when it hit the ground, it . . . changed. Slowly, the lid curved into a saddle shape, the metal creaking loudly and little sparks of yellow light shooting out of it as it morphed. It rolled around on its . . . back, I guess . . . for a second, and four short legs squealed out of the edge of the lid. Then, under its own power, it righted itself onto its feet and a short, straight stub of a tail formed at the side facing me. At the side facing the guy, the shape of the top of a terrier-looking dog head formed and then it sort of . . . well, for lack of a better term, I'll say it *growled* at the guy, although that could have been the sound of the mutating aluminum. I don't know. I've never heard aluminum mutate before. Apparently, neither had the guy, because he jumped back a bit, staring down at the thing.

Do you believe in magic? I heard Davina's voice say to me from the far reaches of the night before.

No, I thought back at her.

The aluminum dog growled again, going for the guy.

"Son of a bitch," the guy grunted, stepping back. That's when the dog jumped up into the air, heading for the guy's kneecaps. The guy darted to the side, and in the air, in midjump, the thing turned back into a lid, and it landed on one edge on the asphalt. We both stared at it for a moment as it wobbled like a twirling coin until it finally stopped, flat and dead and still on the ground.

My voice was weak and strained even to my own ears. "Did that trash can lid just turn into a dog?"

There was a flash of something on his face—anger or terror, I couldn't tell, the break was so brief—and then his lips tightened together and his face was stone again.

"Yeah." He swallowed, then met my eyes. "That never happen to you before?"

"Are you asking me if I've ever seen a trash can lid turn into a dog before?"

"No," he said. "I'm asking you if you ever *turned* a trash can lid into a dog before."

"No," I said. "That was *you.*"

He stared at me, confusion on his face.

I pointed at the lid and repeated myself. "*You* did that."

More silence.

"Well, it certainly wasn't *me,*" I said, my voice almost making it into screech territory as I said the words. My memory flashed on the tingling in my arms, the weird yellow light that had seemed to come from my fingers . . .

"It wasn't me," I said again, trying to sound more forceful, to convince myself. I was almost able to do it. For his part, he just stared at me, seeming just as stunned as I was. After a moment of this odd silence, I remembered that I needed to escape from the crazy guy who just turned a trash can lid into a dog—*it was him, it had to be him*—and I took a few wobbly steps back, and pointed toward the street.

"I'm going to go home now," I said carefully, "and you're going to go wherever it is you go, and leave me a—"

"No!" He grabbed my arm, his grip tight on my wrist, hurting me. "I need to know if you've seen her."

"Seen who?"

And right then, seemingly out of nowhere, another trash can lid flew over my shoulder, knocked him in the head, and sent him spiraling against the brick wall, where he hit his head again and went down, out cold.

"Okay, I know I didn't do *that*." I turned around, stumbling a bit as my shaking legs tried to hold me up, and I looked into the shadows. "Hello?"

Silence. No one was there. I must have been really drunk, except I didn't feel that drunk. Maybe none of this was real. Maybe I was hallucinating.

"Oh, god." I gasped, putting my hand to my mouth, remembering how my mother's sickness had first presented with an insistence on putting the milk under the sink in the bathroom. "Brain tumor."

I felt a roiling in my gut, and the next thing I knew, I puked. Right next to the guy's work boots.

I'm no Stacy Easter, my ass, I thought.

The guy grunted as he started to come to. I glanced around, saw no one there, and did the only thing that made sense at the time.

I beat it the hell out of that alley, and ran the rest of the way home.

4

I was naked and dripping wet from the shower when I heard a familiar banging on my bathroom window.

"Goddamnit, Peach," I muttered, then pulled my fluffy pink polka-dot robe around me and yanked up the blinds just in time to see her pulling her headless broom handle back across the tiny gap between our houses and back into her bathroom. I threw the window open and sat on the radiator.

"We're not twelve anymore, Peach," I said. "You can call me on the phone."

She leaned her elbows on the sill of her open window. "Have you talked to Millie lately? Oh, and I'm out of conditioner."

"Just a minute." I reached under my bathroom sink and pulled out the small bag full of hotel toiletries I kept there. I pulled out a little bottle of conditioner and tossed it across the six feet between us; she caught it handily.

"No, I haven't talked to Millie," I said. "I've been a little distracted since the Confessional. You haven't talked to her?"

"No," she said. "And Nick said she hasn't shown up for work."

"She's missed three days of work? Why would she . . . ?" I shot Peach a look. "You didn't tell him, did you?"

Peach gave me an indignant look. "About her being in love with him? No! What kind of friend do you think I am?"

I stared her down for a moment, and she deflated a bit.

"Okay, fine, *yes,* I told him. He's going to be my husband. We share everything. But I told him not to say anything to her, and he didn't, I swear. He didn't get the chance." She nibbled her lip. "I've left, like, ten messages on her phone. She hasn't called me back. Have you tried to call her?"

"No," I said, feeling a twinge of guilt. I'd been so wrapped up in my own drama with Tobias that I hadn't thought much about Millie. Not that there was much real drama with Tobias at the moment; hard to have a lot of drama when you're pretending the other person doesn't exist. I'd also used a fair amount of mental energy rationalizing the trash-can-lid dog—tequila causes hallucinations, right?—so I just hadn't had much left to worry about Millie.

"I'm worried," Peach said. "Maybe we should go by her house later."

I grabbed a towel off the rack and scrunched my dripping hair in it. "Good idea. All right, I'm going to go dry my—"

"Why don't you come over?" she said. "We can go to CCB's for waffles."

I sighed. "I can't. I've given up waffles. Just until I get the pudge off. Do you know how many calories are in those things? I think I get contact fat just from serving them."

She shrugged; Peach had never had to think about calories a day in her life. "Have you talked to Stacy?"

I felt myself stiffen at the mention of her name. "No."

Peach gave me a sharp look. "You should cut her some slack on that whole thing. It was a long time ago."

I felt a stab go through me, and I toweled my hair with a little too much vehemence as I said, "It doesn't matter. It's over. I'm not upset."

"Okay, whatever you say. But she didn't know how you felt about Tobias back then, and she feels really bad about it."

I stopped rubbing the towel against my head and stared at Peach. "Oh, please. She does not. Stacy has never felt bad for anything she's done, ever." I continued toweling my hair, then stopped again. "And it doesn't matter anyway, because Tobias is a grown man who can do what he wants. Neither one of them owes me anything. There's nothing to feel bad about." I pulled the towel away from my head. My scalp was starting to hurt.

"Well, at any rate, you can't go to Europe now," she said carefully.

I raised my head to look at her. "Oh, no? And why is that?"

She stared at me. "The whole group is falling apart. Millie's upset and none of us know what's happened to her. You and Stacy are fighting."

"We're not fighting," I said through gritted teeth.

"Look, Millie's grandmother is dead. Your mom is dead. My parents are in Florida so they might as well be dead. And Stacy's mom is a nutcase. We're the only family we all have. You're going to just leave and let that fall apart?"

I narrowed my eyes at her. "Is that what this is about? Are you manufacturing drama to keep me here?"

"I'm getting married," Peach said, her lower lip quivering. "Are you even going to be here for my wedding?"

"Of course, I'll be here for your wedding," I said. "They have airports in Europe, you know. Have you picked a date?"

Peach straightened up and stared at me, delivering her statement like a blow. "December twentieth."

"Wow. That's fast. But . . . sure. Okay. I'll be back for the wedding."

Her mouth dropped open. "*Back?* You can't go and come back. Who's going to help me plan?"

I ticked off my fingers. "Nick. Stacy. Millie. A thousand wedding planners in the regional phone book. And your parents are in Florida, Peach. They're not dead. You've got people."

"I need *you*. I can't put on a wedding without you, you're my oldest friend. You're the closest thing I have to a sister. You have to stay here until I get married, and then it's the holidays, and you can't go then. January and February are too cold, and it's even worse in Scotland in the winter. We can talk about it again in April."

"I bought my ticket," I said. "I leave in August."

"Get a refund."

"It's nonrefundable."

"I don't understand why you have to leave all of a sudden like that. It doesn't make any sense."

"I just . . ." I thought about explaining it to her, invoking memories of my mother, who used to sit in her garden staring into space for hours. I know he left her on October fifth only because she spent that day crying in her room every year. But

I couldn't tell Peach all this because she wouldn't allow me to leave her because of a man. Peach was great in a lot of ways, but she would never understand what unrequited love did to you. No one had ever turned Peach down in her life.

"It's just something I need to do, Peach."

"Well, I don't understand *why*."

I huffed in frustration. "You don't have to. We're not family, Peach. We're neighbors. So just back off."

Immediately after I said it, I wanted to take it back, but I couldn't. Silence edged into the space between us as Peach stared down at the ground below, quickly swiping tears away from her cheeks before raising her head to look at me once again.

"I'm only going to get married once, Liv. Europe will always be there." And with that, she closed her window and left her bathroom.

I sat with the bag of toiletries on my lap, just staring until all the products melded together in a blurred lump in my vision. Peach would come around and apologize later. Millie would be fine, we'd all see to that, and Stacy and I would iron over whatever was tense between us. Tobias and I were already getting back to normal, kind of. The chances were good that by the time I got on that plane, Peach would accept it, too. It was about as likely as a winged unicorn flying over my house and pooping rainbows, but there was a chance.

At the moment, though, I was too tired to think about it, so I stuffed the toiletry bag under my bathroom sink and went to take a nap.

★ ★ ★

It was a little after seven at night when I woke up, although with the sun being out so late in the summer, it took me a moment to realize it was still Wednesday, my day off. I lay back in my bed and stared at the ceiling, wrist resting on my forehead. I supposed I could eat, but it was hard to work up any enthusiasm for it. Really, the only thing I had enough energy to do was go back to sleep.

Just as I'd closed my eyes, I heard it. A sound, downstairs. A door opening. I shot up in bed and my heart raced as I tried to remember . . . hadn't I locked the door? Not that anyone in this neighborhood needed to lock their doors with Peach and Ginny Boyle around, but still . . . I thought I had.

"Crap," I said, trying to decide what to do. Maybe whoever it was would just steal my television and leave me in peace. I really didn't care; it was an old TV, and it'd save me the trouble of selling it. I closed my eyes and tried to convince myself it was my imagination, but then I heard more shuffling downstairs and figured I had to at least check it out.

I grabbed my pink softball bat and walked down the stairs; when I got to the foyer at the bottom, I heard a sound in the kitchen, and relaxed a bit as I realized it was probably just Peach. We'd traded house keys years ago, and she had no boundaries. It would be just like her to let herself in if she needed sugar or eggs or something.

"Peach?" I called out, still holding the bat in my hands, but a little lowered. "Is that you?"

The kitchen door flew open and Davina stepped out, her bright peacock-colored skirt whirling around her. I screamed. Davina threw up her arms and screamed, too, spilling a bit of her drink on the floor. She took a breath and raised one hand to the wall to steady herself as she laughed.

"Oh, baby, you scared the hell out of me." She looked down at the floor and said, "Crap, I spilled," and then flew through the kitchen door, leaving it swinging in a wake of blue silk and lilac scent.

I stood in my foyer for another minute or so. I realized my mouth was hanging open and I shut it. Adrenaline shot through my body on every hard pump of my raging heart, and I went into the kitchen, where I saw Davina placing a second glass of scotch down on my tiny linoleum table, presumably for me.

"Sit down," she said, grabbing a sponge off the sink. "I'll be right back."

She disappeared, humming an unfamiliar song as she cleaned up the spill on the other side of the kitchen door, then came back in and sat down opposite me, lifting her glass in the air.

"We need to talk," she said, and downed her glass.

"Talk? About what? You broke into my house. We don't need to talk, you need to leave."

"You look good," Davina said, her eyes bright. She reached out and patted my hand. "You got your color back, which is good. Especially after that incident in the alley next to Happy Larry's."

I felt a chill run down my back. "What are you talking about?"

She laughed. "I'm talking about how I saved you from that guy." She made a flinging motion with her arm, then made some *boom! pow!* sounds to imitate knocking the guy out in the alley. Then, she giggled. "Women's Ultimate Frisbee Champion, University of Louisiana, 1981." She glowed, proud of herself. "I still got it."

"Well . . . what the . . . ? That was *you*?"

"Sure was," she said. "And I saw what you did, too. *Dog!*" She laughed and clapped her hands. "*Very* impressive work, and really advanced for someone who's only been at it for what? A week?"

I swallowed and sat back. "You saw . . . the dog?"

"Sure did."

"But . . . you couldn't have."

"Why not?"

"Because I've spent the better part of the last few days convincing myself none of that happened. That it was a drunken hallucination, a brain tumor maybe. I was making progress with that."

"Ain't no brain tumor, baby. It's magic and you have it." She giggled again, like a little girl. "Isn't it exciting?"

I stared at her. I had a lot of emotions whirling within me at the moment. Excitement wasn't one of them. "Who are you?"

"You know who I am. I'm Davina."

"No, I mean . . . what is up with you? You threw a gym sock at me. What was that about?"

"That was necessary. I had to be sure you were who I thought you were."

"What was in the gym sock?"

She looked to the ceiling for a moment as she composed her answer, then smiled at me. "Think of it as a magical DNA test. It came out positive, and unblocked your power."

"I don't have any power," I said.

"I know an aluminum dog might beg to differ with you there."

"Yeah, and speaking of that . . . why didn't you just come out in the alley instead of throwing things? I was totally freaked out."

"Oh, I couldn't risk that man seeing me with you, baby." She leaned forward. "He's trying to kill me. Who knows what he'd do to you if he knew we were friends?"

"*Kill* you? Why?"

"Well, for the same reason anyone wants to kill anyone else," Davina said simply. "He's crazy."

"Who the hell is he?"

She took another sip, a grim look on her face. "His name is Cain. Avoid him. He's bad news." Her expression brightened. "I want to talk about you. What other magic have you done? Anything fun?"

I stared at her for a moment, trying to figure out what the hell she was talking about, then gave up.

"Yeah. Okay. That's it." I got up and pushed through the kitchen door, walking into the living room, and hunting for my cordless phone. I never put it back on the stupid cradle, and I can never find it when I need it.

I could hear Davina's footsteps coming up behind me. "What's the matter, baby?"

"The matter? I don't know. Trash can lids turning into dogs. Strange men trying to kill you. Either I'm nuts, or you're nuts. Likely, we're both nuts. Maybe you're not even real. Either way, doesn't matter. I need to call someone. Like . . . I don't know. A doctor? Maybe?"

"You don't need a doctor."

I started pawing through my couch cushions, feeling underneath them for the phone. Davina's hand clamped down on my arm, pulling me back. I stared at her dark fingers over my skin. I could feel them there. I looked at her.

"I can feel you."

I reached out and poked her cheek with one finger, and she swatted my hand away.

"I'm *real*," she said.

I pulled out of her grip. "Look, go away. I know you're not real. You're a hallucination, and the trash-can-lid dog was a hallucination, and that guy probably was, too. I'm going to call a doctor, and he's going to give me drugs that make the whole bunch of you *go away*."

Davina stared at me, and took a step back. Good. I went back into the couch cushions and my hands hit something hard and plastic. I pulled it out: the phone. I held it out to her like a weapon, hit the call button. The numbers on the dial pad lit up orange, and I poised my fingers over it to dial . . .

. . . but I didn't have a number to call. I needed the Yellow Pages. Except—crap—it was after five. I wouldn't be able to make an appointment. Did this qualify as an emergency? Should I call 911?

I looked at Davina. She was either real, and had broken into my house, or she wasn't, and I was hallucinating. Both possibilities counted as emergencies in my book.

"Nine-one-one it is," I said, and dialed the 9, but then Davina said, "Don't do that," and touched my arm and I wigged out and tossed the phone up into the air. My hands tingled with extreme heat, and I felt dizzy and disoriented.

"Agh!" I yelled. "Don't do that. You're freaking me out!"

"Calm down, Olivia," she said.

"No. I need my phone. I need to call nine-one-one." I glanced around the floor, looking for where the phone had landed, but I didn't see it anywhere. I was just registering that I couldn't recall hearing it fall to the ground when something flew past my head. I swatted at it and looked up to see a small black body floating above my head with bony wings, wisps of electric yellow light circling around it as it flew . . .

"Bat!" I screamed, pointing, but Davina just stared, watching it fly around. I stared, too, looking closer as it flew in circles overhead. It had bat wings, and a bat body, but on closer inspection, it seemed to be made of some kind of hard plastic.

And there were glowing orange numbers on its chest.

Davina just watched it, smiling as her eyes followed its circular arcs around the room, banging into walls, zooming back, and trying again.

"Oh, Jesus!" I yelled as the thing swooped down at me. I grabbed Davina and used her as a human shield, hiding behind her. "Oh, god, I hate bats!"

Davina angled around and looked at me, her face warm and smiling. "You *have* been practicing. Good girl."

I ducked down behind her. "What the hell are you talking about?" I pointed at the bat. "Kill it, kill it!"

"I can't kill it." She motioned up toward the bat, her face aglow with joy. "That there isn't a bat. Bats don't fly during sunlight. They also don't have glowing numbers on their bellies, and they aren't made of plastic. That there"—she pointed to the bat, which bounced blindly off the living room wall and course-corrected into the opposite wall—"is your magic."

"My what?" I asked.

Davina turned to where I was crouching behind her and pulled me up by my shoulders. She positioned me in front of her and said in my ear, "That's your magic, baby. Isn't it beautiful?"

5

Magic. I straightened, breathed in, and felt a hesitant calm wash over me.

Do you believe in magic?

Maybe.

I blinked a few times, and stepped through the open archway into the living room, leaving Davina a few feet behind in the hallway. I watched the bat fly in circles, bouncing off the occasional wall with a hard clink, leaving puffs of plaster behind with every collision. The harsh *buzz-buzz-buzz* sound of a phone that's been left off the hook grew stronger as it circled over me, and faded as it moved to the other side of the living room. I glanced down at my hands, still hot and tingly, just like with the trash-can-lid dog, and I came to a sudden, calm realization.

I'd just turned my phone into a bat.

I looked behind me at Davina and pointed. "I did that."

"Yes," she said, her voice soft as if talking to a small child. "You did." She patted my shoulder. "Don't worry. It probably won't last too long. You got some good juice there, but it's still early days. We got awhile to go yet before you start to mean some business."

As if soothed by her voice, the bat slowed a bit. Then, suddenly, its wings pulled in and it jolted into complete stillness.

Then my phone landed, with a lifeless plop, on my couch.

"Oh, that's a shame," Davina said. "Such a pretty bat phone."

There was a *tap-tap-tap* on my living room window and we both started, but then I released a breath and said, "Oh, hell." I walked over and pushed the window up. "Hey, Peach."

Peach pulled her broomstick back into her house. She wrapped her fleece bathrobe around her and said stiffly, "What's going on in there? I thought I heard screaming."

"There was a bat in the house." I glanced at the broken phone on the floor. "It's gone now." I looked back at Peach, looking for some kind of regret in her expression; there was none. "Sorry to bother you."

"It's no problem."

There was a long silence, and then I said, "Okay, then," and reached for the window to close it, just as Peach leaned even farther out her window and waved pointedly in Davina's direction. "Hey, Davina!"

Davina moved in next to me and waved back. "Nice to see you again, Peach."

Peach turned her smile on me, but it didn't reach her eyes. "I figured you wouldn't mind, Liv, I gave your aunt my key when I saw her out there earlier this afternoon."

I nudged Davina with my shoulder and whispered, "Aunt?"

Davina shrugged. "By marriage."

"I couldn't very well let her sit outside on your porch all day in this heat," Peach went on, her eyes shimmering with hurt.

"And what a surprise to find out you have an aunt none of us knew anything about."

I sighed. "Peach, it's . . . complicated."

"You don't have to explain anything to me," she said. "I'm just your neighbor."

And then she shut her window and went back inside.

I shut my window and turned to Davina, who was looking through it at Peach's house.

"Nice girl," Davina said. "She told me you two were like family. I think that's nice."

I held up my hand to get her to be quiet, and amazingly enough, she shut up. In my head, I set the tension with Peach aside; I would deal with that later. For now, I had a dead bat phone to think about. I blinked a few times, indulging myself in a distanced, packed-in-cotton feeling. Something was very, very wrong, and my rational mind (*brain tumor!*) was beginning to go to war with my gut (*magic!*) and it was giving me a headache.

"I'm gonna go get my drink." I turned on my heel toward the kitchen.

"Good idea," Davina said, and followed me.

I walked into the kitchen, grabbed the scotch she'd poured for me, and downed the rest where I stood.

"Oh, that's—you're drinking that fast, baby." Davina shook her head back and forth, *tsking* like a metronome. "That is not a good idea."

I handed her my empty glass. "Another."

Davina crossed her arms. "No."

I walked past her, grabbed the bottle of scotch off the counter, whipped the cap off, took a slug, and sputtered for a minute or two as the liquid actively resisted my attempts to swallow it.

"Oh, you're gonna regret that," Davina said under her breath.

I angled my head to look at her. "Am I going to die? Are you, like, an angel of death or something? Coming to get me? And the brain tumor that's killing me is giving me hallucinations? Because that makes sense. Kinda."

Davina took a moment to form her response. "You know what this is. Deep down, you know. But I'll tell you, you keep drinking like that, and you're gonna *wish* you were dead in the morning."

I took another swig. Wasn't so bad this time. My shoulders were starting to relax, and the sharp edges around the memories of the aluminum dog and the bat phone seemed to dull. A little.

"Not a brain tumor," I said. "So, I'm crazy, then?"

"No," she said, the very soul of patience. "You're magic."

I ignored her. "Hallucinations seem like they'd be chemical, though, right? I mean, maybe there's some kind of antipsychotic pill I can take—"

"It's all real," Davina said softly, and I centered my focus on her. She really was beautiful, and she seemed like a basically nice person, gym sock of death notwithstanding.

"Definitely a brain tumor," I said quietly.

Davina raised a brow. "What?"

"You're not real. You can't be—ow!"

I whipped my arm away from her, rubbing the spot on my bicep where she'd pinched me. Hard.

"I'm real," she said.

"And *mean*." I rubbed my arm some more. "That's gonna leave a mark."

"Good. It'll stand as proof that I'm real, and we won't be wasting any more time on this foolishness. You need to get with the program fast, because we do not have time for a mental breakdown right now. Give me that bottle." She reached her hand out for the bottle, but I pulled it back by my shoulder, out of her reach. She huffed in frustration and dropped her hand. "Stop playing games; you obviously cannot drink worth a damn."

I hugged the scotch to my chest. "My brain tumor, my bottle."

And then I thought about my mother and her brain tumor. Her death, which had been extended and heartbreaking and terrifying. And even though I knew—or suspected, anyway—that I didn't really have a brain tumor, that what I was going through was not quite that mundane or straightforward, my stomach flipped inside, anyway, because the imagining of your own impending death brings with it both terror and a dose of clarity.

"I've got something I have to do." I put the bottle down on the counter and started toward the kitchen door.

"Baby?"

I walked out of the kitchen. Davina didn't say anything, but I heard her light footsteps trailing me through the hallway, out the front door . . .

. . . and toward Tobias's apartment.

Five minutes later, just as I was turning the corner onto Rosewood Lane, Davina caught up to me.

"Olivia?" she said, huffing as she hurried to match her pace with mine. "Where are we going, exactly?"

I turned the corner onto Rosewood. "It's not far."

"What's not far?"

We walked the three blocks down Rosewood Lane in silence until I got to Tobias's apartment building on the corner of Main Street. It was a huge Victorian, painted lavender with pale yellow trim and divided into four apartments, one for each level, including the attic. Seven people living in roughly the same amount of space I occupied all by myself.

"What's here?" Davina asked. I darted up the porch steps, found the button labeled SHOOP, and lay on it.

"Who paints a house purple?" she asked, and I shot her a look. She met my glance, her eyes widened, and she said, "I mean, *pink* is completely within the realm of acceptable house colors, but *purple* . . ."

Tobias came down the inside steps to open the front door. He was wearing a white T-shirt and gray sweats and even in my compromised state, I felt twin surges of happiness and dread. For his part, he seemed really happy to see me there, which twisted that mixed-signal knife even more. He waved at me through the glass, then opened the door.

"Hey." He leaned against the doorjamb and looked down at me, his smile wide and genuine. "What's up?"

"I turned a phone into a bat."

His face registered something and he sniffed. "Liv? You didn't accidentally fall in a vat of scotch again, did you?"

"Not accidentally." I stepped aside and grabbed Davina's arm, pulling her up next to me. "Do you see this woman?"

Tobias's eyes landed on Davina, and cooled a bit. "Oh, yeah. Chocolate Belgian waffles, right?"

"That's me." Davina's voice was flat and unamused.

"Okay, so you see her?" I asked. "She's all . . . real, and everything?"

"I see her." Tobias focused on me, the distant expression in his face morphing into concern. "You okay?"

"Could still be a tumor," I muttered.

"It's not a tumor," Davina said.

"Well, of course *you'd* say that," I said.

Tobias kept his eyes on Davina for a moment longer, then turned to me, putting his hands on both my shoulders. "Liv? You okay?"

"No," I said. "I turned a *phone* into a *bat.*"

"We've had a few drinks." Davina reached her hand out to him. "I'm Davina Granville. Liv's aunt."

Tobias held my eye for a moment before reaching out to take her hand. "Nice to meet you. Tobias Shoop."

"Davina's the Women's Ultimate Frisbee Champion, University of Louisiana, 1981." I busted out into giggles. That seemed really funny to me all of a sudden.

"Yeah. You're cut off." Tobias put his hand on my elbow and pulled me inside, then held the door open for Davina and jerked his head toward his apartment in invitation. "Come on. I'll make you guys some coffee."

"I think I'm gonna go on home," Davina said. "I've got some things to take care of. She should be okay with you, for tonight. You'll keep her safe?"

Tobias hesitated for a second, then said, "Yeah."

"I'll see you tomorrow, Liv," Davina said, then disappeared into the dusk.

Tobias shut the door, double-checked that it was locked and turned to look at me, his eyes sharp and sober. "Liv?"

"I'm sorry," I said. "About the other day. The thing with Stacy, and . . . you know." I rolled my eyes. "Just everything before that. I don't want us to be mad at each other anymore."

He hesitated for a bit, watching me. I stayed frozen, barely breathing, waiting for him to just say *something,* damnit. But after all that hesitation, he just said, "Come on upstairs and I'll make you some coffee."

He stepped back in the foyer to let me by, and I led the way up the stairwell to his apartment. I'd been there a few times, although usually we hung out at my place because it was bigger. It was one long open room, with finished walls all the way up to the top where they met in a steep angle, and dark-stained support beams spanning across overhead. Four window seats sat in the cutout windows on each side of the length, and bookcases filled every bit of wall space between them. At the north end was a wall that separated his bedroom and bathroom from the big kitchenette, living room, and dining area. All told, maybe eight hundred square feet. The perfect amount of space for one person. Or two.

He grabbed a blanket off the back of his couch and wrapped it around my shoulders, then sat me down. The couch was really ugly, some kind of plain brown corduroy thing, but it was so soft and welcoming that I sank into it, sighing. Then he went to the kitchenette. I stared out the window at the streetlights while the coffee brewed, and it seemed like just seconds later when he was holding out a mug to me. Possibly, I may have nodded off for a minute.

I took the mug and held it under my nose, breathing in the comforting scent. Tobias sat across from me on the old shipping trunk he used for a coffee table, rested his elbows on his knees, and looked at me.

We sat in silence for a while, and he said, "I don't think I've ever seen you drunk before."

I snorted and looked up. "It's been that kind of a week."

He leaned forward, elbows on his knees, eyes on me. "I want you to tell me what's going on."

I let my eyes drop to the floor. "Nothing's going on." *Except that I might be crazy. Or possibly dying.*

Or worse.

"You know you can tell me, right?" he said. "Whatever's happening to you, no matter how crazy it sounds. I'll believe you."

I thought about that for a bit. Reversing the situation, would I believe him if he told me that his fairy godmother had shown up and given him magical powers that made him turn household objects into living critters?

No. But then, I wasn't as good a person as he was. Still . . .

"Nothing's going on," I repeated, meeting his eye steadily.

He went quiet for a moment, then stood up. "Come on."

I looked up at him. "We're going somewhere?"

He jerked his head toward his kitchenette. "I'm gonna feed you before you puke eighty-proof all over my couch."

I glanced back at the couch as he grabbed my arm and pulled me up. "Yeah, I don't think anything's going to make that couch worse."

He led me to the kitchen island counter, where I sat on a stool. He moved around the kitchen, grabbing flour and eggs and oranges and something from the spice rack, and it looked like dancing, his movements were so smooth. I had watched him cook at work, and he was always in command, moving fast and lithe, but at home, he cooked like it was fun. He smiled and teased me and it felt like it had always been, the two of us comfortable in our little bubble where we were always us and nothing would ever change.

"Okay," he said as he drizzled the hot syrup over the tops of the two plates of waffles, "these are cinnamon orange Belgians with an amaretto pecan caramel sauce. It's my own recipe, so if you hate it, lie."

He placed the plate in front of me, and I looked up at him.

"Waffles? Really?"

He put a fork in my hand. "The best you've ever had, yeah."

I raised the fork, and could see Tobias watching me with a big smile out of the corner of my eye. I cut off a bite, put it on the fork, and then hesitated.

"Something wrong?" Tobias asked.

"No." I lowered the fork down an inch, then another. The warring voices inside my head said, *You've already had eighteen hundred calories today, and that was before the liquor,* and the other said, *oh my god they smell so goooooooood . . .*

"What's the matter?" he asked.

I white-knuckled the fork. "I've given up waffles. Well, most food, really, but specifically waffles."

"You love waffles."

"I know."

"This doesn't make any sense."

"It's just that I was already at my calorie limit for the day before I had the liquor, and I want to go to Europe in my skinny jeans."

"What the hell are skinny jeans?"

"They're the jeans that you buy that are too small so that someday you can wear them and feel awesome."

He put his fork down and stared at me, openmouthed. "There are so many things wrong with that sentence. I don't even know where to start."

"It's okay. This is advanced self-loathing. You'd have to be a woman to understand it at this level."

He pinched a bit of the denim above my knee. "What's wrong with these jeans?"

His touch sent tingles up my thigh, and I pulled my knee back a bit. "They fit."

"Jesus Christ." He snatched my plate away from me and started cutting into my waffles with his fork.

"I don't want to be super-skinny, I just think if I lost—"

"Doesn't even matter what I say here, does it?"

"—twenty pounds or so . . . What? Why are you looking at me like that?"

"This is my standard expression when I'm staring into an abyss."

"Don't blame me. I'm just a product of my misogynistic environment."

He stabbed a bite of waffles expertly with the fork. "Fucking hell."

"I don't—" But I couldn't finish what I was saying, because

he shoved the bite in. The first thing I noticed was the warmth, followed by the sweetness of the caramelized pecans, then I chewed and the waffles crunched a bit before giving way to the pastry inside, fluffy and light and wonderful and accepting. I unwittingly made a vaguely sexual sound, then put my hand to my mouth. "Pardon me. Little foodgasm there."

He grinned, then dug back into his waffles before looking at me again, the smile replaced by a look of revelation. "Is that why you don't eat at work anymore? You're on a diet?"

I cut off another small bite with the side of my fork. "You noticed that I stopped eating at work?"

He nodded, then lowered his eyes. "I thought it was because you were too pissed off at me to eat my food."

There was a long moment of quiet, and I could feel the comfy confines of our bubble beginning to stretch.

So I popped it.

"I love you."

He raised his gaze to meet mine. He didn't look surprised, or freaked out, or anything, really, which meant he already knew. Which was fine.

"That's what's causing all the problems between us," I went on. "It's why I keep getting upset. It's why I decided to go to Europe. It's why the Stacy Easter thing tweaked me so bad. And tonight, when I was thinking about the brain tumor, I just realized how much it doesn't matter."

Tobias's face darkened with concern. "You have a brain tumor?"

I sighed. "No. But for a few moments tonight, I thought . . . maybe. Maybe it's a brain tumor, maybe I'm going to die. And when I thought I was dying, I thought of you. I wanted to come right over here and spend what time I had left with you. And you know, whether I'm dying or getting on a plane, whether you love me back or not, I'm still leaving, and I want us to have time to say good-bye. The drama doesn't matter, and I don't care about it. I just want to be able to say good-bye, and I want to leave feeling like I did it right."

I stepped off the stool and gathered my plate and his, bringing them to the sink. I had just turned on the water when he grabbed my arm.

"Don't even think about arguing with me," I said. "You cooked, I clean. Them's the rules."

He whirled me around so fast, I hardly knew what was happening until the kiss was already underway. At first, his lips were soft and insistent upon mine, but then it caught fire, his tongue making magic against mine as his arms pulled me tight against him. My hands clawed at his back and he lifted me to sit on the counter, my legs open as he pressed against me, clutching at my shirt, balling the fabric in his fist as his other hand cradled the back of my head. It was the kind of kiss that makes your heart pound so hard you're dizzy when it's over, and when he finally pulled back from me, it took a moment for me to catch my breath. He put his hands on the counter on either side of me, holding himself up as he rested his forehead on my shoulder. Then he pushed himself back from me and I could tell by the expression on his face that I was probably going to want to hit him in a moment.

"What *is* it with you?" I said. "I swear to god, if you tell me you're married or a secret agent or something, I'm gonna brain you with that frying pan."

He raised his eyes to meet mine. "If I told you there was a good reason why this is a bad idea, would you just trust me and not ask why?"

"You mean, if you said that, but didn't *tell* me the good reason?"

His eyes met mine, and the look in them was pleading. "Can you please trust me? Can we do the dishes and go watch a movie and table this for just a little while longer?"

I nibbled my lip, and thought about it for a long moment. Could I trust him that whatever his reason for the extreme mixed signals was good and right? Trust him, even though he either couldn't or didn't want to tell me, despite the fact that neither of those realities was a good sign? Trust him, even though if Peach or Millie or Stacy came to me and said the man they loved was behaving like this, I'd tell them to beat him with something that gave a very satisfying *thunk* sound with every hit, and leave him conscious only so that he'd know it when they dumped his ass? Could I do that?

I guessed I could. For a little while, at least.

I hopped off the counter and said, "You dry." He smiled back in stark relief and we did the dishes, then watched the movie until I fell asleep chastely on his shoulder. I only woke up a little when he carried me into his room and laid me on his bed, and went back to the couch. I curled up into his bed and swallowed my disappointment that he hadn't joined me until, finally, I fell asleep again.

6

I woke up, sober and alone, in Tobias's bed at five-thirty the next morning. A dull predawn glow made his windows visible in the dark, but just barely, and I stared at them for a while, thinking.

Then I forced myself out of bed and traipsed quietly into the living room. I slid my shoes on then walked over to where Tobias lay lightly snoring on the couch. I sat down on the leather trunk and watched him for a moment, musing over the fact that he even smiled when he slept. I reached out and touched the hair at the base of his forehead, shifting it gently aside. A small, unconscious smile graced his lips and my heart constricted. He was beautiful, and I loved him, and I was beginning to suspect that he loved me, too, but he was also at that moment the least of my problems.

Ten minutes later, I was at Betty's apartment above CCB's, knocking on the door, filled with cold determination and an atypical clarity. She pulled the door open, wide awake in her fluffy red robe. Her hair was matted against one side of her head and there were pillowcase creases on her cheek.

"I love you, Livvy," she said, pulling me inside, "but it's the butt crack of dawn. Someone better be dead or on fire."

I shut the door behind me with a quiet click as she shuffled into the little kitchenette. "Do you have an empty coffee mug I can borrow?"

"An empty coffee mug?" She stared at me for a moment. "That couldn't wait until a reasonable hour?"

I shook my head. She watched me for a moment, then shrugged and got a red ceramic mug out of the cabinet and handed it to me. "This had better be good, or I'm going to have to kill you with my bare hands. And I'm old. That could take awhile."

"Is this special?" I asked. "Any sentimental value or . . . anything?"

She shook her head. "I got them six for ten dollars on clearance. I'm pretty sure they've got lead in them."

"Okay." I pulled it in toward my chest and closed my eyes, then opened them. "You might want to stand back. Just in case it breaks or something."

Betty stepped a few paces back. I closed my eyes and hugged the mug to me, concentrating on the tingling in my hands. I felt the energy intensify a bit and I tried to focus it into the mug. I imagined it turning into a furry, cute, harmless squirrel and for a moment, I thought I felt something like burning in my palms, but when I opened my eyes and held it out in front of me, it was still a mug.

"You can keep it if you like it that much," she said.

"No. I'm just . . . I'm trying something, and I need you to see it. I need someone I know and trust to check me on this, and since all of my other relationships are kind of a mess at the moment . . . that's you."

She put her hand over her heart and gave a wide, ironic smile. "I'm the only one left, so I get woken up at the butt crack of dawn? I'm touched."

I felt tears come to my eyes, but I blinked them away. "You'll still love me even if I'm crazy or dying of a brain tumor or carrying some kind of alien mutant virus, right?" I still hadn't quite worked out all my theories.

Betty's irony faded, leaving a slightly worried expression in its wake. "Alien mutant virus?"

"You'll understand it better once you've seen it." I swallowed back the weird swell of emotion and tried to concentrate on the task at hand. "I just need you to stand there and watch me. Don't take your eyes off the mug, okay, in case it doesn't last too long. Can you do that?"

Betty released a breath, seeming even more nervous than I was. "Absolutely."

"Okay." I took a deep breath and looked at the mug, unsure of what to do now. What was different from the other times?

Intensity.

Okay, then. I closed my eyes and thought of Tobias. I thought about the first time we'd met, working a busy Tuesday night together, instantly in sync as if we'd been working together for years. I thought about how he'd smiled at me the night before while making waffles. The tingling ran up my arms, intensifying. I clutched the mug to my chest and thought of what it would be like to kiss him, to make love with him, and I was overwhelmed with the want of him, and the tingling intensified.

And then Stacy Easter walked into the fantasy, crooked her finger, and he dropped me in a heartbeat.

And that thought pretty much killed the tingling.

"Damn." I opened my eyes, and looked around. Both of the other times I'd done it, I'd been seriously freaked out. Was it sparked by fear? Maybe. I looked at Betty. "Do you think you can scare me?"

Betty smiled. "Oh, honey, I'm not very— BOO!" and she lunged at me. It startled me a bit, but it wasn't enough. I closed my eyes and tried to clear my mind, opening it to receive something that would adequately freak me out, if I just kept my mind clear—

It's your magic, baby. Isn't it beautiful?

I saw Davina's face, smiling brightly as she watched the bat phone fly around her. Then she looked at me, and spoke, but it wasn't her voice, it was the guy from the alley, Cain.

Is your father Gabriel Ford?

No, I said, and the bat phone lunged at me. I ducked and fell to the floor.

This is your destiny, baby, Davina said, in her own voice now, as she moved toward me. *It wasn't right, them not letting you be what you are.*

My arms felt rubbery, tingly, hot, the energy buzzing through my body, and I cried out, afraid and desperate to get away.

I hadn't felt myself fall, but when the water hit my face, I sputtered to consciousness flat on my back on the floor of Betty's kitchen. I swiped at my eyes, yelled, "I'm okay!" and the water stopped. I looked up to see Betty standing over me, the cold water pitcher she kept in her refrigerator at the ready. I put my hand on my forehead, dizzy. My heart was still beating so fast and so hard, I could feel it. It almost felt outside of my chest. It almost felt—

It almost felt like it was crawling down my stomach.

I lifted my head and looked down. A red ceramic bunny nose twitched at me, pushing out from the back of the mug. The handle at the other end had contracted in on itself to form the tail. Above the face of the bunny, two flopped-over ears stretched out from the rim of the mug. The body of the mug was rounded, and it puffed in and out, like the thing was breathing. The foot of the ceramic mug had sprouted bunny feet. The top of the mug was still open, sort of as if the top hump of the bunny's back had been sliced off, but it contracted and moved as though a full back were there, invisible muscles working to propel the mug bunny as it hopped down my leg, where it dropped down, landing with an awkward clunk on Betty's white tiled floor. I shifted up and away from it until I was sitting with my back resting against the refrigerator, watching the mug bunny as it stuck its little nose under the cabinet and sniffed around. I looked down at my fingers, and could see the fading wisps of yellow light dancing around them, like strands of smoky yarn. I shook them out, and the strands danced away, then dissipated.

"I think I'm gonna need the day off work," I said, unable to take my eyes off the mug bunny.

Betty knelt down beside me and we were both silent for a long time, just watching the bunny. "Well, I'll be damned."

"Yeah," I said, trying to figure out a way to explain it. "So . . . I'm thinking . . . alien mutant virus?"

"Nope," Betty said.

I looked up at her. "Well, it can't be a brain tumor. Unless it's contagious and we're sharing delusions. But that . . ." I shook my head. "No, that doesn't make sense, either."

"It's not a brain tumor."

And then I looked up at her, noticing for the first time that she seemed neither amazed nor surprised that I had just turned her ordinary coffee mug into a living, breathing critter.

"Betty?" I said, suspicion in my voice. "You know something about this?"

Betty put her hand on my shoulder. "Livvy, I think it's time we had a talk."

I sat in Booth 9, staring at my hands folded in front of me on the table. Betty sat across from me, apparently waiting for me to start, but I didn't know *where* to start, so I just sat there, my mind so beyond reeling it was blank. Next to me, on the padded booth seat, the mug bunny I'd made continued to squeak and toddle around in the orange shoebox Betty had given me to put him in. Every now and again, just to be sure it was all real, I looked at him, and he'd twitch his little red ceramic nose at me.

Yep. It was real.

"Okay," Betty said finally. "Let's get started." She went behind the counter, then came back with two empty coffee mugs. She set them down on the table and took her place across from me.

I picked up the mug and looked at it. "Anything in particular you want? Squirrel, mouse, a tiny ceramic cat, perhaps?"

"Shhhh," she said, and closed her eyes. She took the mug from me, cupped her hands around it, and set it on the table. After a moment, a blue light began to swirl inside of it, and a moment later, it was filled with a dark, steaming liquid.

"Arabica roast, cream and sugar, just the way you like it." She smiled. "It's what I do. I make breakfast food. All of us have powers, mostly little things like this, or what you do, but aside from that, we're perfectly normal. Human. And we live perfectly normal, human lives. Okay?"

I blinked at her. "Us?" I said, finally. "How many are there?"

She shrugged. "Not many. I once heard it was about one in a hundred thousand people, but I don't think there's ever been a real survey. A lot of us like to stay hidden, blend in."

"So, there are more . . . people like us? In Nodaway?"

"Hmmm. Don't think so. Just you and me, far as I know." She leaned forward. "You look hungry. Would you like some pastry? I'm especially good with pastry."

"No." My limbs were still buzzy and my brain was still numb, and I didn't think a muffin was going to cure that. "No, thank you."

"Wanna see something cool?" Without waiting for my answer, she closed her eyes, swirled her hands around, and there was an electric zapping sound, followed by a blue light. When I glanced down, a dark, flat pastry glistening with butter and sugar sat on the table in front of me.

There was pride in Betty's smile. "Genuine Grecian baklava. Melts in your mouth. Try some."

"It doesn't come on a plate?"

"I make the food, not the plates. But the table's clean."

"That's not where all the food here comes from, right?" I asked, suddenly suspicious of the baklava. "I mean, you don't just—" I made a whooshing movement with my hands that was supposed to symbolize the magic.

"Oh, hell no." Betty leaned back and smoothed her hands over her hair. "Doing it that much would probably kill me. A girl only has so much juice. No, we do things the old-fashioned way here. Plus, I'm day magic, like you, so I wouldn't be able to feed anyone at night. We can't do it unless the sun's up."

"Oh." I thought back to all my incidents, and realized they had all happened during the day. "Why is that?"

"Beats the hell out of me, that's just how it works. The religious whacks believe it has something to do with eternal natural balance, blah blah blah. I think it's genetic." She shrugged, then smiled brightly. "How about some Danish?" She swooshed her hands over the table, some blue electric light *zip-zapped,* and two Danish bounced off my head and onto the floor. "Sorry, Livvy. Bad aim there."

I stared down at the Danish on the floor, still trying to process. "Right."

"It's not as scary as it seems," she said. "I mean, I knew one girl growing up whose only power was the ability to change the color of tomatoes. So, you make inanimate objects come to life. It's really not that big a deal."

I pondered that for a moment, then said, "It's a big deal."

"Eh." She broke off a bit of Danish and stuffed it in her

mouth. "So . . . are you sure you're not hungry? Not to toot my own horn, but this stuff is amazing."

"No." I shook my head. "Thank you."

"Suit yourself," she said, and took another bite.

Zip-zap, and an English muffin appeared on the table in front of me.

"Sorry," Betty said, grabbing a napkin, wrapping it around the muffin, and tossing it on the seat next to her. "It gets a little out of control sometimes when I'm tense."

"*I'm* the one who just found out my life is a lie. Why are *you* tense?"

"Because I have to tell you about it. This was not the plan. Your mother was supposed to live long enough to be the one dealing with all of this."

Zzzzzzttt. Five glazed doughnuts landed on the table out of thin air. Betty put her hand over her mug, swirled it around, and I could smell her favorite orange spice tea in the steam that wafted over the table. She took a sip and set the mug down. "Okay. Let's start with you. Do you have any questions?"

I picked up the orange shoebox and set it between the baklava and the doughnuts. "One or two."

"Right." She smiled. "Well, let's start with the obvious. Liv, you're a Magical. Meaning someone with power that extends beyond normal human experience. Congratulations."

"Wow." I wrapped my hands around my steaming mug of coffee, not quite ready to drink it, but appreciating the warmth of it in my hands. "Can't tell you how helpful that heads-up would have been a week ago."

She met my eye, her patience obviously waning. "Would you have believed me if I had told you a week ago?"

I thought about that, and conceded. "Fair enough."

"Okay, then." Betty sighed. "Let's start from the beginning." Pause. "Your father is not Some Guy Named Dave."

I nodded. I'd sort of put that together. At the same time, I didn't want to say his name, so I just kept quiet and let Betty speak.

Betty nodded. "When you were just a baby, your family was in danger. Real, serious, gonna-get-you-all-killed danger. Your father decided to split the family up; it's easier to hide two people than four. He brought your mom and you here to me, and he took your sister and went somewhere else."

I blinked a few times, my mind running back through what she'd told me. "I have a sister?"

She nodded. "Holly. She was a cute little thing."

"Where is she?"

Betty shrugged. "I don't know. The last time I saw either one of them was that night your father brought you and Amelia here to me."

I looked at her for a long moment, remembering the mournful date my mother inexplicably spent staring off into space every year. "October fifth?"

Betty's eyebrows knit. "I don't know. It was in the fall, I think. Why?"

I shook my head. "No reason." I put my hand to my forehead. "I'm a little dizzy."

"Understandable," she said. "Have a doughnut."

I shook my head. "Wait. Okay. So, people were after us? Why?"

"There was something special about Gabriel's power, although Amelia never told me exactly what. But it was dangerous enough that he split the family up to keep you all safe."

"So he . . . he never left her?"

Betty looked at me. "He left. Have you seen him for the last twenty-eight years?"

"No. I mean . . ." I shook my head, trying to get it all clear. "He loved her? He didn't leave *her*?"

Betty's expression cleared. "He loved her, and you. I've never seen a man so unhappy in all my life as your dad was when he left here that night." She sighed, closed her eyes, and said, "Move the bunny."

"Hmmm?" I said, and then there was a blue *zip-zap* over the mug bunny's shoebox. I pulled it out just in time for a huge chocolate cake to splat down in the center of the table.

"Wow," I said, setting the mug bunny on the seat next to me.

"Yeah," Betty said, and dug in with one finger, stuffing her cake in her mouth and closing her eyes again. "Mmmm. I make the best chocolate cakes ever. Have some."

"No, thanks."

Her eyes whipped open and flashed with threat. "Have some."

I dug one finger into the cake, and then put it to my lips. At first, I tasted it tentatively, somehow expecting it to zap me with blue lightning or something, but it was just cake. It was perfectly moist, and held the slightest hint of something exotic—

cinnamon? nutmeg?—and was, hands down, the best chocolate cake I'd ever tasted in my life.

"Mmmm, good." I licked the last bit off my finger.

"See? Nothing happened to you. It's not scary or dangerous, it's just who we are."

I thought about Tobias, making me waffles last night, using a waffle iron and batter, the way God intended. "I liked who I was."

Betty dug another chunk out of the cake. "Yeah, well, those days are gone, honey." She raised her eyes to meet mine, and her look was serious. "So now, let's talk about you."

7

I swallowed a chunk of cake down. "Me?"

She leveled her eyes at me. "We bound your power when you were a baby, but now it's here, and we need to deal with that."

"Wait—you *bound* my power?"

She stared at me like I was stupid. "You were supposed to be a normal kid. We couldn't very well have you running around making turtles out of plates, now, could we?"

"No." I sat back. "Guess not."

"Eventually, your power was going to come out. This was never not going to happen. To be honest, I was expecting it all to hit the fan when your mother died; emotional trauma can do it. That's why most Magicals get their power at puberty. And it may not be a big deal, really. Just because you got your power, it doesn't necessarily put you in more danger than you were in last week. It's just that if the people who were after you guys find out you've got power, they might come after you again. So we need to have this talk just so you know to be careful and all that."

"Oh, shit," I said.

Betty's eyes widened. "What?"

"There's a woman, Davina. Last Friday, she showed up here

and threw a stinky gym sock at me, telling me I was magic and that I should be what I am, or something like that."

Betty's eyes widened. "And you're just telling me this *now*?"

"I thought she was insane. We get insane people in CCB's every day. But last night, she came to the house, and talked to me about the magic, and I turned my phone into a bat."

"You turned a phone into a bat in front of someone?" She shook her head. "Way to bury the lead, kid."

"There's more . . ."

She put her hand to her forehead. "Oh, Christ in a bucket."

"Sunday, I bumped into a guy in the alley outside Happy Larry's, and I turned a trash can lid into a dog in front of him." I swallowed. "Davina said his name is Cain, and that he wants to kill her."

Betty stared at me for a while, then pushed up from the table. "Pack your stuff. We're going to the airport."

I stood up as well. "Wait. Let me think a minute."

"Think while you're packing. You're going to Europe in a few weeks anyway, we'll just change your ticket when we get there and send you now."

"Wait. How did you know about Europe?"

"Tobias told me. He asked me if I really thought you would go, and I said no, but right now, I say yes. You go."

"I can't go now."

"Why not?"

"Because we don't know what these people want, or who they are. Davina actually seems kind of nice. A little crazy, but nice. And she protected me when Cain surprised me in that alley. As for Cain . . . well . . ." I felt a shiver go through me at the memory of him in that alley. "Okay, he might be dangerous, but running away isn't the answer. If they found me here, it's just a matter of time before they find me somewhere else." I took a deep breath. "We're just going to need to figure out another solution."

Betty stood there for a moment, her eyes sharp on mine, and then she sat down again. "Any ideas, Mary Poppins?"

"Well . . . you said you bound my power. Couldn't you do that again?"

Betty stared at me for a moment, then shook her head. "No."

"Why not? You did it before."

"No. Your *father* did it before. Gotta be a blood relative, and even then, things get complicated past the age of reason, about seven or eight. There's free will to be messed with and that's where things get dark with magic. It's not a good place to go."

"But it's *my* free will," I said. "*I* will it. And complicated doesn't mean impossible, right? I mean, the spell worked well into my twenties. That means it can work again."

"It's got to be a blood relative, Liv. You're kind of short on those."

"I have a father and a sister out there somewhere," I said, feeling my heart rise at the thought. *Family.* "I'll just find them."

"It's not easy finding people who don't want to be found. I tried when your mother died, I wanted to tell them, but I couldn't find them. And I hired a real private detective. From Buffalo."

I met her eye. "Okay, but I'm not going to Europe. Not yet."

"Okay." She reached across the table and patted my hand. "We'll think of something else, then. In the meantime, though, you're officially on sabbatical. I want you home, safe, and out of the public eye until we get a plan together."

There was a long moment of silence between us, then I dug out a chunk of chocolate cake and stuffed it in my mouth. "Oh my god, Betty, this is really, *really* good."

It took a moment, but eventually she smiled, then picked off a small chunk for herself. "I know."

I sipped my coffee, which was still hot, and out of the corner of my eye, I caught a glimpse of the sparkly magic square.

"Hey, Betty?" I pointed to the square. "Is it really magic?"

"Hmmm?" She looked at the floor, not seeming to see what I was pointing at.

"The sparkly square," I said.

She laughed. "The what?"

I pointed. "That sparkly square. When I was a kid, you told me it was a magic wishing square. And then you told me it wasn't. But I made a few wishes on it and they came true, and in light of recent events, I thought . . . maybe . . ."

"Magic linoleum?" She shook her head. "No. That's just crazy."

It takes awhile to accept that you have magical power, and here's why: It's insane.

It's insane to actually believe that your father was not Some Guy Named Dave, but rather Some Magical Guy Named Gabriel.

It's insane to believe that you can create little woodland creatures from trash can lids, phones, and spare coffee mugs.

It's insane to believe that your boss can conjure baked goods up from thin air, that a stranger in town can bust open your power by throwing a ratty gym sock at you, and that another stranger in town might possibly be here to kill people.

It's *insane.*

And it only took about fourteen hours for me to accept it as truth. Fourteen hours of sitting on my bed, staring at a little red mug bunny and a destroyed, lifeless bat phone. I didn't eat. I didn't sleep. I didn't go to the bathroom. I didn't even really think that much. I just . . . stared.

Mug bunny, meet dead bat phone. Dead bat phone, meet mug bunny.

The truth finally settled around me only once I was in the dark, on my bed. I could just barely see the outline of the mug bunny scooting around my bed, glimmers of reflected moonlight shimmering off the smooth ceramic, and one moment, I was watching it, removed from everything. Then it tumbled off the side, and something inside me shot to life. I gasped and caught it and drew it to my chest and snuggled it, and that's when I knew. That was the moment when I accepted that this was all real, that there were people in the world that had magical power and I was one of them.

"Huh," I said out loud to no one in particular. I patted the mug bunny, and realized I was starving. I put the mug bunny in its shoebox on the floor so it wouldn't get hurt, and I stumbled downstairs in a haze, glancing at the clock on the wall in the kitchen as I went into the refrigerator; it was only nine-thirty. It felt like it should be later, that somehow, days should have passed.

Nothing in the fridge appealed to me, and then I remembered the bag of conjured pastries Betty had sent me home with.

I wandered out into the hallway, but they weren't there. I searched the living room: nada. Finally, I went out onto the porch, flicked on the light, and there was the big brown paper bag Betty had stuffed full for me, sitting on the porch railing.

Huh. I couldn't even remember leaving them there. Then again, when I'd stumbled back from CCB's that morning, I'd been in something of a daze.

I sat down on my porch swing, pulled the top Styrofoam container out of the bag and opened it.

Chocolate cake. Eight gazillion calories of glorious, chocolaty goodness. Then a thought hit me, and I wondered if conjured food has the same calories. What if it had *no* calories? A momentary shiver of glorious wantonness shot through me, and then I came back to reality.

Even I couldn't stretch my imagination that far.

"Liv!"

I looked up to find the source of the voice, and there was Peach, running in place on the sidewalk in front of my house. Her blond hair bounced behind her in a ponytail, and her running outfit clung to her perfect curves as she jogged effortlessly in place. I hesitated at the thought of talking to her while digging into chocolate cake with my bare fingers like a crack addict sucking on a dirty pipe.

If only I'd thought to grab a fork . . .

I set the cake down beside me. "Hey, Peach."

She kept jogging in place, then said, "I'm sorry about before."

I shrugged. "It's okay."

"No, it's not. I was being jerky, and I suck. I'm sorry."

I looked at her and smiled. "Apology accepted."

She grinned back, slowing from jogging in place to just moving her legs a bit. "Good." She waved me toward her. "Come on, run with me and we can talk about everything. I was almost done, but I can squeeze in another mile or two without dropping dead."

I busted out with a sharp laugh. "Seriously? You think I'm going to run a mile?"

She rolled her eyes, smiling. "Fine. We'll power walk. But I tell you, exercise is the best thing when you're feeling like hell. You breathe in the air and your heart gets pumping and it's just . . . whoo! Invigorating. Know what I mean?"

I stared at her. I had just been contemplating downing an entire chocolate cake in one sitting. Of course I didn't know what she meant.

"Yeah, you're probably right, but I don't think so."

"Okay." She touched her neck with two fingers, glanced at her wristwatch, and slowed down the jogging to walking in place. After a few seconds, she stopped moving altogether, then rested both palms on the tree, stuck one leg straight out behind her, and stretched.

"So, are we doing Confessional on Saturday? I really think we should. If you want, I can host, I just have to get all of Nick's landscaping crap out of my living room." She switched her stance, stretching yet another muscle group, although I couldn't tell which one. "Did I tell you about the solar walkway lights he bought when Dunlop's went out of business? Two *freaking* thousand of them, to sell in a town that gets six weeks of sunlight a year."

I stared down at the chocolate cake by my side. Was I really so insecure that I couldn't snarf a little cake just because Peach was a health nut? I was just about to pick it up when I heard wood creaking, and looked up to check where the swing hooks were attached to the porch ceiling. Jeez. You know it's bad when your house starts making commentary on your weight.

"Anyway, of course, he ran out of room in his storage space, so guess where the extras ended—*ow*!"

I jolted at the *thunk* sound. Peach pulled back from the tree, rubbing her shoulder, then bent over and picked up what looked like a pale wooden lime from my yard.

"Walnuts?" she said, picking it up and twirling it in her hand. She glanced up at the tree. "This isn't a walnut tree . . . is it?" She stepped back, staring up into the branches of the tree.

"No. It's an oak," I said, and then I heard it again . . . that creaking. I got off the swing, and the creaking continued. I looked up at the tree, and saw in the light of the streetlamp what looked like long fingers of dark gray smoke swirling oddly around one branch. Then, out of thin air, another walnut appeared and flew down straight at Peach, who jumped out of the way at the last minute. She looked at me. "Are you throwing *walnuts* at me?"

I shook my head, then looked up and down the street; it was quiet, almost ominously so, and the hair on my arms shot up.

"Peach, come up here on the porch, please," I said, trying to keep my voice firm but calm as the creaking sound started up again, louder this time. The trunk of the tree behind her seemed to be shaking now, and the gray smoke was starting to spread through more branches.

"Not if you're throwing things at me. Jeez, Liv, I said I was sorr—*ow*!" A walnut bounced off her head, and she looked up into the branches of the three. "What the hell? Is there a bird or something in there?" She stopped talking suddenly, seeming to freeze where she was, then said slowly, "Liv, is your tree smoking?"

The creaking got louder, the sound approaching violence, and the smoke began to swirl around the branches, weaving between them with will, like snakes.

"Peach, get up here!" I yelled, but Peach just stood there, staring up into the branches, dumbfounded.

I dashed inside and grabbed my biggest umbrella from the holder by the front door, then shot it open as I ran down the front steps to grab Peach. I got her arm just as the walnuts started coming down in force, pelting us in the back and legs as we ran back onto the safety of the porch. We stood there, hands clasped together, staring in disbelief as hundreds of walnuts crashed down onto my yard, bouncing off the ground with unnatural force as they hit. After a few moments, it stopped as suddenly as it had started, and the smoke that had surrounded the branches of my tree seemed to be sucked back into it in a *whoosh*.

Peach was stock-still for a long time, her eyes wide and her mouth shut, and then she turned to me, releasing my hands.

"I think there's something really wrong with your tree, Liv," she said, her voice shaky. I recognized the feeling, that sense of shock as you tried to reconcile something you just witnessed with everything you know about how the world works.

"Yes, there's definitely something wrong." I glanced up and down the street, then gave her my umbrella, which was pock-marked and beaten to a point where I was pretty sure it would never close again. It would get her next door, though, and once she was gone, I could try to figure out what had just happened.

"Why don't you go on home, Peach? I'm gonna call my tree guy."

"Sure." She blinked twice, as if she was still trying to process what had happened, and then flipped the dented umbrella up over her head. "Let me know what you want to do for Confessional on Saturday. I really think we should all . . . you know . . . get together." Her voice shook a little bit, and I patted her shoulder.

"Everything's okay," I said, my voice soft and reassuring. "Go on home."

"Okay." She nodded like a child, and then held the battered umbrella over her head as she made her way next door, giving my oak tree a wide berth as she walked past it toward her house. A moment later, her front door shut and I heard a strange *blurp* sound, like a pop played backward on a sound system. I looked back to the walnuts, which were disappearing one by one, into quickly dissipating puffs of gray smoke.

Blurp-blurp-blurp. Gone.

I stood on my porch for a few minutes, breathing in and out, trying to make sense of what had just happened. It was magic, that much was obvious, but it wasn't the kind of magic Betty and I had. This was malevolent, magic intended to harm, maim, or kill.

Possibly, intended to kill *me*.

I stood there for a moment, lost in thought, and had just started for the front door when something in the corner of my eye made me tense up. I twirled around, and there in the pool of streetlamp light at the end of our lane, stood a woman in a red dress, her ash-blond curls flowing freely around her face in the light breeze.

"Millie?" I whispered. There was no way she could have heard me, but still, she turned and disappeared from the light as soon as I spoke her name. I darted down my porch steps and ran down the road after her. Either she hadn't been trying to elude me, or she wasn't used to the bloodred spike heels she was wearing, but I caught up to her before she'd gone half a block.

"Mill!" I grabbed her arm and turned her to face me. "Mill, what's . . . ? Wow."

Her eyes were made up dark and smoky, and the deep red lip stain brought out the fullness of her mouth. Even her nails were perfectly manicured in the same red. I looked at her again, squinting my eyes at her.

"Millie?"

She smiled sweetly, the same old Millie smile, and I recognized her again. "Yes, Liv, it's me."

"Oh my god." I took a step back to survey her. "Holy crap, Mill."

She gave a little half-twirl, like a shy little girl, and her dress swirled around her legs. "It was time for a change. Do you like it?"

Do I like it? I'd heard stories about women who'd lost a lot of weight and subsequently lost their friends through jealousy, and my mind went to that as I checked out Millie. There was no doubt; she was beautiful. The dress was perfect for her slightly thicker frame, and the little black shrug she wore over her shoulders added an extra sexy element to the outfit. She looked amazing. But did I like it?

No. I wanted to, but something in my gut just wouldn't let me.

I met her eye and smiled. "You look incredible."

She nodded, barely able to contain her exuberance. "I do, don't I?"

"Yeah." I hesitated a moment, then motioned back toward my street. "Hey, did you just see what I just saw over there?"

She blinked, twice. "What?"

"Um . . ." I wasn't sure how to explain it in a way that wouldn't sound completely insane if she hadn't seen anything. "Peach, under the tree in front of my house. All the walnuts fell on her at once. It was . . . really weird."

She worked her face into a frown, but there was a glint in her eye she couldn't hide. Millie wasn't a great liar anyway, but at the moment, she was even worse than usual.

"No," she said, her voice going high with feigned innocence. "I didn't see a thing."

And that's when it hit me; maybe Davina hadn't unleashed just my magic. Maybe she was some kind of magic-freeing fairy godmother, going from town to town and loosing whatever magic had been tied up there.

Maybe I'm not alone.

I took a step closer and touched Millie's shoulder.

"Mill, has anything strange happened to you lately? Like, maybe, a weird, middle-aged black woman throwing a gym sock at you that makes you sneeze? And makes . . . you know . . . maybe other things happen?"

Something flashed in her eyes; she knew what I was talking about, or something about it, anyway. I felt the hope rise within me, and then . . .

"Sorry, Liv." She gave a mild shake of her head, and a shrug of the shoulder. "I have no idea what you're talking about."

"I don't care if it sounds crazy," I said. "Whatever you want to tell me, I'll believe you."

Millie took a moment, eyeing me carefully, and I held my breath, waiting for her to tell me that something strange had happened to her, too. That we were in it together.

That I wasn't alone.

"All I know, Liv," she said, "is that the tree in front of your house is an oak, not a walnut."

I pulled back from her a bit. There was something about the cold enjoyment in her eyes that worried me. This was the same Millie Banning standing before me who I'd known since I was six years old, the same Millie who had helped me stuff my first bra, who had helped me care for my mother, and then bury her, mourning her loss as much as I did. But in a lot of ways, it also wasn't Millie. It was New Millie, and I wasn't entirely sure how I felt about her.

"Okay," I said after a moment. "Hey, we're doing Confessional at my house on Saturday afternoon. Are you coming?"

A deep twinkle shone from her dark eyes. "Oh, yes," she said. "I'll be there. With bells on."

8

I got out of bed early after a night of fitful sleep, then ambled downstairs and watched the early-morning cartoons while I ate my breakfast of coffee, an orange, and a strawberry Pop-Tart. The only thing that was different from every other day off was that now, I had company. It was a magically conjured mug bunny, but hey—beggars and choosers and all that.

"How are you feeling this morning?" I asked the little mug bunny, who tottered around the living room while Wile E. Coyote ran off the edge of the cliff with an anvil in his arms.

"Don't look down," I said.

Wile E. looked down, looked back at me with an expression of tragic realization, and then plummeted immediately out of frame.

"He never listens to me." I took another bite of my Pop-Tart, then picked the bunny up and offered him a bit of it; he didn't appear interested.

"So, is it that you don't eat," I asked him, "or are you maybe a vegan?"

Considering that it had been over twenty-four hours since I'd made him, and he hadn't eaten anything and seemed no worse for the wear for it, I guessed it was option number one.

"I'm feeling edgy," I said to him. "I need to get out of here. Wanna go to the falls?"

In Nodaway, "the falls" referenced a little brook in the woods. One part of it sort of jumps down a bit of a decline, but by no stretch of the imagination is it a true waterfall. Apparently, it was bigger when the town was founded, but even so, when you exist within a hundred miles of Niagara Falls, it's kinda ballsy to add "Falls" onto any town's name unless there are . . . you know . . . *falls* there. Still, it was a nice walk for shaking out your sanity, and my sanity desperately needed some shaking out.

I tucked an old sweatshirt into the bottom of my worn army-navy messenger bag, and set the mug bunny inside. Immediately, it curled up and seemed to go to sleep. I threw on my sneakers, gray sweats, and L'EGGO MY EGGO T-shirt, pulled my hair back into a half-assed ponytail—who was going to see me, anyway?—slid my bag over my shoulder, and went out my front door just as Tobias was turning from the sidewalk onto my walkway.

"Hey," he said, smiling up at me as I froze where I was at the top of my porch steps.

"Hey," I said. "I was just about to take a walk. To the falls."

"Mind if I join you?"

"Not at all." I smiled at him, feeling shaky and tense but somewhat comforted just by the sight of him. "I'd like that."

"Great." He motioned for me to join him, and I fell into step beside him. As we navigated the sidewalks of the village, then the dirt at the edge of the two-laner that passed for Nodaway's highway, we spoke on innocuous subjects, town talk mostly. Maurice Greeley had been in the day before showing off his granddaughter, that kind of thing. Then, when we hit the path in the woods, we started talking about the waffles he'd made for me the other night; I asked him for the recipe, and he told me, and I retained none of it. Then, deep in the woods, we talked about nothing, just went silent and walked together. We reached the falls and sat on the big, flat rock overlooking the inconsequential brook. For the first time in a while, I felt peaceful and at ease.

And then, Tobias spoke.

"So," he said, "I guess your power came in, then?"

I froze, not sure how to respond, and then finally, I said, "My . . . power? What, you mean, like . . . my electricity? It wasn't out."

He looked at me, his expression frank, and I felt my heart clutch in my chest. "Oh. You mean . . ."

"Yes."

"You knew?"

"Yes."

"About the magic. About the . . . things I can do."

"I know about magic, yes."

I shook my head, trying to absorb this. "You knew."

"Yes. Day or night?"

"Day. You *knew?*"

He nodded. "How does it manifest?"

I joke-punched his upper arm. "Bruises. That's how it manifests. Don't skip ahead. You *knew?*"

"Get mad at me later," he said. "Right now, I need answers. How does it manifest?'

"I'll be mad at you now if I want to be mad at you now," I

grumbled, but at the same time I reached into my messenger bag and pulled out the mug bunny and handed it to him. "I turn household objects into woodland creatures, household pets, and common vermin."

He flipped the mug bunny upside down, inspecting the bottom, and the little feet flailed wildly. Then he turned it back upright, and handed it back to me.

"Cute."

"Yeah. It's a growth industry." I tucked the thing, wriggling in objection, back into my messenger bag, and took a moment to breathe and sort out my building fury before turning to look at him again. "So, all that, 'whatever you want to tell me, I'll believe you' stuff. That was about getting me to admit to the magic."

His expression was impenetrable. "I have a job to do. It's important to that job that I know what's going on."

"It's important to making waffles that you know about my magic?"

He shook his head. "No. To protecting you."

"Protecting me? That's your job?"

"Yes."

"So all that 'there's a good reason why this is a bad idea' stuff . . . that was about the job? Of protecting me?"

He met my eye, and for the first time since we started the conversation, I could see some evidence of regret. Not a lot, but it was there. "Don't sleep with the job. Things get messed up when you get emotionally involved."

"I'm a job. Great." I digested that for a minute, then said, "Wait, who hired you?"

"I was hired by your sister to protect you," he said. "She was worried that someone might come after you."

A rush of excitement ran through me, and I jumped to my feet. "My sister? You know Holly? Where is she? I need to find her, I need a blood relative to—"

His eyes met mine, steely dark and businesslike as he said, "She's dead."

I slumped back to sit on the rock, and it took me a moment to catch my breath. Tobias put his hand on my back and ran it down my spine, then lifted it up to do the same again, but I pulled away from him.

He dropped his hand. "I'm sorry."

I huffed. "Sorry for what? That my sister's dead? Or that you lied to me?"

"That your sister's dead," he said.

I glared at him. "You son of a bitch."

"I'm not sorry I lied to you. I did it to keep you safe, and I'd do it again. That's the job."

"Stop saying that," I said. "It's creepy. I'm not a job, I'm a person, and you . . ." I dropped it, unable to sort my feelings. All I knew is that they were unpleasant, but packed for the moment in numbing cotton. Eventually, the cotton would dissipate, and I'd have to feel it, but for the moment, I was okay.

"How did you end up working for my sister?"

"I work for a . . . kind of a security firm, I guess you'd call it. She hired the firm, the firm sent me."

I looked at him. "You never met her?"

He shook his head. "No."

"Tell me everything you know about her."

"Her name was Holly Monroe—"

"Wait, I thought her name was Ford."

He met my eye. "So was yours. When your parents split the family, your mother took the name Kiskey for you and her, and your father took Monroe for him and your sister."

"Right," I said. "The hiding."

He nodded.

"She's dead?" I could feel the cotton dissipating, and I reached for more. I needed my numbness right now.

"Three months ago," Tobias said, his voice quiet.

"How?"

"She was found in the woods. The official word is that she died of exposure, but how a healthy thirty-one-year-old woman dies of exposure in April in Tennessee . . ."

I looked at him. "You think she was killed."

He shrugged. "She was worried enough to hire us to protect you. And then she died mysteriously, so my guess is, she was right to worry."

"Wait. She knew about me?"

"Only your first name, and your mother's first name. She was three when the family split in two, so I guess your father didn't see the point in lying to her."

"Oh! My father! Do you know—?"

I stopped off the look on Tobias's face. He moved a bit toward me, as though considering touching me, but then seemed to think better of the idea.

"Your father's been missing for ten years. Presumed dead."

"Of course." I took in a deep breath, and the understanding came in waves, bringing the hurt along with it. I hadn't realized how badly I wanted my family until that moment. The pain of losing them, even before I'd gotten the chance to know them, promised to cut deep as soon as it got through the cotton. I chose instead to focus on the other pain, and turned my angry gaze on Tobias.

"That's why you showed so much interest in me, why we hung out so much. I was a job."

He hesitated, then said, "At first, yeah."

"And then?"

He looked at me, his eyes dark and intense, and despite the craziness of the whole situation, my heart fluttered with the sudden understanding that my instincts hadn't been wrong about him. He cared about me. Unfortunately, the realization was of small comfort.

"So it wasn't just me," I said. "You did want me."

"I couldn't," he said. "Objectivity is crucial. It can be the difference between keeping you safe and getting you killed."

"Well . . . why didn't you just have them send someone else?"

"They wouldn't," he said. "When a client dies, payments cease, and when payments cease, so does the job."

"But you're still here."

"I'm on leave," he said simply.

"Oh." I stared at the stream, watching the water move gracefully over its bed of stones, wishing it could carry me along with it. "So, you knew this was coming. The magic, I mean."

He sighed. "I knew you had a sister that had magic, that you might have it, too, and that you might be in danger. That's all."

"You knew I had a sister. You knew when she died. And you didn't tell me?"

"I couldn't tell you."

"Why the hell not?"

He let out a sharp, angry laugh. "Well, for one, you wouldn't have believed me."

I had to concede the point. "Maybe not, but—"

"And second, it wasn't the right thing to do. Knowing more than you need to puts you in danger. I couldn't tell you, I was right not to tell you, and given the same choice, I'd make it again."

"Right. I keep forgetting. I'm a job." I got up, slung my messenger bag over my shoulder, and started on the path back home. I could hear his footsteps crunching the twigs on the ground as he followed me.

"Job's over, Tobias. Go home, wherever that is. Not that you'd tell me."

He grabbed my arm, turning me to face him. "We're not done here."

"You may not be," I said, feeling the edges of anger jabbing into me like fiery steel, "but I am."

I tried to wrench my arm out of his grip, but he held on tighter.

"You're hurting me," I said.

He loosened his grip, but didn't let go entirely. "I need you to tell me everything you know about Davina. She's not your aunt. Who is she?"

Blind fury fueled my strength and this time, when I pulled my arm away, he let me go.

"I don't know. A fairy godmother or something. But I can tell you this—out of everyone in my life, she's the only one who has told me the truth. God!" The anger bolted through me, red and hot, riding the waves of the hurt. "How could you, Tobias? How could you know that I had power, that I had *a sister* out there somewhere and not tell me?"

"Part of keeping you safe was making sure you didn't know."

"Yeah? Well, part of being my friend is choosing me over your goddamn job. You just let this whole thing slam into me sideways, without a word of warning." I took in a sharp breath as I realized something. "You *knew* I had a sister when she was still alive. I could have met her."

"That wasn't my call."

"Don't hide behind that. You know it was wrong, you know it, I can tell by the look on your face. Jesus, Tobias. I thought you were my friend. I thought you would put me first."

His eyes went dark with anger. "I put your safety first."

"That was the *job,*" I said. "I'm talking about *me.*"

He went quiet, and my ability to deal crumbled. Hot tears flooded my eyes and I turned away, not wanting him to see. I started down the path, my feet crunching the twigs on the forest floor as I walked away, and I could hear the echo of his footsteps behind me as he followed.

"Liv, wait."

"You're relieved from duty. Go away."

He darted in front of me and blocked my way. "Something's going on. I don't know what, but I think you're in danger, and right now, that's more important than you being pissed off at me."

"I've got Betty and Davina. I'll figure it out." I walked around him and continued down the path, but again, he followed.

"You want to be pissed off at me, fine, but don't be an idiot. Whatever is going on, it's killed your sister, and is likely the reason that your father disappeared. Not taking that seriously because of your fucking pride is just stupid, Liv, and you're not stupid."

"Oh, I'd beg to differ there," I said, giving him a sharp look. "I fell in love with you, didn't I?"

He shut his eyes, released a breath, and opened them again. "We'll get to all that, I promise. But right now, we've got bigger problems."

"No, *I* have bigger problems," I said. "You just need to find a new job."

I continued down the path, but this time, there were only my stomping, crunching footsteps, a fact that filled me with warring factions of relief and distress. I kept moving until I was sure I was completely out of earshot, and then I allowed myself to cry.

It took me the rest of the day to figure out what I needed to do. I spent most of those hours in bed, hanging out with the little red mug bunny and watching streaming TV on my laptop, barely noticing the story lines as I tried to work out my next move in my head. I slept so much that day and night melded together, and when I ate, it was coffee and a Pop-Tart. No matter how I angled everything around in my head, though, wondering what I was going to do, I always came to the same answer. The only answer, really.

Move on.

On Saturday morning as I was toweling my hair dry after

my shower, I heard the door downstairs open, and Davina's voice called, "Baby? You awake? I brought coffee."

I looked at the mug bunny, who was sitting on my bed in his little shoebox. "I bet they knock in Europe." I tucked the mug bunny in my arm and brought him downstairs with me.

"We need to talk," I said when I got to the bottom of the steps. Davina stood in the hallway, a cardboard drink tray in her hand sporting two cups of coffee and some kind of pastry bag. She was smiling, and she looked really pretty in her brightly colored peasant skirt matched with a bright yellow silk shirt, so exuberant next to me in my old jeans and faded purple T-shirt.

"What's going on?" she asked.

"I'm about to disappoint you." I moved toward the front door, holding it open; I didn't expect this to be a long conversation. "You seem like a nice person and everything, really. But this whole magic thing . . . I don't want it."

"What do you mean?" She stared at me for a long moment, then set the coffee tray down on the half-moon hall table. "What's going on?"

"I'm getting rid of the magic."

"Getting rid of it? Why? Did something scare you?"

"Did something scare me? Um, yeah. Every time I pick something up, I'm afraid it's going to sprout wings or whiskers. I have to go out and buy a new phone because I turned my old one *into a bat*. I have no idea what you even feed a ceramic mug bunny. And, I got pelted by magic walnuts the other night." I lifted the right pant leg of my sweats and showed her the fading bruises, then let it drop. "Whatever's going on between you and that Cain guy is your deal. I really don't think he's out

to kill you, but that's between you and him. As for Millie . . ."
I thought about Millie, standing in her red dress at the end of
the street after magically pelting Peach with walnuts, then I
looked at Davina. "You didn't throw your stinky gym sock at
Millie, did you?"

"I'm sorry. You lost me at magic walnuts. Who's Millie?"

"An old friend. Sort of on the short and pudgy side, used to
be a normal person, now she's a bombshell with anger issues?
You don't know her?"

Davina shook her head, then crossed her arms over her chest
and eyed me. "You think she has magic?"

I felt a moment of unease, and then let the front door shut.
"You know, forget the walnuts. It doesn't matter. I probably
imagined the whole thing. The point is, I'm getting rid of my
magic, and then, I'm leaving. I'm going to Europe, and I'm going to take pictures of myself with goats. So, thanks so much
for everything, but you can go do your fairy godmothering with
someone who wants it." I recognized the edge in my voice, and
added, "You know. No offense."

She watched me for a moment, then said, "Mmm-hmmm."

"Mmm-hmmm what?"

"Nothing, it's just . . ." She shrugged, obviously trying to
come up with a nice way to say whatever she was thinking.
"Wherever you go, there you are."

"What the hell is that supposed to mean?"

"It means that your problems will go with you to Europe,
or wherever you end up. Your problem isn't the magic, baby.
It's you."

"So help me god, if you tell me that I had the power within

me to change my life all along and all I have to do is click my heels three times, I'm gonna pop you one."

She laughed, a hearty, lively laugh that somehow, despite the circumstances, made me feel better.

"I'm going to have to take that chance. Because don't you see? You want to do something with your life. This *is* your chance to do something with your life, something important. You have *power*. And not just any old everyday power, either; even among Magicals, you're unique. Power like that, you could do some very important things with it."

"Like what? Turn plates into groundhogs?"

Davina's eyes widened in excitement. "Oh, no. There's so much more to what you can do than that."

"More? Are you insane? I can barely handle this." I held up the mug bunny in my hand. "I'm making woodland creatures out of household goods, and you tell me now that there's *more*?"

"Oh!" Davina laughed and clapped her hands together. "He's cute!"

I lowered him back down. "Not the point."

"Oh, come on. Relax. Hello, little guy." She petted him on the side with her index finger and smiled up at me. "Is it a little guy or a little girl?"

"I don't know. I didn't think to check." I lifted him up and looked underneath while he protested with much twittering and scrambling of little ceramic feet. "I don't know. It just says Gibson." I turned him back upright and he calmed down.

"Gibson," she said. "I like that. That's a good name."

"I'm not naming him." I set him down on the ground, where he clacked across the front-hall floor toward my living room, bouncing into a wall on his way. "I don't want him. I don't want any of this." I swallowed hard, finally saying out loud the plan that I'd had in my head. "I'm going to find my father and have him bind my powers again. Then I'm leaving."

Davina watched me for a moment, her eyes hard. "Oh, that's the plan, is it?"

"Yep." I wished I felt as confident as I was trying to sound.

"I see. And you know where your father is?"

"No." I looked at her, feeling like a surly teen. "That's where you come in. I was kind of hoping you might know something about that."

"I do," she said, and I had just enough time to work up a decent surge of hope when she said, "He's dead."

My heart plummeted. "You know that? For sure? How?"

"I don't know, not for sure. But he's been missing for ten years and I just don't think your plan is exactly . . . realistic." Davina reached out and touched my arm. "I'm sorry. I really am. I knew your father, he was a good man, and it was a great loss to the community when he died—"

I gave her a sharp look, and she changed course.

". . . I mean, *went missing,* but I'm afraid for you that this determination to find him is going to bring you nothing but heartache."

"I'll take that chance." And then I had a thought. "Unless I don't need to find him. Hey." I pointed a finger at her. "You did this to me. You can undo it. Un-whammy me."

Davina crossed her arms over her chest and gave me a doubtful look. "Un-whammy you?"

"Yes, get out your stinky gym sock and take it back."

"Doesn't work that way. And what's more, I wouldn't do it if it did. I gave you a gift, and I don't mind saying, I think you're being a mite ungrateful about it."

"Fine." I pulled the door open again. "Then it's back to Plan A. If not my father, then there's got to be a grandparent or a cousin or someone out there I can find who can do this. I don't mean to be rude, but I've got things to do. So, it was nice seeing you, but . . ."

She stood where she was for a moment, then said, "So that's it?"

I nodded. "That's it."

"You don't even care what kind of danger people are in?"

I paused, leaning on the doorknob. "Who's in danger?"

She hesitated, and said, "I'm not sure. But this thing with your friend and the walnuts . . . you said it was at night? After dark?"

"Yeah, but I could have imagined all that." I thought about the gray smoke, the walnuts falling from the oak tree. "Okay. Maybe not."

"It must be him," she said quietly, a troubled look on her face. "He's started it, then."

I felt a shiver of unease, and I shut the door again.

"Who's started what?"

She looked at me. "Baby, this may come as a surprise to you, but this whole thing? Is not just about you. I came to find you because I wanted to get to you before he did, and it's a good thing I did, but now . . ." She bit her lip and said, "He's doing the same thing he did in Tennessee."

I touched her arm. "Who?"

She met my eyes. "Cain."

"Cain?" I said. "The drunk guy from the alley? The one you knocked out with a trash-can Frisbee?"

She shook her head. "Don't underestimate him. He's much more dangerous than he seems. If he finds out who you are . . ."

I felt a shock of panic go through me. "He knows who I am," I said. "He asked me if my father was Gabriel Ford. I said no because I didn't know who my father was, but he obviously did."

Davina closed her eyes, released a breath through her nose. "Why didn't you tell me that before?"

"I didn't think it meant anything. It means something?"

"It means everything." She grabbed her coffee cup out of the carrier and walked into the living room. I grabbed mine, and followed her.

"Davina, who exactly is this guy?"

She cleared off a space on the couch, sat down, then looked up at me, a grave expression on her face.

"This guy," she said on a grim sigh, "is the man who killed your sister."

9

"You mean . . . Holly?" I said.

Davina's eyebrows raised up in surprise. "You know about her?"

"Yeah." My chest tightened a bit, and I said, "So it was that guy, Cain? He killed her?"

Davina nodded solemnly.

"And now he's here for me?"

"Well . . ." She sighed. "Yes."

I tried to process this information, but couldn't get anywhere with it. I knew I should be feeling something, but mostly, I was just hollow. "I don't understand any of this. What is so special about us that people are trying to kill us?"

"It's power, baby. Power is everything. All the killing, all the evil, all the tragedy in the world, it's all about who's in charge. The only thing that kept magic people marginally safe were the facts that the powers were usually fairly tame, and they couldn't be stolen. You were either born to it, or you weren't. As long as Magicals stayed closeted and didn't present a threat, it was okay. But then, your father got his power and he was . . . different."

I leaned forward, hungry for details. "Different how?"

"He was the first known Magical who could manifest his power by will." She met my eye. "Do you understand what that means?"

"Nope."

"It means that there was no limit to what he could do. Most Magicals have innocuous powers. Some can make flowers grow faster. Some can maybe make things fly, set things on fire without a match. Simple things. Harmless, mostly. But imagine someone who could decide what power they wanted, practice a bit, and make it a reality." And here, her expression grew dark. "Imagine if there was a way for a non-Magical to force that person to will that power away."

I felt a shiver go down my spine. "But I thought . . . you know . . . free will, and everything. I thought that was important."

"It's important to the people who care about what the darkness does to their soul," she said, her voice low. "Some people care about the power more. Cain's one of those people."

"Okay, now . . . who the hell is Cain?"

"He's a conjurer . . . a witch, sort of. Someone who uses natural elements and potions to create magic, but who is not magical by nature." She gave a small, humble nod. "I'm a conjurer as well, although I really just dabble. I'm not nearly as powerful as he is."

I took a moment to absorb this. "So, Cain found Holly and killed her?"

"I still don't believe he intended to kill her. He's crazy, but not homicidal. It was an accident, I believe, an unintended consequence of stealing the power from her." She raised her eyes back to mine. "But now, see, we've got a problem."

"*Now* we have a problem? Didn't have one when he killed my sister, but *now* . . . ?"

She nodded. "Since taking your sister's magic, Cain has been slowly losing his grip. The transition from day to night, from no power to power, it's taking a toll. But it's not like he's going to give up the power so . . ." She eyed me. "He's figured out another solution."

I thought on this a moment, then finished her thought. "Me. If he takes my day magic, he doesn't have to deal with the transition."

Davina nodded. "I knew he was searching, and so I searched, too, and I found you. That's what the test was about, the gym sock? The sneezing? I had to be sure it was really you. And then, you turned out to have day magic. You're exactly what he needs."

"No, no, I'm not anything," I said, standing up. "I'm going to find my father and have my powers bound and—"

Davina stood up as well. "It's too late for that. Cain's found you, he's not going to let you go." She grabbed my hands and held them in hers, nice and warm and comforting. "But there's good news here."

I stared at her. "Hmmm. Missing father. Dead sister. A crazed conjuring killer after me. Somehow I missed the silver lining."

"Well, for one, he won't try to take anything from you yet. You're not strong enough. You would die before he could get enough juice out of you."

I swallowed. "*That's* the bright side?"

She smiled, her expression calm and loving, and I felt my heart rate slow down a bit.

"You can fight him. With Holly, we didn't know what he was after, but now, we do. If you build up your magic, if you get strong enough, you can defeat him. You can take Holly's magic back from him, and then he won't be able to hurt anyone anymore."

I thought on that for a moment, then said, "Yeah, I like my plan better. My plan has European goats in it."

Davina sighed. "Your plan will take forever, if it works at all, which is unlikely. And the longer you hesitate on this, the more damage he's going to do."

"What do you mean?" I said. "You said he could only take me if I was strong. If I just don't use the power, if I don't get strong—"

"Walnuts," she said.

"Walnuts," I repeated, and then made the connection. "Wait. *Millie's* walnuts?"

"Not Millie's. Cain's. He took her as a conduit, a non-Magical you can run your magic through, but it comes at a cost. He promises them what they want more than anything in the world, and for that they drink a potion that allows him to gain power over them at night. With every conduit he takes, and he could take quite a few, he is able to draw on their life force to stabilize and increase his own power." She looked at me. "Do you know what it is Millie wants?"

I thought for a moment, but it didn't take long to figure

it out. "Nick. She was attacking Peach." I rubbed my hands between my eyes, trying to ward off the headache that was forming there. "And I have them all coming over this afternoon for Confessional."

"Well, if it's the afternoon, during sunlight, it should be okay."

"One of my best friends is trying to kill another one of my best friends," I said. "It's not okay."

"Well, if we don't do something, it won't just be Millie," Davina said. "He'll do it to others, to gain power, to frighten you." Davina made a disgusted sound, then looked at me, resolute. "But now, we know exactly what we're up against. If you get strong enough, fast enough, you can fight him. And I'll be here, to help you, all the way."

I stood behind the easy chair, my hand over my beating heart. All I wanted was out. I wanted the power gone and my life back to what it was before. Or, whatever was left of what it was before. But if Cain was messing with Millie, how could I just stand back and let it happen?

Davina went to the coffee table, got my cup, and put it in my hands. "Drink this. Relax. Everything's going to be okay, I promise."

I took a sip of the coffee and almost melted with the decadence of it; real cream, real sugar. I took another sip, then had a thought and looked at Davina. "So . . . how are you involved in all of this? What's it to you?"

Davina released a heavy sigh. "Cain and I were both conjurers. We traveled in the same circles. I had known your father, and I went to Tennessee to keep an eye on Holly. I led him right to her." Tears came to her eyes and she blinked them away. "This is my fault. I just want to fix it."

I stood there in silence, staring at her. My head was reeling. It was too much information, too fast, all of it floating like a bunch of puzzle pieces in my head that I was helpless to even try to put together.

"Well," Davina said after a bit. "I have to get going."

I glanced at the clock on the wall and straightened up. "Oh, okay."

She put one hand on my arm. "We'll figure this out. You finish that coffee, and have your friends over this afternoon. You're fine for now, so try not to worry."

"Oh, sure. No worry. No problem." I took another sip of my coffee as I walked her to the door. Damn, it really was good. "When will I see you again? You're coming back, right?"

She smiled. "Of course, I'll be back. We'll figure this out. He won't hurt you; I won't let him."

She gave me a hug and left. I closed the door behind her, sipped my coffee, and decided that I should have stayed in bed.

I sat hunched on my couch, feet on the coffee table, empty to-go coffee cup on my lap. I was staring dazedly out my living room window that looked directly into Peach's living room window when Stacy walked in, as usual without knocking. I heard her heavy construction boots thud through my hallway, and she plopped into the easy chair across from me.

"So, what are we serving? Do you need any help?"

I stretched my foot out and nudged the open box of Pop-Tarts her way. She nodded, grabbed a package, and ripped it open.

"Having a good day, are we?" she asked, breaking off a piece of one tart and popping it in her mouth.

I looked at her, my eyes taking a moment to focus on her, as they hadn't focused on anything since Davina had left, some three hours before.

"No, we're not," I said. "My life is kind of a big mess right now."

She sighed and set the tarts down on the coffee table. "Okay, let's have this out. I'm sorry about Tobias. When I slept with him, I didn't think you'd care, but then you guys started hanging out so much more—"

I raised my hand up and made a cross in the air, like a priest. "You are absolved. Tobias is officially the least of my problems right now."

"Really?" She sat back, eyeing me with deep suspicion. "Because I don't think it's a coincidence that you haven't spoken to me since the last confession."

"I sent you an e-mail about this week," I said.

"An e-mail is not talking."

I looked at her, reading some atypical softness in her expression. "You're being oddly sentimental."

"I'd walk in front of a train before doing anything I thought would hurt you. You know that."

I felt a surge of affection flood through me. "Yeah. I know."

She picked up the tart again, and pulled at the wrapper. "Good."

The doorbell rang.

"Come in!" I hollered, and a few moments later, Peach and her perfume wafted in, carrying a Tupperware container filled with what looked like big Peanut M&Ms, only pastel-colored.

"Hey," she said, her voice uneasy as she got a load of me and Stacy.

"Tart?" Stacy said, nudging the box toward her.

Peach sat in the love seat, her posture straight, her makeup perfect, her Tupperware container resting perfectly on her knees. The living room was quiet for a little while, except for the sound of Stacy's Pop-Tart wrapper as she broke off bits and chewed. Finally, Stacy nodded toward the Tupperware.

"Whatcha got there?"

"Oh. Right." She pulled the top off the container and set it in the middle of the coffee table. "Jordan almonds. Mom says we have to wrap them up in groups of five. Not four, not six. Five. I have no idea why, but she insists—we must have five Jordan almonds per guest." She made a face. "I think they're kind of disgusting. What do you think?"

Stacy and I both reached out and grabbed one, then popped them into our mouths. We chewed for a bit, and then right as I said, "Oh, god, no," Stacy said, "Elope to Vegas."

"Yeah, that's what I thought," Peach said, then smiled. "What I want are these." She reached into her big tote bag, pulled out a bright orange folded paper bird, and set it on the table next to the almonds.

"What the hell is that?" Stacy asked.

"It's an origami crane," Peach said, her face lighting up. "See, you get a thousand of them, and decorate the reception hall with them."

Stacy raised one brow. "A thousand?"

"They're good luck, if they're folded by people who love you."

Stacy and I exchanged looks, and then I said, "So that would be us, then?"

Peach shrugged. "I guess . . . if . . . ." She trailed off. "I mean, if you don't want to . . ."

I reached out and picked up the dented orange crane. "Of course we want to, Peach."

"I mean, the wedding's not until December," she said. "There's plenty of time."

Stacy smiled at her. "You got it, babe."

Peach smiled back, and for the first time since last week's disastrous confessional, we felt a little like us again. I sat up straight and leaned forward.

"Okay, guys, I can't confess this week because . . . well . . . what's going on with me is just . . . I can't talk about it. But I need a favor from each of you, okay?"

"Absolutely!" Peach said, and Stacy said, "Long as it doesn't involve eating any more of those almonds."

"No. It doesn't." I looked at Stacy. "You're good at research, right?"

She shrugged. "I'm a librarian. Research is pretty much the gig. Why?"

"What if I needed to find someone? You know, maybe someone who doesn't want to be found?"

She snorted. "Then you call a detective."

"I tried," I said. "No one will take my case."

Her eyes narrowed. "Why not?"

"Because all I have is a name."

She angled her head and watched me, her eyes sharp. "Who are you looking for?"

"My father."

"Wow," Peach breathed.

"You want me to find the famous Some Guy Named Dave?" Stacy shrugged with mock confidence and snapped her fingers. "Piece of cake."

"His name is Gabriel Ford. I don't know when he was born, or where. All I know is that he went missing ten years ago."

Stacy and Peach exchanged a glance, and Peach said, "Jesus, Liv. You have had a lot going on."

"It gets better. He had a daughter, my sister, Holly, who was three years older than me. They changed their last name to Monroe, and were living somewhere in Tennessee."

"Wow," Peach breathed. "You have a sister?"

"Had. She died a few months ago."

"Oh, honey." Peach touched my shoulder. "I'm so sorry. How crazy is that?"

"Pretty crazy," Stacy said, keeping her eyes on me.

"Can you do it?" I asked.

"I can try," she said. "Can't make any promises, but I'll give it a shot."

"Thanks." I reached out to pat her hand in thanks, but when I touched her, a sharp shock of static electricity zapped us both, and we yanked our hands back as we both cried out in pain.

"Shit," Stacy said, shaking her hand out.

"Ouch. Sorry." I rubbed my fingers together, trying to get rid of the residual sting, then turned to Peach. "And now there's you."

Peach smiled. "You bet, honey. Anything you need, just say the word."

"I need you to cool it with Nick," I said. "Take it down a notch with the wedding planning. Maybe make it secret again, just for a little while."

Peach's smile dropped. "What?"

"It's not for me. It's for Millie." I paused, trying to think of the best way to express that Millie had gone magically insane. "I don't think she's dealing with this particularly well."

"Well, I'm sorry about that, but what you're asking me . . . is kinda nuts. We just came out publicly. I'm still trying to win over his crazy mother." Her eyes widened, and she looked at Stacy. "Sorry, Stace."

Stacy waved her hand dismissively. "It ain't slander if it's true."

Peach made a sad face, then turned back to me. "Look, I didn't know how Millie felt about Nick, but even if I did . . ." She looked from me to Stacy, then back to me. "He chose me. That's not my fault."

"I know," I said, trying to pick my words carefully. "I'm not saying forever, I just think . . . maybe tone it down for a little while, until Millie stabilizes."

"Stabilizes? Have you talked to her? What's going on?"

There was a noise in the hallway, and Millie stepped into the living room, cutting all conversation dead. She was wearing a different dress this time, a soft, shimmery thing of that same deep red, with a surplice neckline, ruching at the waist, and a skirt that danced around her legs even when she stopped moving. Her eye makeup was smoky, and it made her look both older and younger at the same time; her mouth was a pouty red, and gave the impression that she'd just come from a lazy afternoon of drinking the blood of innocents.

"Sorry to startle you guys," she said. "The door was open. I came in during the heartfelt please-find-my-father thing, but I didn't want to interrupt."

Peach gave a quick, shocked laugh. "Oh, my god. Millie! You look amazing!"

Millie's smile was wide, but as she looked at Peach, it didn't reach her eyes. "I know."

Stacy, unfazed, held out the box of Pop-Tarts to Millie, who shook her head and said, "No, thanks. I just came by to confess something quickly, and then I have to run. You know, things to do." She locked her focus on Peach again. "I've been a very busy girl."

"Suit yourself," Stacy said, and set the box of tarts back on the coffee table.

"Mill," Peach said, standing up. "I've been trying to call you all week. I think we need to talk."

"Really?" Millie scrunched her nose. "I don't. Well, no, that's not exactly true. I think I need to talk, and you need to listen, Peach. See, here's the thing. Ever since we were kids, you've always been the pretty one, the one who got all the attention. I was the smart one, and that was okay. I knew that someday, someone would see how sharp I was, how efficient, how much

I could anticipate his needs and meet them before he even had to ask. I just knew it would happen, if I was patient, if I waited long enough."

"Told you so," Stacy muttered.

Millie either didn't hear her, or didn't care; she kept her eyes locked on Peach. "I waited a long time, and that was okay, because I knew he would see me, eventually. But instead, like everyone else, all he saw was *you*." Her eyes glittered with malice, and I felt a chill go down my back. This wasn't Millie; whatever Cain was doing to her, it had not just given her power, it had somehow changed who she *was,* and it was creepy as hell.

I stood up. "Come on, Millie. Let's go out on the porch and cool down for a minute." I reached to touch Millie's shoulder, but she stepped back and waved me away.

"I don't need to cool down. I need to confess." She turned her cold eyes on Peach, and they flashed with rage and no small amount of insanity. "I need to confess that last night, after a long evening of going over the quarterly taxes, Nick and I had sex on his desk."

"Oh, god, *ew.*" Stacy said, putting her hands up over her ears.

Peach blinked a few times, as if she'd been struck, and then she shook her head. "No. You didn't."

"Oh, I'm sorry. Do you know differently? Was he with *you* last night?" Millie's voice was saccharine and cold as her thick lashes fluttered at Peach with mock innocence.

"No," Peach said, her color rising. "He was . . . working late, but there's no way . . . he would never . . ." She looked at me and Stacy, desperation in her shaking voice. "He wouldn't cheat on me. He just wouldn't."

"And yet, he *did,*" Millie said, watching with unmasked glee as Peach's eyes filled with tears.

I stood between Millie and Peach. "That's enough, Mill. I don't know what the hell's going on with you, but it needs to stop."

"I see it differently," Millie said. "I think it took too goddamn long to start."

And with that, she turned around and walked out, heels clicking and hips swaying, like a woman who knew she was in charge. She shut the door quietly behind her, and I turned my attention to Peach, who stared after her, face awash in shock and hurt.

"Peach." I touched her, and when I did, a huge spark of static electricity went off between us. She cried out and stepped away from me, rubbing her shoulder.

"Jesus, Liv!" she said, tears falling freely now. "What the hell is wrong with you?" Then she grabbed her bag and ran out the door. I watched after her, shaking out my hands, which were tingling again.

"You know, I think maybe we should put a moratorium on the confessionals," Stacy said from behind me.

I turned around to look at her, and she shrugged.

"Just a thought."

10

"Didn't I fire you?" Betty said when she unlocked the front door to CCB's to let me in later that night.

"You put me on sabbatical." I walked into the empty dining room, sat at the counter, and placed my head in my hands. "Turns out waitresses don't go on sabbatical."

Betty glanced pointedly out the front windows to the dark night beyond, and I held up one hand to stop the lecture. "I know. It's past sunset. But I couldn't stay in the house." I let out a whoopee-cushion puff of air. "It's been a rough day. I had the Confessional with the girls this afternoon, and it took a bad left turn."

Betty made a face. "Of course it did. There's never any good to be had from confessions. I've been telling you that for years. You'd think seventy-three years of wisdom would count for something. Jeez."

I reached out and grabbed her hand. "Let me close with you tonight. I can mop. Count the till. Anything. I promise, I won't go outside again until daylight. I'll sleep on your couch. I just need something to do to take my mind off things."

"It's all done. You're just lucky I was still down here. What the hell were you thinking, walking over here at night?"

"What's the difference?" I said. "My house, out on the street, here. If he wants to get me, he'll get me. Holing up at night isn't going to make much of a difference."

We both went silent for a moment, and Betty gave a small shrug conceding the point.

"I need chocolate," I said. "You didn't happen to zap up any chocolate cakes today, did you?"

She shook her head. "Gotta place your order before sunset, sweetie." She watched me for a moment, her expression softening. "So, Millie told you girls about what happened with her and Nick, I take it?"

"How did you know about that?"

"Livvy, *everyone* knows. She's been blabbing it around town all day. Nick's gone into hiding, apparently; no one's seen him since yesterday. I don't blame him. Peach is a sweet girl, but I wouldn't want to be on the business end of that woman scorned. It's the pretty, perfect ones who go nuclear and take out a city block."

I let out a highly stressed sigh. "Look, work or chocolate. Give me something mundane to distract me."

Outside, the revving of a car with a blown muffler got our attention, and Betty went to the front door to watch, more out of habit than any strong curiosity. "There's no work for you to do, but I think I've got some Ho Hos in my cupboard upstairs."

I followed her. "Ho Hos? Really?"

"Don't mock. You get to be my age, you learn that sometimes life calls for bad snack cakes."

I stood on my tiptoes to try to see the source of the noise

pollution, even though there was really only one possibility. "Frankie Biggs, I'm guessing?"

"Gotta be," Betty said. "No one else in this town drives a car that loud. I can't believe the damn thing's still on the . . ." She trailed off, went silent for a moment, then said, "What the hell?"

"What?" I opened the front door to get a better look and saw the headlights of Frankie's car swerving down the street, accompanied by an oddly familiar popping sound. Betty and I both stepped out into the street to watch, just as Frankie's blue '72 Barracuda became visible under the streetlight at the end of the block.

"Christ, is it *smoking*?" Betty said just as I took another step out toward the street, my heart beating in response to my mounting panic. The Barracuda jumped the curb at the opposite side of the street, then swerved back onto the road, a cloud of whirling gray smoke circling around it. The car wasn't moving very fast, maybe thirty miles an hour, but it wasn't the speed that was bothering me at the moment. What had my attention were the pool balls flying at it, seemingly from nowhere, bouncing off the car as it went down the street. Pockmarks appeared all over the body of the car. The back passenger window was shattered, and the front windshield was spidercracked all through.

"Shit, shit, shit, *shit!*" I muttered as I glanced up and down the street, my mind racing as I came to the conclusion that only one person in town cared enough about Frankie Biggs to want to hurl pool balls at him.

"Amber!" I yelled, starting down the sidewalk. Betty grabbed at me, but I pulled my arm out of her grasp. I could feel it, that same gut-level sickness I'd had when I watched that same gray smoke attack Peach with walnuts outside my house. It was a bit different this time, though, because beside the blind panic there was now a new emotion; deep, roiling fury. I stomped as I headed down the sidewalk, pissed with Cain for messing with my town, with Millie and Amber for giving him a way in, and with myself for being unable to stop him.

"Amber!" I hollered again, and started running for the corner as the Barracuda swayed under the attack. I glanced back in time to see the blue-striped ten ball crash through his passenger side window, and even over the tragic muffler, I could hear him holler in pain as the car jerked dangerously toward CCB's.

"Betty, call nine-one-one!" Betty darted inside, and I ran faster toward the corner. The Barracuda jumped the curb again, the metal screeching as it scraped against the concrete. Another pool ball shot out from the whirling swarm of smoke and crashed through the windshield, finally shattering it, and I watched in sickness as the ball cracked against Frankie's forehead. He slumped over the steering wheel, his dead foot falling off the accelerator but unable to hit the brake. The car lurched straight for me, and I barely got out of the way before it shot past me and crashed into the redbrick wall of the vacant corner building that used to be Decker's General Store. With the final collision, the gray smoke began to clear, and I heard the familiar *blurp-blurp-blurp* of the pool balls disappearing as I ran toward the car.

"Frankie!" He was slumped, bleeding, and definitely unconscious when I reached him. I stretched my hand through the busted driver's side window and felt his neck for a pulse; it was there, and it was strong, probably still pounding from the adrenaline of the last few minutes. Given that he was definitely alive, in no more immediate danger, and I could already hear the distant whine of emergency sirens, I thought it best not to move him. I pulled my hand out and spun around, scanning the immediate vicinity for any sign of Amber, or Cain, but whoever had attacked Frankie seemed to have disappeared along with the gray smoke.

Which, honestly, was okay by me, because what the hell was I going to do about it, anyway?

"What happened?" Betty said as she caught up to me, then glanced at Frankie bleeding in the front seat. "Oh, crap."

I pulled her aside, toward the vacant general store, so we'd be out of the way when the EMTs arrived. "Did you see it? The gray smoke?"

She stared at me. "I'm old, not blind. But who was throwing the pool balls?"

"They were magical," I said. "The other night, Peach and I got attacked with magic walnuts. Same gray smoke, same disappearing projectiles."

"Walnuts?" Betty seemed surprised for a moment, then gave a knowing nod. "Millie?"

"Yeah. How'd you know?"

"Her grandmother had walnut trees all over the property, and Millie got hit in the head by one when she was four. She had to go to the hospital and everything. She's been traumatized by walnuts ever since." She shook her head. "But Millie's not a Magical. I would know. And, even if she was, why would she attack Frankie?"

"She didn't," I said. "This was Amber Dorsey."

Betty shook her head. "Now, I *know* Amber Dorsey isn't a Magical. Too angry. She would have gone all Carrie-at-the-prom way before now if she had the power."

"I don't think she has any." I raised my voice to be heard over the approaching ambulance. "Have you ever heard of people taking conduits?"

Betty thought for a moment, then nodded. "I've heard of it. Never seen it. But who . . . ?"

"Cain, that guy I told you about, from the alley at Happy Larry's? He's a powerful conjurer. With night magic."

Her expression darkened. "That's not good."

The ambulance screeched to a halt and EMTs popped out of the back, rushing toward Frankie's car. Right behind, a sheriff's car pulled up, lights blazing, and Mickey Taylor hopped out, heading straight for us. Betty smiled and waved him over. I grabbed her arm and stepped in close.

"Wait, what do we tell him?" I asked, my voice low.

"As much of the truth as we can," she said.

Mickey walked us into CCB's, where Betty told him that we saw Frankie's car swerving, and it looked like someone had pelted the car with pool balls, and that he might want to talk to Amber Dorsey about it, although we didn't actually see her. Everything she said was absolutely true, and yet not at all supernatural. I mostly just nodded and kept my mouth shut. Mickey took it all down on his notepad, saying he'd call us if he needed any more information. After locking the door behind him, Betty walked back to where I was sitting at the counter and sat down next to me.

"That was really good," I said. "You were incredible."

"Not my first rodeo." We were silent for a moment, until she sighed. "Conduits? You're sure?"

"Pretty sure," I said.

She nodded acceptance, her expression grim. "If this Cain is preying on people with scores to settle, then we've got serious trouble. You know how many people want to kill each other with pool balls and walnuts in this town?"

I sighed. "I'll hunt around town, see if I can find Cain. Maybe I can . . . I don't know. Talk to him."

She gave me a dull look. "Oh. Good idea. Go search out the man who wants to kill you. That can't end badly."

"He doesn't want to kill me," I said. "He wants my magic. The fact that it'll kill me is incidental. And besides, he's night magic. I'll just look for him during the day."

"He can still knock you out and tie you up until it's night-time."

I opened my mouth to argue, but she kind of had a point. He might not be able to do magical damage during the day, but he'd been strong and fast enough to pull me into that alley. I couldn't afford to forget that there was basic human damage that could be done, too.

"Point taken. So what do we do?"

"Tonight, we sleep. You'll stay on my couch. Tomorrow . . ." She sighed, watching me with dark eyes.

"What?"

"This Davina," she said carefully. "Do you know where she's staying?"

I shook my head. "No."

"But you trust her? Are you sure?"

The hairs on the back of my neck prickled. "Yes. I've got no reason not to trust her. Right?"

"If you trust her, that's enough for me." Betty watched me for a moment, her eyes calculating something. "Can you bring her here to me tomorrow night? I'd like to talk to her. Compare notes, find out what she knows."

I hesitated for a moment, not sure how I would find Davina, but somehow certain that she'd show if I needed her. "Yeah. Sure. I think that's a good idea."

Betty reached out and in an atypical show of physical affection, put her palm against my cheek. "You're a good girl, Livvy. Don't you worry. We'll figure this all out."

I smiled. She lowered her hand and started toward the side door that opened into the stairwell to her apartment. I followed, feeling like an obedient dog, grateful to be led.

"So, is this one of those life situations that calls for bad snack cakes?" I asked.

"I'd characterize this as more of a vodka-straight situation," she said, closing the side door behind us, "but you make do with what you've got."

I went home the next morning, let Gibson out of his shoebox so he could wander around my room—hell, ceramics need exercise, too, right?—and took a shower. It wasn't until I'd dried off and changed that I realized Gibson was missing. I searched the second floor, then panicked at the stairs as I raced down them, trying to comfort myself that there was that strip of carpet down the middle of the hardwood to give him a soft(er) fall, but still.

"Gibson!" I hollered, hitting the first floor running. I heard a clunk coming from the living room and ran in to find him, bumping against the couch. I grabbed him and held him up, running my fingers over him to check for damage. Amazingly enough, he'd managed to tumble down the steps and waddle into the living room with only a little chunk taken out of his handle. Tail. Whatever. It twitched at me as I held him, and I touched the rough spot of bare white ceramic where the paint had chipped off.

"Poor baby," I said, then wondered aloud, "Does it hurt?"

He didn't seem to react at all when I touched the chipped spot, and I realized that what I had on my hands was a blind and likely deaf ceramic mug bunny with no pain sensitivity, and no sense of self-preservation as a result. If I didn't figure out a way to keep him safe, I'd have a shattered Gibson on my hands. I searched the basement, found the huge cardboard box that they'd shipped my computer monitor in, and lined it with old towels. I set him in it and he toddled around, bouncing lightly off one side and then righting himself so he could bounce into the other.

I sat back on the couch, watching him wander happily through my handiwork, and my mind drifted to how the hell I was going to find Davina. She wasn't staying with Grace and Addie, we'd figured out that much, but the fact is, if she'd been staying at any of the places in town, talk of her would have filtered into CCB's by now; no one new came to town without everyone knowing about it. Yet both Davina and Cain had been here for over a week, and not a word was making the rounds about either of them. Wherever each of them was staying, it was either somewhere out of town, or in town with someone who didn't talk.

My bet was out of town. Which, considering that Buffalo, Niagara Falls, and Erie, Pennsylvania, were all within an easy drive of Nodaway, meant it could be weeks before I'd find either of them, and I didn't have weeks to kill.

There *had* to be a way to get a message to Davina. I closed my eyes and lay down on the couch, soothed by the muffled sounds of Gibson exploring his new space, and thought.

Then, it came to me.

Peach's crane.

I reached over to the coffee table, grabbed the slightly crumpled orange crane she'd left the day before, inspected it, and decided there were crazier ideas than this one. I found a pencil under the couch and used it to jot "My house" on the underside of one wing, and "Tonight" on the other. I held it up to my face, staring it down and wondering what else it needed. I went through the house, out the back door to the patio by my mother's garden of wildflowers, then closed my eyes and tried to work up the magic buzz. For a minute or so, I felt stupid and self-conscious, but then the energy started to build and I immersed myself in it, working up a decent flurry into my palms. I cupped the crane in my hands and concentrated on sending the magic into it. Then I released it and, much to my surprise, it flew gracefully out of my hands and flapped around me, its little body working as if an invisible origami-obsessed child was pulling it, the way the design intended.

"Cool." I laughed, full of accomplishment and satisfaction. Maybe my magic wasn't so useless after all. Of course, there was still part two to consider; I'd given it form, but who knew if I'd be able to give it function? I whistled for it to come close and it did.

"Good boy," I said. "Now go find Davina."

It fluttered around my head, bounced into my shoulder, and flapped back up to hover near my head.

"Okay, I should have known it wouldn't be that simple." I reached out and took it by its base. Its wings flapped carefully, not panicked, just moving. I held it in my hand and pooled my magic again, visualizing the thing locating Davina, wherever she was, and delivering the message. Then I opened my eyes and released it. It flapped upward into the calm, sunny day, and I watched as it disappeared around the corner.

"If you want to keep this whole thing secret," Tobias said, as he emerged from the driveway at the side of my house, "then it may be a good idea to shoot off your magical paper airplanes from inside the house."

I glanced at him. "It was a crane."

"Oh. Well, in that case, I take it all back."

I turned to face him, watching him with my arms folded over my stomach as he crossed my backyard to meet me. "Hover much?"

He moved toward me, his eyes locked on mine. "I just happened to be in the neighborhood."

"Spying on me?"

"Making sure you're okay."

"Potato, po-tah-to." I sat down in one of the blue Adirondack chairs. Tobias took the other one. We were quiet for a long time, and then I said, "My mother used to come out here all the time."

He was quiet for a minute, then he said, "It's pretty."

"Yeah. I don't think she ever noticed the garden," I said. "She just stared off into space, mostly."

"Is there some subtext I'm missing here?" He leaned forward in his chair, resting his elbows on his knees. I could see the strong muscles of his arms go taut as he did, the only outward sign that he wasn't entirely relaxed.

"She would come out here, stare at the garden, but not look at it. She was missing my father, and my sister. I always thought he didn't love her, or me, and she could never get over it. But it turns out he left *because* he loved her, and me. That's what she couldn't get over."

Tobias was quiet for a bit, and then he said, "Sometimes leaving is the right thing to do."

"And sometimes loving someone does more damage than not loving them."

He nodded and leaned back. "Ah. Subtext."

I let out a small laugh as a bubble of affection for him overrode my tension. Our eyes caught and held, and his face broke out into a smile. Just the sight of those overlapping front teeth made my heart skip, the arrhythmic beat accentuating the truth that I'd known for a long time.

I was in a lot of trouble with this guy.

"For the record," I said, "I'm still mad at you."

He nodded. "Okay."

"And I don't like you spying on me."

"Duly noted."

"Not that that will stop you."

"No, it won't."

"But you're right," I said. "I need help, and you might be able to help me."

There was no hesitation. "What do you need?"

Looking directly at him hurt a bit, especially when I met his eyes, but there were bigger things at stake here. I needed help, and this was no time to be emotionally skittish.

"First, I need answers to some questions," I said. "Are you a Magical?"

He nodded.

"Day or night?"

"Day."

"What's your power?"

He took a deep breath, let it out, then said, "I can freeze things."

I thought about this for a bit, then said, "Like . . . what? 'Wonder Twin powers activate, form of an ice bridge'?"

His discomfort was palpable, but I had to give him credit; he didn't skirt anything. "Not freeze like cold-freeze. I can stop things from moving." He glanced toward the oak in my yard. "If I wanted to, I could paralyze a whole squirrel. Or just one leg." He glanced at me quickly, then nodded toward Mom's garden. "I could stop those flowers from pulling water up from their roots. That kind of thing. If I can see it, I can stop it dead in its tracks."

I took this in, my mind extrapolating to all the places a power like that might go. "It sounds like that kind of power could be dangerous."

He didn't say anything for a while, but his arm muscles tightened again. "Anything can be dangerous if you're not careful with it."

"Your security work," I said. "Was this with a normal firm, or was it . . . special?"

He watched me for a minute, then said, "Special."

"But you quit?"

He shrugged. "It's not the kind of job you quit. I'm on leave. If they need me, they'll come get me."

"And what happens then? They just come and fetch you, and you go?"

"Something like that." He raised his eyes to meet mine. They were dark, and a little tired. "Liv, I can stop a heart beating, and no one would ever know it wasn't your standard heart failure. I'm the kind of guy people keep an eye on."

I felt a coldness creep over my skin. "So you're like . . . what? A magical assassin?"

"No." He shook his head, caught my expression, then shifted forward on his chair, his eyes intent on mine. "Liv, *no*. It's security, what I do. I swear. I protect clients." He took my hand in his, squeezed it as he met my eye. "No one has ever asked me to kill anyone."

Even as he spoke the words, though, there was a hint of tension in his voice, and I gave voice to their subtext.

"Yet," I said. "No one has asked you . . . yet."

He stared at me, and I could see the gears churning in his

mind, wanting to argue, until finally he relaxed, as though accepting that he couldn't.

"Magicals like me end up in one of two places, Liv. Either working in . . . *security,* or living in hiding. Just having the kind of potential we have, if you run away, well . . . they chase you. Either way, you're never really free."

"Jesus," I breathed. "That's a hell of a way to live."

"There's a power structure in every community," he said quietly. "Just because we're magic doesn't mean it's all puppies and rainbows."

"So what happens if they come and get you? Do they give you time to, you know . . . say good-bye, or anything?"

He gave me a dark look, followed by a small, sad smile. "I'm very low-man-on-the-totem-pole with these people. They've got bigger things than me going on. There's a good chance I could live out my life here, forever, and never hear from them again."

"But there's a chance—" I began, but he cut me off.

"You said you needed my help with something?"

"Right." I took a breath, and directed my focus to the problems at hand. "There's a guy in town. His name is Cain. He's the guy who killed Holly, and we think he's probably after me next."

Tobias's eyes widened, and I could see a flash of anger in them. "And you're just telling me this *now*?"

"I'm not in danger at the moment. I'm not quite ripe, in the magical sense."

He seemed to understand, and relaxed a bit. "Oh."

"I need you to find him. Don't *do* anything, just . . . find him. He's either in town or nearby, probably not staying anywhere under his real name, but who the hell knows? He's a little over six feet, dirty blondish, scruffy, cranky, and Southern. When I met up with him, he was at Happy Larry's. That should be enough to lead you to him, especially if he's here in town."

"You got it." He gave me a direct look, presumably to show me he meant business. "Meanwhile, you start packing."

"What?"

"Change your ticket to Europe. Get the next flight out of Buffalo. I'll follow up with you when we find this guy."

I shook my head. "No."

He stared at me as if I was crazy. "Why not? Now, five weeks from now, what's the difference?"

"First of all, if he found me here, he'll find me there. At least here, I have friends who can help." I took a deep breath. "Second, it's not just about me. He's taking conduits."

Tobias's eyes widened; he obviously knew what conduits were. "Who?"

"So far? Definitely Millie. Possibly Amber Dorsey. There could be more, but the bottom line is, I'm not leaving Millie like this. I'm not leaving until she's okay, and that's it."

He watched me for a while, his entire being vibrating with tension and worry, and then something in his eyes softened, and he seemed to relax, just a bit.

"Okay," he said simply. "I'm going to poke around, see what I can find out about this guy. I'll come back tonight, let you know what I've found, if anything."

"That's fine, but you can just call me in the morning. I've got plans tonight."

He tensed. "Where are you going?"

I rolled my eyes. "To Betty's." I left out the part where I'd be with Davina. This boat was already rocky. "I'll be fine. We'll talk in the morning."

He hesitated for a moment, then nodded. "Keep your cell phone with you. Don't turn it into a bat."

"Oh, ha," I said.

He pushed up from his chair, and I got up from mine. He looked at me, not moving, and I met his eyes. We held the gaze for a long moment, and my heart started skipping as all the feelings I'd been denying for so long rushed forward, making their presence undeniably known.

Not the time, I thought, and then he said, "We'll deal with the rest of this later, okay?"

I wasn't quite sure what he meant by "the rest of this," but I was willing to let it go, for the moment. I nodded, and watched his back as he crossed my backyard and disappeared down my driveway.

11

I stood on my patio for a while. Fifteen minutes or an hour, I couldn't tell, just staring at the corner Tobias had disappeared around, my mind going a mile a minute, trying to assimilate everything that was happening to me into something that made sense.

I wasn't having a lot of luck.

"Liv?"

I looked up to see Peach standing in my driveway, her eyes red, crumpled tissues in her hand.

"Oh, honey," I said, and held my arm out to her. She sniffled and walked up to me, letting me hug her as she cried.

"That son of a bitch," she said, her words muffled into my shoulder as she spoke them.

"Come on inside," I said. "I'll make some tea."

When I came into the living room with the tea, she was slumped down on my couch, playing ruefully with the Tupperware full of Jordan almonds she'd laid on her stomach, scooping up handfuls and letting them fall through her fingers, like big chunks of sand. Peach was petite, but her presence had always made her seem bigger somehow. Now, she looked shrunken, tiny, and spent.

I set her mug on the coffee table in front of her, then took my seat in the floral love seat, waiting for her to start. Eventually, her eyes still on the almonds, she did.

"I asked him," she said. "It was true. Everything Millie said."

I stayed quiet, not sure how to respond. I'd expected that it was true, but also, had some suspicions as to the level of Nick's culpability. I didn't know the extent of Millie's magical influence. Could she have coerced him magically, somehow? Nick may have been kind of a jerk when we were kids, but as an adult, he had always seemed like a good guy to me, and I couldn't imagine him hurting anyone this way, but especially not Peach.

"The wedding's off," she said. "I told him I never wanted to speak to him again."

I hesitated a minute, then said, "What did he say? Did he . . . explain why?"

She snorted angrily. "He doesn't know why." She swiped at her eyes. "What is it with men? They always treat these things like accidents. *It just happened, baby. It's not my fault. I didn't want to, I slipped and my dick just fell into her, over and over again, and . . .*" She trailed off, her voice crackling with pain and despondency.

"Maybe . . ." I began, but I didn't know where to go with it. Under any other circumstances, I would be leading the charge to castrate the son of a bitch. But I couldn't help but feel like this particular thing might be a special circumstance. If it was beyond Millie's power to coerce Nick, it probably wasn't beyond Cain's, and he could only continue to control Millie if he held up his end of the bargain, and she got what she wanted . . .

But then there was the possibility that Nick was just a horny son of a bitch, too, in which case, he got what he deserved. But there was no way to explain any of this to Peach, who sat there, sniffling and playing sadly with the Jordan almonds.

She flicked her hand out a couple of times. "And the worst part? It's making me sick. Last night I had the *worst* headache, and now, my stupid hands are falling asleep. He doesn't get the right to do this to me, goddamnit." She clamped her fist around a handful of Jordan almonds, as if trying to crush them. "And now I've got a living room full of his stupid solar walkway lights. Bastard. Oh!"

She made a surprised sound and bolted upright, throwing the almonds in her hand back into the Tupperware dish. She shoved it onto the coffee table and stared at it, her eyes wide and horrified.

"Peach, what . . . ?" I began, but then stopped as I saw what she was seeing. The almonds were *moving*, sort of shaking, like eggs about to crack open. I glanced down at my hands; they were tingling, a little, but they were almost always tingling a little now, to the point where I wasn't always aware of it. Had *I* somehow made the almonds dance without realizing it?

Peach blinked a few times, then looked at her hand. I looked closer at her hand, too, and caught the last little wisps of light fading. Unlike my yellow light, this was pinkish in color, and it faded very quickly, almost fast enough that I could convince myself I hadn't seen it at all.

Except I knew I had. And I knew what it meant. I wasn't sure exactly how, but Peach had magic.

Crap.

"Jesus!" Peach crawled back into the corner of the couch,

staring at the bowl on the coffee table as if it were full of spiders. "What the hell?"

Goddamnit Cain, I thought. *Doesn't she have enough to deal with right now?*

"Peach." I said her name forcefully and carefully, and waited until she pulled her eyes away from the almonds and locked them on me before I said anything else. "You haven't made any kinds of . . . vengeance deals lately with anyone? Like a scruffy Southern bad boy type?"

She shook her hand out absently as she looked at me like I was crazy. "Vengeance . . . what? What the hell are you talking about?"

"Scruffy Southern bad boy type," I said. "Let's focus on that. Name of Cain. Have you seen him, talked to him, sold your soul to him for vengeance against Nick? Say, in the last day or so?"

She blinked and shook her head. "No. I've been home eating Cheetos and drinking wine since I left your place yesterday. What the hell are you talking about?"

I relaxed a bit, realizing that Cain's power was at night, and was accompanied by the gray smoke. Mine, however . . .

. . . was light.

"Oh my god," I said.

For the moment, the despondency in Peach's expression was replaced by genuine concern. "Liv, you're looking kind of pale. Are you feeling okay?"

I stared at her. I couldn't have taken her as a conduit. I didn't know how. But *something* had happened, something weird.

I needed to talk to Davina.

"Yeah, I think I'm going to vomit." I grabbed Peach's arm and pulled her out of the love seat. I spoke fast as I led her through my front hall to the door. "It's a twenty-four-hour thing, I'm sure I'll be fine soon, but I don't want to give it to you. That's the last thing you need."

I guided her to the front door, but she stopped and turned to face me on the porch.

"What's going on with you, Liv?" she said, suspicion deep in her voice. "You've been acting really weird lately."

I sighed. "I know. I'm sorry. There is something going on, but I can't talk about it right now. I promise, though, when I can, I'll come find you."

She hesitated for a moment, then let it go. She had problems of her own; there was no need to bug me about mine. "Okay. I'm going to go home and get drunk on Boone's Farm. If you hear crashing sounds later, it's just me throwing his stupid walkway lights into the street from my roof."

"Go rest that throwing arm, babe." I pulled her in for a hug and said, "I love you."

"Love you, too," she said, and finally, she left.

I shut the door, then walked into the living room, over to Gibson's box in the corner. I picked him up and cuddled him to me, and for something hard and ceramic, he was oddly comforting. I held him out and looked into his little blinking blind eyes.

"Oh, Gibson," I said. "I think we're gonna need a bigger boat."

* * *

A little after nine that night, there was a knock on my front door. I put Gibson into his padded cardboard box, lest he get another crack in his butt, and walked over to get the door. When I opened it, Davina held up a bottle of wine, grinning as she motioned toward the orange notepaper crane that danced in the air around her head.

"*That* is adorable." She stepped inside and handed me the wine. "And this is your reward."

I took the wine from her and put it on the half-moon table. "I wouldn't need to send you cranes if you told me where you were staying, or gave me a cell phone number. Do you even have a cell phone?"

"The crane is genius." Her eyes followed its trajectory around her head, her expression glowing with pride. "It actually found me! And it's still got life in it. What time did you make it?"

I shrugged and thought. "I don't know. About two, I guess."

"And it's still in the air." She smiled, watching the crane. "Lovely work. Your power's growing. That's good, baby. That's very good."

I grabbed her arm to get her attention. "Yeah. Not good. My neighbor made Jordan almonds dance this afternoon. Little wisps of pink light *zip-zapping* around her fingers. A lot like my yellow light."

She eyed me for a long moment, then said, "I guess it's starting early."

"Hmmm? What? What's starting?"

"I can't be sure, but if you're beginning to leak—"

I did not like the sound of that. "*Leak?* I'm leaking now?"

"It's rare, but it happens. When a Magical gets more power than they have the control to handle, they can leak onto non-Magicals. Sometimes. A little. The effect is usually temporary, and as long as your neighbor stays calm, it probably won't get anyone hurt."

I was just starting to calm down at "the effect is usually temporary," but then I heard the rest of the sentence. "Wait, *probably* won't get anyone hurt?"

"It's magic. You never really know what's going to happen with magic." Davina frowned. "But it's not good news. You're gaining power faster than we anticipated. We're running out of time."

My heart clenched in my chest. "So . . . so . . . so, what are we gonna do? I haven't even gotten close to finding my father yet."

She grabbed my hand and patted it. "Even if the binding was a good idea, which it's not, we don't have time for it, baby. We need to move. We need to build your powers, get you ready to fight."

I put my hand to my forehead. "My brains are scrambled. I can't think about fighting. Not now. We have to go." I started toward the door.

"Where are we going?" Davina asked.

"To see Betty, over at CCB's."

I pulled the door open, and Davina grabbed it with her hand, holding it there. "Who's Betty, and why are we going to see her?"

"She's my boss at CCB's. She's magic. She wants to meet you, so she can figure out how to help."

Davina narrowed her eyes. "There's someone else with magic in this town?"

"Yes. She makes pastries. *Zip-zap*-baklava. They're amazing. Anyway, I told her about this thing with Cain and—"

"You what?" Davina seemed annoyed. "You can't go around telling people things like this. This is very sensitive information."

"Don't worry. We can trust Betty." I decided not to tell Davina that I had also told Tobias; she seemed annoyed enough about Betty, and there was no need to add fuel to that fire. "Anyway, we need to go to CCB's tonight. Betty wants to talk to you, find out what's going on."

"Oh, sure," she said, slowly. "We can do that. But first, I want you to tell me . . . have you had any more contact with Cain?"

"No," I said. "I haven't seen him, and I haven't heard anything about him, which is strange because whenever there's a new man in town, usually, I hear about it."

She nodded, her expression thoughtful. "Let's go talk to your Betty. Maybe she'll have some ideas on what we should do." She headed toward the door. The crane followed her automatically and I grabbed it gently by one wing.

"You want me to . . . I don't know. Undo it?"

Davina watched me, interest in her eyes. "Think you can? You know that's an important part of your growth, learning to take the power back."

"I know," I said. "It just feels too much like . . ."

"Killing?" Davina nodded. "I know it does. But you know it's not, right? That thing lives on your power. It's no different from clipping your nails or cutting your hair. It's all just a part of you that you don't need anymore."

I glanced back toward the living room, where Gibson thunked around in his cardboard box. I held the crane's wing in my fingers, closed my eyes, and rallied my energy, feeling it flow through my arms, amazingly at my control. Then something occurred to me, and I looked to Davina.

"Hey, wait," I said. "It's night. Why is this working?"

"You generated the power during the daytime," Davina said. "You can take it back whenever. It's just a little bit of power in that thing. No big deal."

"Oh." I concentrated on the crane again, looking it in the . . . well, I guess . . . face. I stopped rallying my energy. "Go hang out with Gibson."

I released it, and the crane flew into the living room to hover over Gibson's padded box. I turned to see Davina staring at me, smiling.

"You're a softy, baby," she said, chuckling. "That's gonna hurt you someday."

"I know," I said, stepping out onto the porch and shutting the door after us. "Let's just go to CCB's and get this over with, then we can come back and drink the wine."

"That's fine," Davina said. "Let's go."

We stepped out into the night and made it about half a block when Davina grabbed my arm.

"What?" I said as she yanked me into the narrow driveway between two houses at the end of the street.

"Shh." She held her finger to her lips and seemed to be listening. I listened, too. Didn't hear anything. I waited a few more moments, and was about to ask her what was going on, when she looked at me, her eyes wide. "We need to get out of here." She pointed to the darkness behind the houses. "What's that way?"

"Um . . . the woods," I said.

"Okay."

She grabbed me by my wrist and pulled me along behind her. We crossed through the backyard and into the woods. It was dark, the moon was only about half-full, and I stumbled along behind her as weeds and twigs crunched under feet.

"Davina, what—?"

"Shh!" she said, and we broke into a run. She moved through the woods like she already knew them, and I had trouble keeping up with her. Finally, we came to a thick copse of trees, and she pulled me behind one.

"You stay here."

I didn't have time to argue. She left me there and walked into a clear space, turning around as if looking for someone.

"You can't have her!" she called. "She's under my protection!"

There was nothing. No response. No sound. Not even twigs crackling under anyone's feet.

It was then that it first occurred to me that just because Davina had told me the truth about a few things, that didn't mean she *wasn't* absolute batshit. I waited for a few moments, then started to move out from behind the tree, but Davina made a motion with her hands, telling me to get back. I sighed and retreated; if she was crazy, I could indulge her for a few minutes until she felt safe, and we could go to Betty's and then . . . I don't know. Find a doctor, get a prescription, and—

It sounded a little like wind at first, the eerie whistling when air moves a little too fast. The air around me, however, was still and dead. I watched Davina's form in the moonlight, and had she not been wearing bright yellow, I might not have seen it. But, slowly, circling around her, there appeared to be something . . . kinda smoky. My heartbeat ratcheted up; she wasn't crazy.

Crap.

And that's when things started to move. The smoke swirled around her, furious, fast enough to move her hair and send her skirt billowing around her. She turned in circles, too, her eyes wide with fear, but when she spoke, her voice was firm.

"You can't have her!"

The trees around us started to rustle as the smoke spread out. There was the crack of wood overhead, and I looked up to find a baseball bat–sized branch flying toward her in the grip of the smoke. I ran out from behind the trees to get to her.

"Davina!"

"Olivia, get back!" she yelled, and then the branch came down on her head, and she fell to the ground with a dark thud.

"Davina!" I ran to her, the smoke continuing to circle around us, blowing my hair into my face. I skidded to her side and touched her face; she was out cold.

"Davina, Davina, Davina," I said in a panic. "Oh, shit, this is *not good.*"

I heard something behind me, the faintest crackle of a twig, and I grabbed the branch that had hit Davina and jumped to my feet, waving it blindly around me.

"Get away from us!" I screamed.

There was no answer. There was nothing but smoke, whipping the air up around me, smelling thick and hot and acrid. I circled around, trying to guard her body, and then there was a pull on the branch and it was out of my grip, flying away from us in the smoke as it retreated. A second later, I heard the thud as the branch fell somewhere far enough away that I had no hope of retrieving it. Once again, the night was silent, and all I could hear was my heart banging in my chest, and my own panicked breath wheezing in and out.

I waited, standing guard, but really, what the hell was I going to do if Cain stepped out of the shadows and attacked? It was night. I was helpless, and Davina was down. I thought about Tobias and felt in my pocket for my cell phone, but it went dead right after I turned it on.

"Damnit, I have to learn to charge this stupid thing!" I cried to myself, my voice sounding high and panicked. I tucked the phone back in my pocket and turned around and around, trying to catch sight of Cain in the dim moonlight, hoping Davina would wake up before I might have to defend us, because if it was left to me, we were dead meat.

Then, finally, I saw him. His outline was faint and dark, but as he moved closer, I knew it wasn't my imagination. It was Cain, and he was heading straight for us. I glanced around at my feet, kicking at the small branches there, looking for something, anything I might use as a weapon. There was nothing. I closed my eyes tightly for a second, just a second, and when I opened them, he was right there, looking down at Davina.

"Get out of here," he said, not taking his eyes off her.

"No," I said, my voice audibly shaking. "I'm not leaving her."

He looked at me. "This is between me and her. It's got nothing to do with you."

I had nothing. No branch, no power, nothing. Except the knowledge that, according to Davina, he couldn't kill me yet and still get what he wanted. I stepped over Davina, putting myself between her and Cain.

"You want her? You're going to have to go through me first."

His eyes narrowed to slits. "Why are you protecting her?"

Before I could answer, I heard a creaking above us. A second later, there was a thud as a big branch, probably loosened by all the gray smoke havoc earlier, fell to the ground between us. I lunged for it, and grabbed it at the end like a baseball bat. I splayed my feet on the ground, bracing myself as I gripped the branch in my hands. Cain watched me, his stance calm and seemingly unworried by any threat I might present. I swung as hard as I could. There was another thud as it connected with his shoulder, sending him sprawling backward.

"Son of a bitch!" he grunted.

I swung again, and the branch made a whooshing sound as Cain dodged the blow. "You're not getting near her!"

"Put that damn thing down." There was a growl in his voice

that might have scared me on a normal day, but at the moment, all I saw was red. I swung again and missed, and as I was setting up to go for him again, he lunged at me, sending the branch flying as his shoulder connected with my midsection, throwing me to the ground, knocking the wind out of me. My head connected with something hard, probably a rock, and for a moment sparks exploded in my vision. When my sight came back, I scrambled backward, glancing around frantically until I saw Cain. He was standing nearby, not advancing on me, but simply watching me.

"You okay?" His voice sounded mildly concerned, which I had to admit, threw me a bit. Then I remembered; *he* needed *me,* and that gave me leverage.

"Get away from us," I said.

"She's not your friend," Cain said. "She's—"

Davina groaned loudly, and I turned away from him.

"Davina?" I could see the outline of her form putting her hand to her head. I looked back to Cain, then scrambled on all fours to Davina's side.

I touched her gently on the shoulder. "Are you all right?"

She sat up. "I . . . I think so."

"Good." I looked back behind me, but Cain was gone, and I could hear the faint crackling sounds of twigs crunching under his retreat. My heart started beating furiously then, and my shaking got more violent. My arms and legs felt weak, and I sat on the ground next to Davina, trying to breathe.

"Baby?" Davina said, concern in her voice. "What happened?"

"You lost consciousness," I said as though that were news.

She rubbed my back. "Olivia? You're shaking. What did he do to you?"

"He . . ." I began, but realized . . . he didn't do anything. No gray smoke, no magic. He knocked me down in self-defense; that was it.

Only because he needs you, I thought. *Otherwise, you'd be dead.*

"I don't know. You were knocked out, and then I hit my head on a rock . . ." I swallowed, the panic taking over now that he was gone. "I'm just a little freaked out."

"It's okay," Davina said, rubbing her head. "That was quite a storm he set on us."

"Yeah. Are you okay?"

Davina moved her neck slowly from side to side. "I think so. You?"

I checked myself, then nodded. "Yeah."

"Good. Help me up?"

I got to my feet, then reached down and helped her to hers. She glanced around and let out a long breath.

"He's gone." She grabbed my hand and squeezed it. "Thank you. You saved my life."

"No problem. Can we go now?"

"You bet, baby." She watched me for a long moment, and then she nodded in the direction of my house. "Let's go."

12

The walk home was short, but it was long enough that by the time we got back, the cold hollow inside me had filled itself with fury. Once we got inside, I settled Davina on the couch, grabbed my cell phone out of my pocket, and flipped it open.

"What are you doing?" Davina asked.

"I'm calling nine-one-one," I said. "You need to go to the hospital and I need to report that asshole and have him put in jail."

I flipped it open, but it was still dead. Damnit. I walked over to the charger and plugged it in. "I always forget to charge this stupid thing." I glanced around. "And my other phone's a dead bat."

"Calm down, Olivia. We need to talk."

"With the *police,*" I said. "We need to talk with the police."

"One thing you need to learn," she said, her eyes suddenly hard and angry. "Police don't work for people like us. The police belong to *them.* We"—she motioned her hand between us—"need to take care of our own."

"He attacked us," I said. "If he's so magic let him magic himself out of a goddamn jail cell. Just give me a minute, and my phone will charge, and—"

Davina took in a breath, and her face looked strained as she closed her eyes and put her hand to her head.

"I'm sorry," she said. "I just need a minute."

"I'll get you some water and some aspirin." I went into the kitchen and filled a glass with ice water and grabbed a bottle of Advil. When I got back to the living room, Davina was lying on the couch with her eyes closed. I was going to step out, let her rest while I fumed quietly to myself, but she opened her eyes and reached for the water.

"Thank you," she said.

"No problem." I gave her the water and put the bottle of pills in her hand, then collapsed into the easy chair. Davina sat up to drink the water and take the Advil, then fell back again and let out a long breath.

"Oh, that's much better," she said.

"Okay, you ready to explain to me why we're not having his ass thrown in jail?"

Davina looked at me, and a small smile graced her lips. "Because he didn't break any laws."

"He *attacked* us. We don't have to tell them about the gray smoke. We'll say he hit you in the head with a branch. That's the truth."

"It doesn't matter." She smiled up at me. "You handled him just fine."

"No, I didn't, and I'm not fine," I said. "I just don't understand why we can't call the police."

"*No,*" she said, her voice firm. "I'm serious. Police don't work for people like us. If we call the police, and they see—or sometimes, just *think* they see—something weird, the next thing you know, we're gone."

I felt a chill run down me at the word. *"Gone?* What do you mean?"

She stared at me, her eyes hard, and then she said, *"'Thou shalt not suffer a witch to live.'* Exodus 22:18. You think people don't believe that?"

"Well, sure. Crazy people."

Her eyes got beady with anger. "They use religion, they use science, they use national security, whatever they need to use to justify it, but if you think there aren't a million little Salems happening every minute of every day, then baby, you're just being naive."

I took that in for a moment, then shook my head. "No. This is Nodaway, it's not like that here. Betty's been here for, god, thirty years—"

"And she's open with her magic?" Davina asked. "Everyone knows about it?"

"Well . . . no. I mean . . ." I sighed, regrouped my argument. "Look, I know the sheriff. His name is Mickey Taylor, and he's really nice and he's known me since I was a kid. I went to school with his son. He would never hurt me, or let anyone else hurt me."

Davina closed her eyes and shook her head as though lamenting my stupidity, but when she looked at me again, her expression was kind. "That's how it *used* to be. That's not how it is *now.* You can't trust anyone, and things are only going to get worse."

"Worse? Worse than being attacked by a homicidal maniac?"

She met my eyes and said simply, "Yes."

"I don't understand how—"

"You think he's bad now? Imagine how he'll be when he gets your magic. He could have this kind of power at his disposal, day and night. Someone like that . . . well, you just can't stop someone like that. Not the police, not anyone."

Except . . . maybe . . . Tobias. I thought about it for a moment, but then decided not to tell her about Tobias right now. She was already very agitated, and I didn't want to make things worse. I could tell her tomorrow. "Okay. Fine. No cops. So, what's your big idea, then?"

"We need to get you strong, and you need to fight Cain."

I shot up from the easy chair. "Are you insane? I can't fight him. I do the magical equivalent of balloon animals, Davina."

Her voice was raspy as she spoke. "Right now, yes. But soon, you're going to have all manner of power."

"How do you know that? Just because my father's power evolved, or Holly's did, doesn't mean mine will. What if this is it, this is all I do? I can make a chicken out of a Tupperware dish; how is that going to defeat a guy like Cain?"

"Well, you're right," she said thoughtfully. "If all you can do in the next few days is make balloon animals, then . . . well . . . we'll figure something else out."

"Like what?" But I'd barely gotten the words out before it hit me, so clearly, like the solution had been there all along, only I hadn't seen it. I pulled back from her and said, "What if I gave *you* my magic?"

She stared at me blankly. "What the hell are you talking about?"

"You. But you wouldn't have to force me to give you my magic, I'd do it willingly. Godspeed and god bless, take it."

"Oh, really? And have me end up like him? Going crazy every twelve hours, living on potions to keep me hanging on?" She shook her head. "No, thank you."

"Well . . . what if . . . ? What if you just took it and spit it out? Like with snake venom? You're a conjurer, like him. You're smart. Can you do that?"

Something flashed over her face and I grabbed her hands.

"You can! You know something."

She sighed. "I don't. Not really. There's a possibility that I could do something like that but . . ."

"That's great, let's—"

She held up her hand. "This stuff is very dangerous, baby. Your magic . . . if someone takes it from you, you'll be weakened. You could die. Holly died, and I will not see that happen to you, I will *not*!" She sighed, reached for my hand, and smiled. "Don't worry. You can do this. I will help you, I'll—"

I hopped up off the couch. "You don't understand. I *can't*."

Davina smiled. "You did well tonight. You were very brave."

"We're only alive because he didn't want to kill us yet." I took a deep breath. "I know myself, Davina. I know what I'm capable of, and I'm telling you, I'm not the kind of girl who fights magical battles. I wanted excitement in my life, sure, but the kind that involves flirting with some guy wearing a kilt, not . . . not this."

"Life isn't a drive-through," Davina said. "Sometimes you get things you didn't order."

"Okay, I don't need a motivational poster right now." I breathed deep, trying to allay the panic, not getting very far. "Look, maybe it only kills if it's taken unwillingly. I mean, I leaked magic to Peach, right? And that didn't hurt me at all. Hell, I didn't even know I was doing it. If I can do that, I bet I can find a way to give it to you. Maybe not all of it, but enough that I won't be useful to him anymore."

"Calm down, Olivia." She patted the space next to her on the couch. "We don't have to figure it all out tonight. There's time. We've still got some time."

I sat down next to her and stared into space, suddenly exhausted. I let my head loll back on the couch, and didn't realize I'd fallen asleep until I felt a pat on my knee, and my head shot up.

"What? Huh?"

"Time for me to go, baby," Davina said, smiling softly. "And time for you to go to bed."

"Why don't you stay here tonight?" I said, rubbing my eyes and yawning. "I have an extra bedroom. Actually, I have four."

"No, no, I feel much better now, really."

She started to get up, and I hopped up to help her stand, but she managed it on her own, pretty easily, considering how wobbly she'd been on the way home.

"Wow," I said. "You heal fast."

"Yes." She smiled brightly. "I'm feeling much better now."

"Are you sure you won't stay?" I said, walking her toward

the door. "It'll take me two seconds to put fresh linens in one of the guest rooms."

"No, no, I'm okay. I'm going to walk. The fresh air will do me good."

"But . . ." I glanced out the panel windows by the door. "What if he's still out there?"

"Oh, I'm pretty sure he spent what he had tonight," she said. "I'm not worried."

That makes one of us, I thought. I followed her to the door. "Hey, where are you staying? I can call you tomorrow, maybe we can go out to lunch."

"That's a fine idea," she said. "Just send the crane for me. I liked that."

And with that, she headed out the door. As soon as she was out of sight, I glanced up and down my street, and then heard Davina's voice echoing eerily in my head.

Thou shalt not suffer a witch to live.

I shuddered, then shut the door and hit the dead bolt.

I woke up early the next morning, tossed and turned for a while as the animated orange paper crane flew around my room, possibly still looking for Davina. When the sun finally rose, I caught him in my fingers and whispered for him to stick close to Gibson, sort of a Seeing Eye crane. I let him go, and he floated down to Gibson's box, covered Gibson protectively with one wing, and . . . I think . . . fell asleep.

I headed out to CCB's at seven, and found Betty behind the counter. I sat down near the cash register, and she quickly finished pouring coffee for Ray Skipp, then zipped over to me.

"Hey," she said, her voice low. "How are you? I was worried when you didn't come by last night."

"I know, I'm sorry." I met her eye briefly, but couldn't hold it for long. I'd been jumpy all morning, and I couldn't shake it. "We got . . . detained."

Her expression got serious. "I don't like the sound of that."

"You're not going to like the reality of it, either," I said. "So let me just say, we're fine, Davina saved us."

"Saved you? From what?"

"Well . . . he kind of . . . attacked us."

"Excuse me? What the hell happened?"

I told her the story, abbreviated but hitting all the major points, and when I finished she was watching me, her expression grim and determined.

"I don't want you spending time with Davina anymore."

"It's not her fault."

"It's been nothing but trouble since she got here."

"Betty—"

"I don't trust her."

"Stop it." I leaned forward, keeping my voice down. "She ran right out in the thick of it, all his dark magic, gray smoke everywhere. She almost got herself killed trying to protect me."

"I don't care if she swallowed dynamite and shot rabbits out of her ass, you are not to spend any more time with her. I don't trust her."

"Well, *I* do. I even wanted to give her my magic, and she—"

"You *what*?" Betty's whisper was harsh. "Are you crazy? What if your magic is exactly what she wants?"

"She wasn't going to *take* it, take it. Just spit it out, like a snakebite."

Betty made a face. "Ew."

"It doesn't matter, anyway, she refused. Too dangerous." I put my hands to my pounding head. "Look, Betty, please. It's been a hell of a few days, and I need you to just trust me, okay?"

She watched me for a long moment, then slowly nodded, although her shoulders didn't seem to relax at all. "Fine. If you say she's all right, I believe you."

"Okay." I craned my neck from side to side, trying to get the kinks out. "So, have you found out where Cain is staying yet?"

Betty shook her head. "I went to all the B and B's, even though he doesn't seem the B-and-B type—"

"He's not," I said.

"—and no one's seen him. I canvassed all the motels within fifty miles, and even asked Happy Larry if he'd seen him around. No joy."

"How is that possible? Fresh meat doesn't stay hidden in this town, even cranky, scruffy meat. There are too many girls in this town who'd go crazy over something like that." I pressed my fingers to the bridge of my nose, then sighed and looked at her, pulling on the best smile I could muster. "Thanks for trying, Betty. Keep your ear to the ground."

"It's never anywhere else." She watched me and sighed. "Speaking of which, how is everything shaking out with Millie and Peach?"

I sighed. "It's not. Hey . . . is it possible . . . ? I mean, could she have overridden his will?" I lowered my voice to a whisper. "Is there such a thing as magical rape?"

Betty thought for a moment, then slowly shook her head. "Like I said, most people get innocuous powers. Change the color of a dress, make a pencil fly, that sort of thing. Messing with free will, that's dark stuff. If there are people who can do that kind of thing, I've never had contact with them."

"What about a conjurer? Might someone like that be able to make a potion, slip it in Nick's drink?"

"I don't know," Betty said, although she looked doubtful. "Maybe. I guess. But . . ."

She trailed off, and I prodded her. "What?"

She leaned forward, her elbows on the counter, her eyes compassionate and sad. "Have you ever heard of Occam's razor?"

"Yeah. The simplest explanation is usually the correct one, right?"

"Well, the simplest explanation here is human nature. Men—especially men who are about to get married—are known for this sort of thing. You don't need to slip anything into their drinks. You just have to be . . . tempting. Millie tempted him, he was human, he messed up." She leaned back and wiped down the counter absently with her towel. "I'm seventy-three years old, Liv, and I've seen this happen a lot. Never once has there been any magic involved."

"Right." Still, I couldn't help but feel like there was something more here. But then, maybe that was just because I didn't want Peach to be suffering like this. I sighed and put my head in my hands. "I'm gonna go stand on the magic square and wish it all away."

She patted my hand. "You go do that, honey."

I pushed myself up from the counter and walked over to the square near Booth 9. I sighed and looked down at it, my feet just outside its edges. *I wish*—I thought, and then I heard my name. I looked up, and Andrew Garvey, the elementary school principal, was holding up an empty coffee mug, looking at me expectantly. I glanced down at my sweatpants and my Mason's Plumbing T-shirt that read, WE FIX ANY CRACK, and looked back at Andrew.

"You bet." I walked around the magic square, grabbed a carafe from the industrial coffeemaker, and caught Tobias's eye through the pass as he delivered a waffle order up for Betty.

He looked pissed.

"Great," I muttered to myself.

"What are you doing here?" he said.

"Serving coffee." I delivered Andrew's coffee and then headed back into the kitchen, where Tobias was manning the grill while Kenny headbanged on his iPod, supervising the waffle irons. Tobias shot a look at me and whistled loudly to Kenny, who raised his head.

"Take over for me, Ken. I'm on break."

Without skipping a headbanging beat, Kenny walked over and monitored the grill. Tobias took me by the elbow and led me out toward the back dock. On the way, I grabbed a small ceramic prep bowl full of raspberries off the counter and then followed dutifully until we were sitting, once again, in the two nylon camping chairs in the back. I sat down, pulled out a raspberry, and popped it in my mouth. Man, they were good.

"I thought you were going to stay home," he said.

"I was," I said. "But, you know, best laid plans."

"This isn't a joke," Tobias said. "I was going to come by and see you after my shift."

"Why?" I said, sitting forward a bit. "Did you find something?"

"Not much. I made some calls to friends, just preliminary stuff. His name is Cain Taggart. From Hastings, Tennessee. He's a conjurer, although he didn't show up on Magical radar—"

"You guys have Magical *radar*?"

The edge of Tobias's mouth quirked up a bit. "I mean, they only first heard of him recently."

I sat back, flushing at my own stupidity as I chewed on another raspberry. "Shut up. I don't understand how this world works."

He smiled. "Don't worry about it. Few people do. Anyway, he dropped off the surface about two months ago, and no one has seen or heard from him since." He cleared his throat. "I also looked into your friend Davina." He gave me a look. "She didn't show up anywhere at all. Are you sure her real name is Davina Granville?"

I stared at him. "I didn't check her driver's license or anything, no. But she says she's just a small-time conjurer. Maybe she's just never done anything to show up on your radar."

Tobias shrugged. "Maybe."

I set the raspberries down on the ground and leaned forward, looking at Tobias. "I trust her. She almost got herself killed last night protecting me—"

"Last night? What happened last night?"

"Cain attacked us," I said, then held up my hand as Tobias

sat forward. "I tried to call you, my cell phone was dead, and by the time I could contact you, we were home safe and I was exhausted. I'm telling you now. Please back off, okay? If I have to deal with one more well-intentioned but overprotective person in my life, I'm going to throw myself headfirst into the falls."

Tobias smiled. "Well, that would be bad."

"I know," I said. "I could get wet. And possibly even a little muddy."

This time, the flush was his, appearing at the base of his neck. I felt myself warm up all over, and this time, I didn't think the tingling I felt was from any paranormal source. I reached down and grabbed the bowl of raspberries again, cupping it in my hands.

"So," he said after a while, his voice just as calm and in control as always. "You're okay, then?"

I looked at him, and our eyes met again, and there was more tingling, all over. *Oy.*

"Yeah," I said, my voice soft. "I'm fi—"

And that's when something small hit my face and bounced off.

"What the . . . ?" I pulled back a bit and swatted at the air by my face. "What was that?"

"I think," Tobias said flatly, "it was a flying raspberry."

I hopped up out of the chair and looked inside the ceramic bowl I'd been holding; it was empty. I glanced around and a number of raspberry butterflies zoomed around the patio, their wings seeming to be made of some kind of raspberry juice vapor, my yellow light flickering around them as they flew. I checked my fingers and I caught the last fading glimpse of the light on my fingers; I hadn't touched the raspberries at the time of transformation, nor did I intend to change them.

Evolving power, I thought, and my throat tightened.

The wayward raspberry that had hit me in the face now flew drunkenly around Tobias's head, then backed up a bit, as if trying to get a good look at us, as though we were the freaks of nature. For his part, Tobias stared back at it, equally mesmerized.

"Huh," he said.

The raspberries flew around us, tightening their circle, occasionally bouncing off my shoulder or the back of Tobias's head.

"So," he said, ducking a raspberry as it buzzed his head, "this is interesting."

"The charm wears off after a while, trust me." I watched the raspberries fly around, wondering what the hell I was supposed to do now. "Davina said I should practice. I guess I should try to undo them? Maybe?"

Tobias motioned toward the swarm. "This is gonna be fun."

I stood up and concentrated, trying to remember what Davina had said to me the other night about pulling the energy back in. *It's mine,* I thought. *I'm not killing anything. I'm just pulling what's mine back to me.* I took a deep breath and closed my eyes, locating the raspberries around me, visualizing them as tiny yellow balls of my energy floating around me. One by one, I pulled the yellow light back in, and one by one, I heard the tiny plops around me. The energy flowed back into me, and for a moment, my limbs buzzed and my stomach dropped, the jolt of power hitting me like a steep decline on a roller coaster. But then I absorbed it, and my body calmed. I was getting stronger, just as Davina had said I would. I could feel the magic inside me, buzzing throughout me, waiting to be of use. And if I didn't figure out how to control it, it would control me.

I looked around at the scattered raspberries on the ground. I concentrated on one, and it took a moment to get it right, but soon, wisps of yellow light surrounded it and I floated it into the air. While holding that one up, I allowed my concentration to spread to the others, finding all of them and lifting them up as well. Slowly, I circled them around and around, until they whirled around us like a Ferris wheel on its side. I let the energy hum for a bit, enjoying the feel of the power, and then, I pulled the magic back into myself and let them drop, one by one, perfectly aimed into the center of the little ceramic dish.

When I finally allowed myself to meet his eyes again, Tobias was staring at me, concern on his face.

"You all right?" he asked.

"I guess." I looked up at him. "My power is evolving, just like Davina said it would."

He nodded. "Yeah."

"I think that means I'm going to have to fight this guy." My legs started to shake. "Tobias, I don't want to fight this guy. I don't want to fight anyone."

He stood up and walked over to me. "It's a little late for that." He put both hands on either side of my face and guided me to look at him. "If you have to fight, you'll fight. But you won't fight alone, ever. Okay?"

I took in a sharp breath, only then realizing that I had stopped breathing in my panic. "Okay."

He leaned forward and kissed me on the forehead. "Go on

home. Lock the doors. Get some rest. I'm gonna follow up on some things after my shift, but I'll be by later tonight, if that's okay."

I nodded. "It's okay."

"It's not too overprotective of me? All the hovering?"

"Yes," I said, "but it's okay. I kind of like it when you hover, sometimes."

"All right then." He smiled. "Call me if you need me."

I took my index finger and crossed over my heart. He hesitated a moment, then gave a little wave and went back inside. I folded up the chairs and tucked them back into the corner of the patio, then headed down the alley to Main Street, just walking home as if I were a normal woman on a normal day doing normal things.

None of which was exactly the case.

I killed the afternoon sitting on my porch swing, watching the neighborhood and thinking. I knew I should have gone inside and thrown the bolt when the sun set, but what difference did it make? If Cain wanted to come after me, what would I be able to do to stop him? Was my little dead bolt going to stop a guy who had both conjuring and magical powers? My guess was that if he wanted me, he would come and get me, and there wasn't much I could do about it if he did.

"Nothing like a little fatalism to make the day complete," I muttered to myself.

Just then, a big white van with the EASTER LANDSCAPING logo on the side pulled into my street.

"Oh, hell," I said as Nick pulled the van in front of Peach's house. He slammed the door, walked up onto Peach's porch, and banged on the door. Nick was short, stocky, and bald as a cue ball, but he was powerful and determined.

"Peach!" he yelled, then stepped back off the porch and looked up at her bedroom window, where her light was on. "Peach!"

The light shut off, and Nick waited for a bit, then when there was no sign of Peach, he shouted again.

"I know you're up there! Come out and talk to me!"

"Crap." I got up and walked out to the sidewalk. "She doesn't want to talk to you, Nick."

He turned and his eyes fixed on me. "Liv!" He rushed over to me, and only then could I see the frantic desperation in his eyes. "Liv, you have to help me. Go talk to her for me."

I eyed him coldly. "Why would I do that? You broke her heart, you big bald asshole."

"I know." He ran his hand over his head, and shook it, as if he didn't understand what was happening. "I know."

I couldn't help it; I felt myself softening toward him. On the one hand, Occam's razor. On the other hand, strange things had been happening lately, and Millie was at the center of it all. That bought Nick a little leeway. A *little*.

"What happened?" I said finally.

He looked at me, his eyes glazed. "I don't know. I've never thought of Millie that way. Never. It just happened, and it was like . . . like I didn't have any control."

"Were you guys drinking anything?"

He shook his head, and lowered his eyes. "Just coffee. I don't know what happened. We stay late and do taxes once every quarter. I get Chinese food and we knock it out and it's always fine. It's always . . . you know . . . Millie."

"But there she was, all sexy in her red dress . . ." I said, but Nick shook his head again.

"I don't like the change," he said. "It's not Millie. I get that she wanted to change, and that's her business, really, but to be honest? I liked her better before."

"But you slept with her now," I said.

He leaned back against his van, obviously confused. "I don't know what the hell I was thinking." He swiped at his eyes, rubbing them briskly before going on. "I love Peach, Liv. She's the one. I never thought in a million years a woman like that would want a guy like me. Why would I do this to her, to myself? I've never cheated on a woman I've been dating, never. But the one woman I really wanted, the one woman I actually . . ."

He trailed off, his voice choked, his misery visible in his slumped shoulders and the tears that welled in his eyes.

Screw Occam's razor. Somehow, this was Cain's handiwork. I didn't know how, but it was, I was sure of it. I reached out and patted his arm. "I believe you, Nick."

He turned his head to look at me, a tiny smile, almost imperceptible through all that misery, on his lips. "Thanks."

"Oh, so you're going to try to sleep with Liv, now? Is that it?"

I looked up to Peach's porch, where she was standing watching us, her body tense with fury.

"Peach," I began, but she didn't hear me. Her eyes were focused on Nick as she barreled down on him, her arms flailing.

"I hate you!" she yelled. I stepped in between them and clasped my hands on her elbows, keeping her from swinging.

"Peach, calm down!"

"I just want to talk," Nick said. "That's all."

"Yeah, well I don't want to talk to you!" she hollered at him over my shoulder.

I angled my head toward Nick.

"Go home," I said. "I'll take care of her."

Nick hesitated for a minute, and was about to get back into his van when I heard a wild cracking sound, and felt Peach jerk in my arms.

13

"Ow!" Peach said, and put her hand on the back of her head. "What the—?"

My heart pounded as the first dose of panic flooded my bloodstream. I glanced around, and saw the smoke behind Peach. I pulled her behind me, pushing her toward my front door, and said, "Inside!"

I heard the distinct wood-creaking sound I remembered from the last time Peach got pelted, only this time it was louder, almost deafening. I looked toward Peach's house and saw a dark gray haze forming into wisps of smoke as walnuts, pasty pale green and lime-sized, began to appear in its midst.

"Get inside!" I yelled to Peach, then looked at Nick. "Get her in my house!"

Nick, however, was staring down the street, at the pool of light under the streetlamp at the corner, where Millie stood in her bloodred dress, her arms raised around her as she walked slowly toward us. Her fingers flashed out from her, and behind me I heard a thunk and Peach gave a little scream.

"Millie?" Nick started walking toward her. I glanced behind us at Peach, who was now surrounded by a tornado cone of flying walnuts and wild gray smoke, trying to bat them off as if they were bees. Nick, meanwhile, continued for Millie, who was making her way toward us, her fingers flicking out from her at unnatural speed, manipulating the magical walnuts that were pelting Peach as she closed in. I had nothing, no magic, not even an umbrella. But I had at least learned one thing: that kind of magic required concentration to maintain.

"Aaaaaagh!" I yelled, and started to run down the street, passing Nick as I gained speed. I launched myself through the air and, landed on Millie, taking her with me as we both fell to the ground. She made an "oomph" sound as she hit, and I hopped back to a crouch, ready to spring at her again.

Millie scrambled to her feet and narrowed her eyes at me. "This isn't about you, Liv. Go home." She flashed out her fingers, and behind me, Peach screamed. I glanced back and saw Peach racing down the street, the walnuts in hot pursuit, continuing to pelt her from all directions. She had her arms up around her head, but the walnuts kept coming at her, moving so fast you could hear them whistling through the air.

When I looked at Nick, though, he was focused completely on what he was doing: reaching out to Millie.

"Millie?" he asked, his voice flat and dull. "Are you okay?"

"Don't touch her!" I said, and kicked at his arm to push him away just as Millie was about to take his hand.

Nick looked at me, his eyes glassy and wild, but losing a bit of that dazed quality as he held his arm where I'd kicked him. "What the fuck, Liv?"

"She's . . . contagious," I said quickly. "She's sick and she's contagious and if you touch her . . ."

Peach fell then, just a few feet away from where we were.

The walnuts were still popping out of the air, throwing themselves at her, pelting her unconscious body. I turned to Millie and grabbed her arm. "Cut it out, Millie!"

She wrenched her arm away from me. "I said, *go home!*" She flashed her fingers and some walnuts cracked against my upper back; it felt like the pelts from a paintball gun, only with a lot more sting. I cursed and rubbed my shoulder.

"Goddamnit, Millie!"

Nick blinked, and looked at Millie. "Millie? What's going on?"

"She already has everything! She doesn't get to have you, too!" And with that, Millie raised her hands, and there was more flashing of her fingers. I looked down the street to Peach's body; gray smoke was swirling around her.

"Nick," I said, but he was looking at Millie. His face wasn't tranced-out anymore, though; he was pissed. He grabbed Millie's forearms and turned her to face him.

"What the hell are you doing?"

Millie's fingers stopped moving, and I released a breath as I looked to Peach, expecting the gray smoke to be dissipating; instead, it was picking up speed.

"I'm not doing anything," Millie said, her voice cold and sweet as she raised her hands, her palms out, her fingers still.

Fury cut through me, and I whipped around in a wild circle, trying to catch sight of Cain, somewhere. He was there; I could feel the thick blackness of his power, darker and nastier than my own, almost as dark and nasty as the anger I was feeling.

"You want me, you son of a bitch?" I hollered into the street. "Then come get *me!* Leave them alone!"

As expected, there was no response. I hunched over and dashed to Peach's side, crouching over her as walnuts came at me from all directions; one zapped me in the head and for a moment, all I saw were stars. One got me in the shoulder; another on the hip. Then there was a concentrated, thunderous sound around me as they fell to the ground, lifeless. I raised my head just in time to watch as, one by one, they popped into puffs of gray smoke that dissipated into the air, as if they had never been there at all.

There was a touch on my shoulder, a gentle one, but still, I jumped and swung blindly at the attacker.

"Liv!" Nick said, jumping back, holding up his hands. "Liv, it's me!"

I fell back onto the patch of grass by the sidewalk and tried to catch my breath. I couldn't speak, I could barely breathe. My heart couldn't get a simple rhythm going, pounding erratically in my chest, and for a moment, I thought the fear alone was going to drop me right there.

Nick looked up and down the street, as if trying to get his bearings. "What the hell just happened?" He glanced down at the ground, where Peach lay on her stomach, and he made a hollow sound and dropped to his knees at her side. Gently, he rolled her over, looking at her bruised, unconscious body.

"What happened?" He looked at me, his eyes bright, almost fevered, as he dialed 911 on the cell phone. His voice shook a bit as he told them that we'd been attacked, and then he flipped the phone shut and tucked it in his pocket. He leaned down over Peach and pulled her into his arms, and she groaned as her eyes fluttered.

"Nicky?" she said.

"Yeah, baby." His voice got stronger, for her, and he'd even managed to inject his usual undertone of easy, good humor. "How ya feeling?"

"Ow," she said. "I'm feeling *ow*."

"I know." He ran his hand over the unbruised side of her face. "There are people coming to help. You just relax, okay?"

"What happened?"

A flash of disturbance ran through his expression, and he looked to me, a question on his face.

"You don't remember?" I asked quietly.

He shook his head, just a bit, just enough to tell me he remembered nothing without alarming Peach.

"Me, either," I lied. Seemed the simplest of all my choices.

He smiled down at Peach. "You're okay, and everything's going to be just fine."

He didn't remember. Probably, neither would Peach. It was only then that I thought to glance up and down the street—a street on which you couldn't open your refrigerator at midnight without Ginny Boyle or Frances Huddy commenting on it the next day—and no one had come out of their houses. I could see the flickering lights from televisions playing on some windows; in front of others were shadows of people passing from one room into the other. My neighbors were home, but no one seemed to have heard or seen or noticed a thing.

I turned my head the other way, toward the spot where Millie had been; there was no sign of her. I remembered her cold laugh, and the joy in her voice when she'd said, *I'm not doing anything.*

It had been a lie, of course; she'd done some of it. But not all.

It was *him,* the son of a bitch. He'd loaned her power, and when she'd pooped out, he'd tried to finish the job, until I got in the way. To kill Peach, he would have had to go through me, and he didn't want me dead.

Yet.

People didn't start to come out of their houses until the ambulance got there, and then all hell broke loose. A crowd formed around us, everyone asking what had happened, and none of us could say. Well, I could, but I didn't; I feigned amnesia to fit in with Peach and Nick, who genuinely didn't seem to remember. The EMTs treated Peach and put her in the ambulance, and Nick went with her. Ginny Boyle told me I looked like hell, and I should go to the hospital with them, but I declined. I had a tender spot on my shoulder, and my lip had split a bit on the lower left side, but aside from that, I was okay.

Well, physically, I was okay. Emotionally, I was a mess. Furious, helpless, terrified. Once the furor on the street died down, and I'd refused the many offers of hot tea, baked goods, and guest rooms in case I didn't want to go home alone, I went back into my house. I walked upstairs to my bedroom, where I found Gibson in his box, snuggled up with the little crane, who perched on Gibson's back, either dead or asleep. I put my finger under the crane's little paper feet, and it stirred, then moved gently onto my finger.

"Good boy," I said, hitting instantly on a name for him. "Good Niles."

I walked him downstairs to my front door. I put my hand

on the doorknob and it took me a moment to find the courage to open it, but I did. I went out onto my porch and whispered, "Bring her here, Niles. Right now," and then pushed my hand up into the air. Niles flew upward, bounced off the ceiling of my porch, and then made his way out into the night. I didn't know if I could even give him orders he would follow at night. I didn't know if he could find her. I didn't know if he had enough magic or life left in him to make it past the end of my street. But sending him out was all I could do, and so, it's what I did.

I stood there on my porch for a while, looking up and down my street, trying to see through all the darkness. I couldn't, so I turned and went back inside to wait.

Davina showed up a little before midnight. I heard the creak of her footsteps on the porch and met her at the door. When I opened it, Niles flew inside and up the stairs to reconvene with Gibson in my room. Davina stepped inside, setting her heavy leather backpack on the floor.

"Well, something must be important, that little guy would not let me sleep—" Her bright expression darkened as she caught sight of me, and she reached out to touch my chin right below where my lip was split.

"What happened?"

"Millie," I said.

Davina pulled her hand back, her face awash in concern, but not surprise. "Walnuts again?"

"He used her. I don't think she even knows what she's doing. He put the whammy on Peach and Nick; they were there for all of it, they don't even remember." I stepped back from her and started to pace as I ranted. "Peach is in the hospital, and so is Frankie Biggs. What's going to happen next? He's going to kill someone. And for what? For me? For magic, power?" I shook my head. "This isn't my fight. I don't want it, I don't need it, but most of all, I can't win it." I took a deep breath. "I want you to snakebite my magic."

Davina's eyes went wide for a moment, and she slowly shook her head. "Oh, no. No, no. I told you, that's dangerous."

"I need this over. Tonight, with Millie . . . I couldn't do anything. I was useless. And even if it was daytime, what would I have done? Turned the streetlights into bluebirds? Seriously, *what use is that?*" Tears welled in my eyes as my frustration and fear took over. "I'm scared. I want this over, *now.*"

"Oh, baby." Davina patted me on the shoulder, but I winced at the tenderness there, and she pulled her hand back. "Sorry."

"I need this, Davina. I need you to take this magic away from me."

She was quiet for a long time, then slowly shook her head. "I don't even know if I can do it. And even if I could . . . it killed Holly when Cain did it. What if . . . ?" She trailed off, her eyes wide with anxiety.

"If it looks like it won't work without killing me, then we'll stop," I said. "But we can at least try, right? I mean, it's got to be easier if I'm willing, right?"

Davina sighed, and shrugged her allowance of the point. "If you're going to survive this, though, you have to be strong enough."

"I made raspberries into butterflies today. I made them circle around me, and then I took the magic back and dropped them all back into the dish. I had total control."

She watched me. "Really? So soon?"

"Yeah. I can do this, and I trust you, Davina. I know you won't let anything hurt me. But as long as I have this magic, he's going to keep hurting the people around me and I can't stop it." My eyes teared up again, and Davina grabbed my hand.

"You're sure you want to try this?" she said, her voice grave.

"Yes," I said.

She went quiet for a minute, then picked up her leather backpack and flung it over her shoulder.

"Then let's go."

"Oh." I followed her to the door, surprised and relieved by her sudden acquiescence. "We can do it now? You don't need to get . . . I don't know. Supplies?"

She patted her backpack. "Since that attack, I've decided to travel fully stocked. I'm not taking any chances with you or your safety." She stopped at the doorway and turned to face me. "You can change your mind at any time."

"I'm not going to." I slid past her and turned to face her just as she pulled my front door shut behind us. "Where are we going?"

"Well . . ." She stepped out to the edge of the porch and glanced around. "We need a clear space, outside where we can catch some moonlight."

"I know just the place," I said, and led the way.

We walked the path to the clearing by the falls in silence. I kept my eyes ahead, listening to Davina's steps behind me to make sure she was still following, but I didn't look back. All I wanted was to get there and get this magic out of me, once and for all. I didn't care if I projectile-vomited pea soup for a week, this exorcism was going to happen. Still, even as my resolve held firm, my dread grew with every step we took. Whatever it was we were doing had killed my sister, and it was going to at least hurt, and likely a lot. But once I didn't have the power anymore, Davina could get out of town and Cain wouldn't have anything to stay for, and then everything here would go back to normal. I could go back to my job at CCB's, and I would be smart enough to be grateful for my boring, normal life.

"It's just a little farther," I said as we came to the last part of the path. We made our way up the incline to the clearing by the falls. I stopped and turned to see Davina surveying the area, her face inscrutable even in the bright moonlight.

"Running water," she said, sighing as she surveyed the brook.

"Is that bad?" I asked.

She shrugged. "I can work around it." She raised one hand into the air, fingers splayed as if she was feeling for energy, and breathed deep. As she exhaled, she curled her hand into a fist that gleamed blue in the moonlight and whispered a few words that I guessed were in the Latin arena—if ever I'd been out of my depth, this was the moment—and then she dumped her backpack on the ground. I looked around.

"So . . . how exactly does this work?" I rubbed my hands up and down my arms, which had gone to gooseflesh. "Is it some kind of rite or something? You don't have to cut me or anything, do you?"

"No, no, nothing like that," Davina said, rummaging through her bag. "I'm going to give you something to drink, and you drink it. I'll do the rest."

"That's it?" I said.

"That's it." She unzipped her backpack and began to unpack it. Vials of this and canisters of that, a leather book thudded to the ground; the thing was full to busting and who the hell knew what all she'd brought?

You really think she's going to spit that power out once she gets it? a voice inside me said. The voice was mine, but I squelched it. I didn't need doubt right now. I'd made my decision, and I was moving forward. It wasn't like I was swimming in options; I wanted that magic gone, for good. Davina wouldn't let me die, I was sure of that.

Pretty sure, anyway.

I watched Davina, who was focused entirely on her supplies. She pulled out a tall metal canister full of white powder and poured it in a wide circle, mumbling more of the Latin-ish stuff as she did. It looked a lot like the stuff Peach put on her carpets to vacuum. I tried to focus on that instead of the increasingly creepy feeling I was getting. It couldn't have been later than two in the morning, which meant I'd have no magic to draw on if anything went wrong. Not that a random woodland creature was going to be of much help if anything went wrong . . .

And that's when I shook my head. Davina was my friend. She was helping me. She was strong, and she understood what was going on. And like she'd said, if it got bad, we'd stop. All I had to do was say the word, and she'd stop. I was sure.

Pretty sure, anyway.

She finished pouring the circle, then stood in the middle, closed her eyes, and spoke a few more words. She opened her eyes again and they glittered in the moonlight as she stared at me across the circle. For a moment, her face had a wild look to it, more like a feral dog gauging its prey than a friend looking at a friend.

"You know," I said, taking a step back. "I think I'm going to need another minute."

She took a deep breath, then smiled. "I know it's scary, baby, but if we're going to do this, we should do it. We are running out of minutes." She started to walk around the edge of the circle, toward me, and I found myself stepping along the circumference, too, keeping it between us. She pointed toward my feet.

"Now be careful," she said. "You want to watch your step around that circle. If it gets broken, this could go terribly wrong."

I stepped back a bit, keeping an eye on the carefully drawn circle. "Wrong how?"

She stopped where she was, and I stopped as well, directly across from her. "What?"

"What happens if it goes wrong?"

"Won't go wrong if you do what I say," she said, her voice deepening.

"Okay, you're officially freaking me out."

She smiled warmly, and her voice softened. "I know. But it's for the best, right? I mean, you want to protect your town, don't you?"

"Right," I said. "So just . . . close my eyes and think of Nodaway?"

She laughed. "Something like that." Her smile faded. "You know, if you want to turn back, it's not too late. But once we start . . . well, then it will be tough."

I thought on that for a moment. Part of me wanted, very badly, to turn back. To run home, to crawl under my covers, and wake up in the sunlight and figure out another solution. But the rest of me knew there was no other solution. The next time someone got attacked, I would no more be able to stop it than I had been able to stop things the other night with Frankie, or tonight with Peach. And the next time, someone might get killed, and if they did, it would be my fault, and the very idea of that was way worse than anything I would be dealing with here, tonight. Davina wasn't going to let me get hurt, and this was the best shot we had at getting rid of Cain. Once I didn't have what he wanted anymore, everything would be okay. I just had to suck it up and get through to the other side; maybe I couldn't save the town from a rampaging redneck asshole, but this much, I *could* do.

"Let's get this done," I said, and took a deep breath, raised one foot, and stepped carefully over the powdered line, into the circle. I didn't realize I was holding my breath or scrunching my eyes until a moment later, when Davina said, "Gonna need to open your eyes, baby."

I opened them, and she handed me a water bottle. It was pink plastic, and had flowers on the side, which just seemed . . . wrong for a potion.

"So, I drink this? And that's it?"

"Yes," she said. "I already said the prayers for your protection, and the circle has been purified. All you have to do is drink that, and I'll take care of the rest."

"How much do I have to drink?" I asked.

"As much as you can. What's in that bottle is your best shot at surviving this process."

I felt tears come to my eyes, and my leg muscles began to tremble. "It's going to hurt, isn't it?"

Davina reached out and touched my face. "I'm going to take care of you. You trust me, right?"

She's not your friend.

It was the memory of Cain's voice in my head now, and there was no way I was listening to him.

"Yeah," I said. "I trust you."

Davina smiled. "Good." She touched the bottom of the water bottle in my hand, nudging it toward me.

"Let's get this over with, okay?"

"Okay." I lifted the bottle, pulled the top open, touched it to my lips, hesitated, and then squeezed. "Oh, god," I sputtered, spitting and choking. It went down like fire, harder than any alcohol I'd ever tasted. Davina rubbed my back and said, "I know, but it's all we've got. Remember, this is what's going to protect you when we get started. You have to drink it or it's just too much of a risk."

The tears splashed down my cheeks, partly from the burning in my esophagus, and partly from the terror I felt, but I thought of Peach being pelted into unconsciousness by walnuts, and I thought of Davina surrounded by gray smoke in the forest, and I forced myself to drink.

The first thing I felt were my arms getting weak and shaky, and the tingling crept up them, starting at my fingertips and going into my chest, bringing along a cold, dark feeling. It was getting hard to breathe, and I was starting to feel a little dizzy.

"Just a little bit more, baby," Davina cooed. "You're doing great."

I put the bottle to my lips and forced a little more down, gagging a bit as I did. The world around me was spinning, and there was yellow light swirling around me in electric wisps, and Davina was sucking it in, her face glowing with the power as it infused her. And that's when I noticed that there was also something swirling around her: dark gray smoke. I started to stumble and it occurred to me, a little late, that perhaps I'd just done something phenomenally stupid.

A flash went up around us, bright red and crackling, and then calmed; the white powder that had made the circle was burning. I tried to speak, tried to ask a question, but my body felt like it was encased in iron, everything cold and too heavy for me to move. Davina grabbed my shoulders and I screamed as the pain slashed through me, like swords of light cutting from my shoulders into my chest.

"Hush, baby," Davina said, her voice thick. "It'll be all over in a minute."

I tried to scream again, but there was no air inside me anymore. I worked up the strength to open my eyes, and saw Davina standing over me, holding me by my arms like I was a rag doll, her eyes gleaming in the flickering firelight with greed and power and not a bit of concern for my obvious distress.

That can't be good, I thought.

I wriggled a bit, but she held on tight. That was when it first occurred to me that I was maybe going to die.

She's not your friend, Cain's voice said again in my memory, and I thought absently, *You're right. She's not.*

But now, it was too late. I was going to die, and I would be leaving what was certainly an insane person behind to do . . . who the hell knew what? I felt pretty certain that saving the town wasn't as high on her priority list as she had led me to believe, though.

Stupid, stupid, stupid, I thought, but then stopped as I realized that beating myself up wouldn't help things. I had to work with what I had, which wasn't much. I closed my eyes again, tried to get past the pain, and did the only thing I could think of doing.

I spit in her face.

14

"Ugh!" she said, releasing one of my arms as she instinctively swiped at her face. I jerked myself out of her grip and shifted in the air as I fell, using the force of my body—for once, I was glad I had some heft to me—to hurl myself toward the flaming edge of the circle. I hit it, breaking the circle with a skid as I hurtled into a world of hurt, and the fire went out instantly. I heard another thud after my own body fell; I figured it was Davina, and gained some comfort from the sound.

"You stupid bitch!" she rasped, and when I looked up, I saw her, clawing the ground, pulling herself toward me like some demented zombie from a bad fifties' pulp cover. I took a deep breath and clawed as well, heading toward the gurgling brook. I managed to crawl across it, the coldness from the water shooting sharp ice picks of pain through me. Finally, after what seemed like years, I made it to the other side and turned to see her, on her stomach, stopped at the moving water, shooting me the most vile look I'd ever received in my life. Lacking the strength to speak, I flipped her off and then fell back onto the ground with a thud.

I dipped into darkness then for a bit, and when I came to I

was breathing, albeit with a lot of pain, my entire body seeming to protest every breath, every heartbeat, by shooting sharp shards of hurt through every nerve. I lay back on the ground, my chest arching as I gasped for air, and when I opened my eyes I could see vague wisps of yellow light drifting back into me. I followed the trails of light to their source, Davina's brightly dressed form splayed on the ground at the opposite side of the circle. After a moment, the light dissipated, and the world was silent and dark around us as we both breathed, at first loudly and with effort, and eventually slower, and calmer.

What the hell was that? I thought, lacking the strength to speak out loud.

You screwed up, was what came back, and although I knew I had felt the words instead of heard them, I also knew they hadn't come from me. Telepathy, however, was not the strangest thing that had happened to me lately, so I went with it. I moved my head a bit, trying to get a better look at Davina. She stared back at me, her eyes gleaming in futile fury.

If you think this was bad, Davina's voice said in my head, *just wait until I recover and come for you again. You will wish you'd died tonight. Just wait.*

"Just you wait, 'Enry 'Iggins, just you wait," I sang in a scratchy whisper through my burned throat. Then I laughed a bit, which sent pain radiating from my lungs to my toes, and my eyes filled with tears.

Ow.

"That's right, baby," Davina said, out loud this time.

I closed my eyes and thought, *Bring it on, bitch.*

"Liv!" A man's voice echoed through the woods, familiar, but I couldn't place it. I could hear hard footsteps racing through the brush. I stayed on the ground, thinking, *Right here!* but was unable to say anything. Singing to Davina had used up what little strength I'd had left.

"Goddamnit, where the hell are you?" He was frightened, whoever he was.

I opened my eyes. It was still dark, and cold, but there was a hint of the coming dawn on the horizon. I must have passed out, for a couple of hours at least. I turned my head, which throbbed in response, and looked for Davina. She was gone, as was her backpack. As far as I could tell, all evidence of her ever having been there was gone. I closed my eyes and tried to make sense of it. She'd had the strength to get up and walk away, and she hadn't killed me?

"Liv!"

Tobias. I recognized his voice, and the relief of hearing it washed over me. I was going to die, sure, but at least I'd be with Tobias when I did. I felt hot tears track down the sides of my face, but I couldn't move. I closed my eyes and listened to the footsteps. They were getting louder, which meant he was closer. Possibly he'd get to me before I died.

That would be nice, I thought, and fell into darkness again, coming out only when I felt the *boom* of Tobias as he skidded to his knees on the ground beside me, each vibration shooting pain through my entire body, but I was too weak to even whimper.

"Liv, goddamnit," he said, running his hand down my arm. It was a gentle touch, but it still hurt like a mother.

I opened my eyes. "Quit it!" I croaked, each word a torture in my ruined throat. I tried to wrench my arm away from him, but it just wiggled a little, and gave me spasms of pain for my trouble.

He leaned over me, his hand gently touching my face. "I need you to stay with me, Liv."

I could tell he was trying to keep a calm facade, but underneath, there was panic in his eyes. If I didn't know I was going to die before, I knew it now. Tears pricked my eyes. "Tobias . . ."

"Stop. You're going to be fine." He shrugged a messenger bag off his shoulder and pulled a water bottle out, then put his hand under my head, angling me up.

"Ow!" I grunted, but he ignored me, pushing the water bottle to my lips and squirting liquid that was *not* water into my mouth. I sputtered it out with what strength I had, finally feeling the desire to live, even though I knew it was hopeless, and I started to cry.

"Liv, listen to me," he said, his voice calm and even. "You need to drink this. You understand?"

I managed to focus my eyes on his face, his beautiful face. His eyes were red-rimmed and frantic, his hair was a mess, and he looked like he could maybe use a shave, but he was my Tobias, and he was always beautiful to me.

A racking pain shot through my body, and I whimpered. "It hurts."

"Yeah. I know." He touched the bottle to my lips and squirted it into my mouth. I sputtered a bit, the stuff tasted like flat beer with dirt in it, but once swallowed it was cool and soothing to my wretched esophagus, and I managed to drink some. I swallowed down as much as I could, then fell back on the ground. The racking pain subsided, but then . . .

"Oh, god, I don't feel right," I said, and Tobias held me while I vomited everything I'd ever consumed in my life onto the ground. After a few minutes, I collapsed against him, the thrumming of his heart next to my ear giving me some comfort through my intense misery. He held me to him, one hand cupping my head as the other wrapped around my middle, pulling me toward his warmth.

"You all done?" he asked after a minute.

"I thought that was supposed to make me feel better."

"It's supposed to save your life," he said "Can you move your toes?"

I looked down at my legs, which still felt leaden and cold. Although breathing was no longer as painful as it had been before, just the idea of moving my toes made me start to cry. "I can't."

"Try."

"It's too hard," I whimpered.

"Liv, come on. Just *try*." His voice was ragged, and I could hear the desperation in it. "Please."

"Okay." I sniffled, concentrated, and wriggled my right big toe a little. "Can I die now?"

"No." He pulled a green hoodie sweatshirt out of his pack and slid it over my head, not bothering to string my arms through the sleeves, then settled me gently back on the ground. I looked up at him as he slung his bag back over his shoulders, the predawn sunlight bathing him in a soft glow that made him look almost unreal. Maybe I had imagined it all. Maybe he wasn't really there.

Maybe I was already dead.

Huh.

He looked around, then put his fingers between his teeth and let out an ear-shattering whistle.

"Ow," I said, and then I heard footsteps. I pulled my focus onto Tobias, who was standing still, but watching a point to my left. Slowly, I forced my head to turn, but all I saw were an old pair of construction work boots, and then a rough, Southern voice said, "She alive?"

"Yeah," I heard Tobias say, his voice tense. "She's not doing great, though."

There was a grunt, then the work boots stopped next to me. A moment later, Cain crouched down and looked at me, his eyes flickering with cold assessment over my face, then my body.

"Can she move?" he asked, not bothering to talk directly to me.

"A little," Tobias said, his voice quiet.

Cain reached out to touch my face, and I wanted to shrink back from him, but I couldn't. Maintaining consciousness was about all I had it in me to do at the moment.

"No," I said, my eyes filling with tears. How could Tobias do this? Bring *Cain* to me when I was at my weakest? What the hell was going on? My vision started to darken, but whether it was a result of my panic or my impending death, I didn't know.

"We have to go back to my place," Cain said, leaning forward to pick me up.

"No," I whimpered, and my body started to shake and convulse.

"I got her," Tobias said. A moment later, the hard earth was no longer under me, and I was being jostled about in Tobias's arms as he carried me out of the forest. I tried to speak, to ask Tobias what the hell he was doing with Cain, but the pain of the movement was too much, and I passed into blackness instead.

When I woke up, I was lying on a futon, staring at a nicotine yellow ceiling in a vaguely familiar studio apartment, although I couldn't place where I'd seen it before. I didn't know how long I'd been passed out, but the light outside wasn't full yet, so it couldn't have been too long. Or, it was so long that it was already dusk.

Or, I was dead, and hell was a studio apartment with nicotine ceilings. At this point, my mind was open to anything.

"Tobias?" I croaked, my throat rough and pained from all the abuse it had taken.

I heard noise, the clanking of pots, pans, utensils, and I lifted my head a bit to look. Cain was rummaging through the cabinets in his kitchenette, pulling out little bottles and tins and setting them aside. They looked a lot like the bottles and tins I'd seen Davina using.

"Where's Tobias?"

"What?" He opened a tin, sniffed it, then shook his head and tossed it aside on the counter.

"Tobias?"

Cain looked at me over his shoulder, then opened another cabinet and continued rummaging.

"He went to get me something I need," he said. "He'll be back later."

"Oh." I laid my head back down on the cushion. I was covered with a blanket, but my body was still shivering involuntarily with cold. "Are you going to kill me?"

I couldn't see Cain anymore, but from the sounds of things, he just continued his business in the kitchenette, ignoring me.

"It's just that, if you're going to kill me, it's kind of mean to bring me here to do it. I had the job half-done for you in the forest."

He made a harsh sound, then said, "Shut up and let me concentrate."

"She tried to kill me," I said, staring at the ceiling while the bottles and tins clanked in the kitchenette. "*You* tried to kill me. I don't understand why people want to kill me. I'm basically a very nice person."

"I didn't try to kill you," he said. "I tried to kill *her.*"

I blinked, trying to adjust my memory to what had really happened, but my mind was reeling. I couldn't put it all together.

"But . . . that night . . ."

"I was following her. She took the opportunity to put on a show for you."

I tried to wrap my mind around it all. The woods, the smoke, the branches flying . . . it had been Davina. "But she was knocked out. How . . . ?"

He made a disgusted noise. "She was never knocked out."

And then, the truth flowed over me like water. It had been Davina all along. She'd used Millie and Amber Dorsey as conduits, and blamed Cain to get my trust. *She* was the gray smoke. Not Cain. She'd never actually been knocked out that night in the woods; she'd faked it to frame Cain. Tobias knew this, and had brought Cain to me to save me, not to kill me.

I took a moment to adjust to this, to temper my intense dislike of Cain and my strong affection for Davina with the knowledge that he hadn't done any of the bad stuff; she had. But the proof was simple; Tobias had trusted me to Cain, and I trusted Tobias.

So that was that.

"God, I'm so stupid," I said.

There was a long pause, then, "You're not stupid. You just wanted to believe. Get someone who wants to believe, half your work is done for you."

I closed my eyes, then opened them again as I realized something. "Hey. This is the apartment above Happy Larry's, isn't it? I was here for a party once in high school."

Cain grunted. I took that as confirmation.

"Happy Larry lied. He told Betty he hadn't seen you."

"A good man knows when to keep his mouth shut."

"Happy Larry is not a good man. Happy Larry is a sleaze-bag," I said. "You paid him off, didn't you?"

"Damnit. Where the hell is it?" Cain opened a drawer, cursed, and shut it again.

I stared at the ceiling and just repeated whatever thoughts

came into my head. "I don't understand anything that's happening."

"Here it is," Cain muttered. I heard water running, and looked up to see him filling a pot. I rested my head back down, and tried to move my fingers. It hurt, but not as much as I thought it would.

"I can move my fingers," I said. "That's good, right?"

"Don't move anything. Just breathe and shut the hell up. You're not out of the woods yet. You like Splenda? Don't much matter, it's all that's in here." He ripped open two packets and dumped them in the pot.

"I hate Splenda," I said. "Any man who doesn't appreciate a woman with curves probably doesn't like women much to begin with, anyway." I remembered when Davina had said that the night we met, how much I had liked her. My eyes filled with tears and I blinked them back, not wanting to deal with Cain's certain surly response to my being a human person.

Cain grabbed a spoon and started stirring. I went quiet for a while, staring at his ceiling, distracting myself by wondering if it was originally white and had just been neglected into that nicotine yellow, or if Happy Larry the Sleazebag had actually thought that was a good color for the apartment. I entertained the idea of asking Cain, but then decided he'd just tell me to shut the hell up anyway.

A few minutes later, he was at my side, holding a plain mug with a blue stripe around the top.

"Hey," I said. "I know that mug. Did Happy Larry steal that from CCB's? He did, the sleazebag."

He put his hand behind my head and held the cup to my lips. "Drink."

"Oh, god, not another putrid—" I began, but stopped as I sniffed. "Wait. That actually smells not bad."

Something that might have passed for a smile if you're grading on a really big curve graced his lips, and he said softly, "Just drink it, okay?"

I leaned forward a bit with his help and sipped it. It was warm, not hot, and tasted of peppermint and licorice, and the feel of it in my ruined throat was incredible. It wasn't terribly sweet, but just enough, and as I drank it down, the pain in my body started to fade a bit. I stopped halfway through, but Cain kept holding me up until I'd finished every last drop, then he gently lowered me down onto the couch.

"I'm not going to throw everything up again, am I?" I asked. "Because that was kind of a mean trick."

Cain walked to the other side of the tiny room, grabbed the pillow and blanket from his bed in the corner, and brought them back to me.

"I don't need those," I said. "I feel a lot better. Just give me a minute, and I'll be out of your hair."

"Shut up." He lifted my head and set the pillow underneath, then flipped the blanket out over me. "You're not going anywhere until you're stronger. Go to sleep."

"Stop telling me to shut up," I said, my lower lip twitching as my mood swung back into the crying zone. "I'm tired and I hurt and I'm scared, *so stop being mean to me.*"

He paused for a moment, watching me.

"You gonna cry again?"

I blinked a few times and took a deep breath. "No."

"Good." His expression seemed to soften a bit, and I looked up at him. We stayed like that for a bit, both of us seeming to accept the gentle transition from enemies to . . . well, not exactly friends, but we were on the same side at least. For the moment, anyway.

He broke the eye contact first, turning to grab the ugly orange recliner and shove it next to the couch. He sat down, flicked the legs out, and said, "Get some sleep. I'll be right here. She's gonna be hurting for a while, too, so it'll be a bit before she tries to get at you again."

"Is that supposed to comfort me?"

He shrugged, leaning back into the chair. "It's what I got."

"Right." I turned over onto my side, hugging the pillow under my head. "Why are you here? What does any of this have to do with you?"

He closed his eyes and rested his head back on the chair, and for a moment, I thought he hadn't heard me, but then he said. "I'm here because of her."

"Because of who?" I asked.

It took him a minute to answer. "Holly."

Holly. "My sister," I said absently. "Davina told me you killed her."

He let out a bitter huff. "She did, did she?"

"Not true?"

He was quiet for a long while, his face stony, and then he said, "No. It's not true."

I let the puzzle pieces slowly rearrange themselves in my head. "She's the one who stole Holly's magic. She was the conjurer.

She's the one who's going crazy, and needs my day magic to balance herself out." I felt dizzy, all the pieces flying around me, and I picked one out of the air. "And you . . . did you know Holly? Were you friends, too?"

He didn't answer, just stared off at a spot on the wall over my head, and my heart cracked a little as the realization hit.

"You loved her," I said, and his eyes shot back to mine. "Holly," I added, as if either of us needed the clarification.

Even through the hard shell he kept around him, I could see the pain in his face, the slump of his body, and my heart ached for him. Or for me. Probably both.

"You loved her," I said again, and again, he didn't argue. "Did she love you back?"

He lowered his eyes, and I could see the answer. *Yes. She had.*

"So . . . you're kind of like my brother-in-law, then."

"Go to sleep."

"No." I took a breath, trying to slow my thudding heart, and with great effort, pushed myself up to sitting.

"You forget the part where I saved your life? Least you can do is listen when I say you need rest."

"I want to know what happened," I said. "To Holly."

He gave me a dark look. "You know all you need to know."

"What was she like?"

"Lie back down. You look like you're gonna vomit again, and I don't want a mess on my floor."

"I just want to know what she was like," I said. "Was she pretty? Was she kind? Was she smart? Funny?"

Just the effort of sitting up was making me dizzy, but the

idea of lying down and going to sleep without learning everything there was to know about my sister from the man who
had loved her seemed unthinkable.

Cain leaned forward, his tone uncharacteristically gentle.
"We'll talk when you're stronger. But for now, you need to rest.
Okay?"

"Okay." I leaned back, slowly, onto the couch and my body
trembled a bit with the effort. My eyes filled with tears, and I
didn't bother to blink them back. A father I'd never known
about was missing, probably dead; a sister I'd never known about
was definitely dead; and the friend I'd thought could help me
make sense out of it all had betrayed me.

Cain shifted in his seat, but I didn't look at him, just closed
my eyes and let the tears flow. Screw him if he didn't like it.

I heard him get up a moment later, and when I looked up,
he was holding a roll of toilet paper out to me.

"Thanks." I took it from him, ripped off a length, and blew
my nose. He sat down in the recliner and kicked the legs out
again. I cried for as long as I needed to, and he didn't say a word.
After a while, the grief dried up, leaving only exhaustion in its
wake. I snuggled into the soft pillow.

"Happy Larry really is a sleazebag," I said, sniffling.

"Yeah," he said quietly, leaning his head back on the chair
and closing his eyes. "He is."

I don't know how long I slept, but it was almost dark when
I opened my eyes again. I could feel the *thump-thump* from the
music downstairs in the bar, but I couldn't hear clearly enough
to tell what song it was exactly, which said some impressive

things about the construction of the building, considering the apartment was right on top of the bar. I stretched for a moment, rolled on my side, and looked around.

Cain was gone, but Tobias was there, asleep in the orange easy chair, his hands clasped lightly over his stomach. I didn't make any noise, just watched him, but apparently the heat of my stare was enough to wake him. He opened his eyes and watched me for a long while, unmoving.

"How are you doing?" he said finally.

I sniffed. "It smells bad in here."

"That's probably me."

"I don't think so." I reached up to my neck, where something was tucked around my throat, into my sweatshirt. I pulled it out, holding it away from me with my two fingers.

A damp gym sock that had been filled with some kind of weird paste.

"Oh, right," Tobias said. "That's a poultice, for your throat. Cain sent me all the way out to Buffalo to get the mullein. I don't even know what the hell else he put in there."

"These people and gym socks, I swear. Smells like a mix of baby butt paste and dead muskrat." I tossed it across the room and lay back down. "Where is Cain?"

"Outside, having a smoke." Tobias kept his eyes on me, and even in the dark, I could see the intensity in his expression as he watched me. "How are you feeling?"

I took a moment to check myself. I wasn't cold anymore. My throat was still a bit raw, but definitely improved. My muscles felt weak and sore, but other than that . . .

"I think I might survive."

Tobias cleared his throat. "For a while there, we weren't sure you would."

"Oh." I swallowed. "Sorry."

His every muscle seemed taut with tension, making him look like an animal on alert for an attack. "Wanna tell me what the hell happened?"

I looked at him, surprised by the sudden ice in his tone. "You know what happened."

He got up from the chair and went to the window, staring out of it as he spoke. "I know that I asked you to stay home and wait for me, and I know that you didn't. What I don't know is if my advice even entered your mind when you were running off to get yourself killed."

I pulled myself up to a sitting position, and it made me a little dizzy, but lying down while getting yelled at made me feel too vulnerable. "Peach got attacked. I panicked. I just wanted the magic gone, I wanted it out of me. So I sent for Davina."

He turned to face me. "Why didn't you send for me?"

"Because . . ."

He waited for a moment for me to elaborate, and when I didn't, he let out an exasperated sigh. "Because *why*?"

I shrugged, annoyance creeping through me as he made me feel more and more like a kid in the principal's office. "Because I wanted it gone, and you couldn't help me with that. Davina could."

He let out a harsh, mirthless laugh. "Yeah. The same way she helped your sister, leaving her dead in the middle of a forest? Is that what you wanted? Because ten more minutes, and you would have had it."

"I didn't know that at the time. I thought Cain killed Holly, and I thought Davina was my friend." I put my hand to my spinning head. "Tobias, I'm in rough shape. Any chance the grilling can wait for a while?"

"Sure." He sat down in the chair, leaning back and pressing the heels of his hands into his eyes. He looked like hell, which made me feel like hell, but there was nothing to do but sit there and let the tension set around us.

"I thought you were dead," he said finally, but when I looked at him, he wasn't looking at me. He was staring at the ceiling. "I saw you lying there . . . you were so still. When I touched you, you were cold and all I could think was that you were dead and I had killed you."

"Tobias, that's ridiculous."

He shifted his focus to lock his eyes with mine. "I didn't want to crowd you. Had you just been a job, I would have shadowed you every minute. I wouldn't give a rat's ass if you were mad at me or if you didn't like it. I would have protected you."

At this, my ire rose. "What, just because I'm a woman, I can't take care of myself? I need a man around to protect me all the time? Sexist ass."

He gave me a dull look. "Not because you're a woman. Because someone wants to kill you, and I have more experience with that than you do."

My ire deflated. "Oh."

He let out a huff of annoyance. "Yeah."

"So . . . I guess I'm the sexist ass in this scenario, then?"

"Yep."

"Just checking." I yawned, unable to help myself, then breathed deeply and immediately regretted it. "Jeez, I need a shower. I smell like stinky gym sock."

He was silent, staring off into space. I sat forward, leaning my elbows on my knees.

"Forgive me for what I'm about to say, because I know every girlfriend in the world says this and it's awful but . . . what are you thinking?"

He watched me for a long moment, then said, "I'm thinking that you're not my girlfriend."

I felt the stab of that hit me hard in the gut, and I took a breath and sat back. "Ow."

"Liv—"

"No, I got it." I blinked hard, and took in a deep breath. "Message received."

"There's no way to make it work," he said, his tone flat. "One of these days, I'm going to disappear, and you'll never hear from me again."

"Stop protecting me," I said. "I'm a grown woman. I get to decide what I can handle and what I can't."

"What if I can't handle it?"

He said it so quietly that I almost wasn't sure if I'd heard him right, but when I looked at him, I knew I had. He was drained, both physically and emotionally, and he was coming off two days of panic and worry and very little sleep, if he'd gotten any at all. I put myself in his shoes for a moment, imagining how I would have felt if the roles were reversed. The very thought of finding him half-dead, of not knowing whether or not he would survive, of believing that I could have protected him but had failed . . . just imagining it made me feel sick.

I was still trying to figure out what to say when the front door opened, and Cain walked in. I hugged my arms around myself, digging my fingers into my sides and trying to concentrate on the physical pain, which was tough, but at least bearable. Tobias shot up off the chair and went out the door, letting it close quietly behind him.

"I see you've been winning friends and influencing people," Cain said wryly.

"Can I go home now?" I looked up at him, trying to focus my anger on him rather than deal with what had just happened between me and Tobias.

Cain watched me for a moment, then glanced toward the door through which Tobias had disappeared. When he looked back at me, his expression was not friendly, exactly, but it wasn't antagonistic, either.

"Yeah," he said. "If you can walk, you can go home."

I pushed myself up from the futon and took a step. My muscles felt wobbly, but I managed to put one foot in front of the other and not fall down, so I chalked that up as success. Cain walked over to me, took my hand and placed it on his shoulder, and I pulled it away.

"You either lean on me or him," he said, motioning his head in the direction Tobias had gone. "But you're not making it down those steps without help."

I sighed and gripped his shoulder, letting him put one hand on the small of my back to help guide me. We stepped outside onto the metal exterior steps that led down the side of

Happy Larry's to the alley. Tobias, who had been sitting on the top step, got up.

"We're going back to her house," Cain said. He and Tobias exchanged a glance, and Tobias stepped out of the way to let us by. I kept my eyes on my feet as we navigated the rickety metal staircase, and managed to ignore the fact that Tobias was right behind us as we made our way home.

15

I was sitting on my couch, freshly showered and in blissfully clean clothes, when there was banging on the front door, and I heard an aged voice hollering, "Livvy?"

Betty.

"In here!" I called out, too tired to even think of getting up to answer the door.

"Liv?" Betty came into the living room and looked at me, her hand over her heart. "I swear to god, if I survive this, I'm going to kill you. I am too *old* for this, Livvy."

She made her way over to the couch and sat next to me, pulled me into a hug, then pinched my cheek, kinda hard.

"Ow!"

"That's what you get for scaring the hell out of me." She leaned back on the couch, hand over her heart. "I need a drink."

"What happened?"

She turned her eyes to me. "Ginny Boyle told us that you were there when Peach got attacked, and then I called and called and called and all I got was voice mail."

"Oh, yeah, sorry," I said. "I turned my phone into a bat."

"So, I came here last night to check on you, and you weren't here." She picked up my cell phone, which was still charging on the coffee table where I'd left it two nights ago. "I left you a thousand messages. Where were you?" Before I could answer, she said, "Oh, god, Stacy!" She flipped open her phone, hit a number for speed-dial and then said, "Stacy, I've got her. Yes, she's . . . fine." She eyed me warily as she said it; I guessed I didn't look quite fine. "Okay, come by in the morning, and you can yell at her then." She tucked her phone in her pocket and sat next to me, grabbing my hands in hers. "Honey, you look awful. Do I smell bacon?"

"Oh. Yeah. Um . . ." I hesitated for a minute, wondering how to explain why Cain was in my kitchen cooking for me, but I was too tired to explain, so I just said, "Cain's making eggs."

Betty froze and her voice went low. *"Cain?"*

"He's okay," I said. "Davina tried to steal my magic last night. He saved my life."

Betty opened her mouth, then closed it, then looked at me, her face all confusion, but I had to give her credit—she didn't argue, and she didn't say *I told you so.* "And now he's making you eggs?"

"Everything's in the wash," Tobias said, stepping into the living room. "I set it to cold, like you said. Hey, Betty."

He sat down in the floral love seat across from the couch, and Betty raised a brow at me.

"One man cooking for you, another doing your laundry." Betty smiled at me. "How do I get your job?"

I managed a half-smile, and Tobias cleared his throat stiffly. Betty looked from me to him, then back to me. Her expression softened as she picked up on the not-too-subtle tension between me and Tobias; her response was to squeeze my hand gently.

"Now eat this slowly," Cain said, coming around the corner into the living room, a plate in his hand. "Little bites. If you hurl, I'm not cleaning it up."

Cain paused for a moment when he saw Betty, then walked over to stand across the coffee table from me. Betty stiffened, making it clear she was not happy about Cain's presence in my house. Cain, either not noticing or not caring, handed me the plate and a fork and repeated himself, as though I was a third-grader. "*Little* bites."

"Betty . . . this is Cain." I said, motioning toward Cain with my fork. "He's a conjurer, a . . ." I hesitated, choosing my words carefully, ". . . friend of Holly's. Cain, this is Betty. She's my boss. Also, she makes magical pastries."

Cain gave a brief nod, and Betty shifted closer to me on the couch. I poked at the food on my plate and my stomach protested, so I turned to Betty.

"How's Peach doing?"

"They let her go from the hospital this morning," she said. "She had a minor concussion, but other than a few bruises, she's okay. Nick's with her next door. Neither one of them can remember what happened." Betty looked at me pointedly. "I'm assuming you know."

I sighed and put the fork down. "Millie. Walnuts. Only it wasn't just Millie. She was surfing Davina's power."

"She'll tell you about it later," Cain said, picking up the fork and putting it back in my hand. "Right now, she needs to eat, and then she needs to rest."

Betty shot an annoyed look at Cain, and turned her attention back to me. "So, I take it Tobias knows . . . everything?"

I nodded. "He's Magical security. Holly sent him to watch over me, a year and a half ago."

Betty straightened in surprise and looked at Tobias. "ASF or RIAS?"

"ASF," he said.

"What's that?" I said.

"Allied Strategical Forces," Tobias said. "Name of the firm."

"Better than RIAS," Betty said. "You can't trust those bastards. They get ahold of you, no one will ever hear from you again."

"RIAS?" I asked. "What's RIAS?"

Tobias looked at me. "Regional Initiative Action Services."

"Oh." I thought for a beat. "So, Magicals are as fond of bullshit acronyms as everyone else, then?"

Betty looked at me. "We're Magical, but we're still human."

"But Tobias is with the good group, the . . . whatsit?"

"ASF," Tobias said.

Betty let out a huff of disgust. "To say they're good is a bit of an overstatement. They're better than RIAS, but that's a pretty low bar." She looked at Tobias. "No offense."

"Trust me, none taken." Tobias stood up and looked at Cain. "I'm gonna take watch out front."

Cain nodded, and Tobias left without looking at me or Betty. I watched him go until the front door shut behind him, and it took a moment before I realized someone was saying my name.

"Olivia."

I pulled myself out of my distraction and looked up at Cain, who motioned toward my plate. "Eat."

"Right." I took a few bites, chewing slowly and swallowing carefully, until the thought of taking another bite made my stomach turn in protest. I handed the plate back to Cain; it looked as though I'd barely touched it.

"I'm sorry," I said. "I can't . . ."

"It's okay." He took the plate back, and Betty said, "So, Cain, you were friends with Liv's sister?"

There was ice in her voice when she said his name, but I was too tired to defend him, not that he needed me to; I got the sense that if Cain was comfortable with anything, it was hostility.

"Yeah," he said simply.

"So . . ." Betty put effort into covering her distrust with sympathy. "Can you tell us what happened there? And what it all has to do with Liv?"

After a moment of assessment, Cain finally sat in the chair across from us and leaned forward, elbows resting on his knees.

"Davina's got one MO; come to town, pretend to be a friend, take what she wants, and step over the bodies on her way out."

Betty reached out and took my hand, but kept her eyes on Cain. "Well, you stopped her. She didn't kill Liv."

Cain shook his head. "Davina's no quitter. She's gonna keep coming at Liv until she gets what she wants."

"So . . . what are we gonna do?" I asked, my voice sounding feeble even to my own ears.

Cain looked at me and said, "Right now? You're gonna

sleep and heal up. I got a plan, but I need you strong to make it work."

"What's the plan?" Betty asked.

Cain picked up my picked-over plate of eggs, and stood up. "We'll talk about it tomorrow." And then he walked back into the kitchen.

As soon as he was gone, Betty spoke, her voice low and panicked. "Liv? What the hell is going on? Wasn't he trying to kill you twenty minutes ago?"

"No," I said. "That was Davina. It was always Davina. Cain was trying to stop her, not hurt me. And then, after the attack with Peach, I just wanted the magic gone, so I called Davina and . . ." I let out a bitter laugh. "God, I was so stupid. I offered her my magic. It was exactly what she wanted. She set that whole Millie attack up just to get me desperate enough to turn to her, and I fell for it."

My entire body started shaking then, little racking spasms of fear I was too weakened to control. Betty rubbed my back and said, "Everything is going to be okay. But Cain's right. You need to rest. Get a little sleep, and you'll be able to deal with everything else."

I nodded, although I wasn't sure I believed her.

Betty got up off the couch and looked down at me. "I'm going to go upstairs and prepare the guest rooms. I'm staying, and I assume"—she nodded in the direction of the kitchen—"*he's* staying, too?"

"He's the man with the plan, and that's more than I've got so . . . yeah," I said.

"And Tobias . . . ?" she said softly.

I shrugged. "I don't know. But there are four guest rooms upstairs, and there's clean bedding in the closet at the end of the hall, next to the bathroom. Thank you."

Betty nodded and headed upstairs. I had a few moments of silence, and then the front door opened, and Tobias walked in.

"All quiet on the western front?"

He nodded, but didn't say anything.

"You look like hell," I said, not really meaning to be so blunt about it, but unable to edit myself.

He rubbed at his face, and I could hear the scratch of the scruff under his hand. "That sounds about right. I haven't slept in two days."

"Up the stairs, second door on the right. Room's yours, if you want to stay here tonight."

He eyed me for a second, then said, "The couch is fine."

"God, I'm not making a pass," I said, feeling a stab of annoyance. "You made yourself clear on that. I'm just saying, this house is lousy with guest bedrooms, and I'm offering you one."

"I know," he said. "It's just that someone should be down here on the couch, keeping an eye out."

"*I'm* staying on the couch," a voice said from behind me. I turned and saw Cain standing in the entryway between the hall and the living room. He, however, wasn't looking at me; he was looking at Tobias.

"She needs sleep," he said. "You want to help her to her room, or should I?"

"Oh, *please*," I said, pushing myself up off the couch. "I'm not an invalid, I don't need—*whoa*."

I put my hand to my head as the world got wobbly, and Tobias was there in a moment, one arm around my waist. I didn't have enough pride left to fuel an argument, so I let him lead me upstairs, and I almost wept with gratitude when we got to my room and I saw my bed.

"I love this bed," I said as I plopped face-first into my bedding. I turned my head to the side, indulging in the soft girliness of the down under my face. "I shouldn't have mocked that guy who married his pillow. I'm having serious romantic feelings for this duvet."

Tobias chuckled as he pulled back the covers and maneuvered me into them.

"Sleep well," he said, and he might have said more, but I was passed out before I could hear anything else.

It was a little after dawn when my eyes fluttered open. The light in my room was dim, but I could see the shape of Tobias, slumped on the floor with his back against the door, his head hanging down as he slept. I could hear his breath, just the slightest hint of a snore, and I sat up to watch him.

His hands were clasped lightly over his stomach, which rose and fell with his breath. His lips turned up slightly at the corners, and I realized that despite all the incredible tragedy he'd experienced in his life, a smile was his default expression. I felt a sudden overwhelming swell of love for him, and then was distracted as my hands began to tingle.

Not now, I thought, and shook them out, then closed my eyes and calmed my heart. When I opened them again, Tobias's head was up, and he was watching me.

"You okay?" he asked.

"Yeah," I said. "You slept by my door all night?"

He cleared his throat and shifted up so he wasn't quite so slumped, then said, "Yeah."

I smiled. "Did I mention I have four guest bedrooms in this place?"

He tapped one knuckle gently against the door. "You underestimate how comfortable this door is."

I scooched to one side of the bed, making space for him. "Come up here. If you're not going to leave my side, at least don't be an idiot. You can't protect me if you've got a spasm in your back."

I patted the empty space next to me. He hesitated for a moment, then pushed himself up and lay down on top of the covers, leaning back into the pillows and letting out a slow sigh.

"You're right," he said, a small smile forming on his face. "This is a great bed."

I lay down next to him, suddenly wide awake, and stared at the ceiling. I listened for his breathing to deepen and morph into the light snore I'd heard before, but after a few minutes went by and that didn't happen, I turned my head to look at him, and found him watching me.

"I don't care what Edward did in the Twilight books, watching a girl sleep is just creepy."

He smiled. "You weren't sleeping."

"Don't think you're going to breeze by on a technicality, Shoop. You go all Cullen on me, I'm staking you through the heart."

He laughed. "Good."

I was quiet for a while, and then I said, "I'm sorry about all this. I know it sucks."

"It's okay," he said.

"It's not." I turned in bed to face him, pushing up on one elbow. "I hate this. I hate having to deal with the magic at all, but to have some crazy woman want to kill me? That's too much. And now you're pulled into it, and Cain—I don't care if he's good, he still creeps me out." I let out a heavy sigh. "And then there's Millie."

"What about Millie?"

"Davina did something to her," I said. "She created this monster where Millie used to be. Millie was sweet and quiet and thoughtful and smart, and now she's just . . . evil. It's like Davina ate her soul or something. Can she do that?"

Tobias opened his mouth to say something, then seemed to think better of it.

I couldn't have that. "Go ahead. Say it."

He met my eye. "Davina gave her a makeover, and she loaned her some power. Everything else that Millie's doing . . . I don't know. I think it's just . . . Millie."

"What? What the hell are you talking about? Have you met Millie? She would never hurt anyone."

"Except, she *did,*" he said. "She seduced Nick. She attacked Peach, physically. Twice. Magic walnuts or a baseball bat, the choice to attack is what matters. Millie's been repressed and angry for a long time. She was a stick of dynamite just waiting to be lit."

I shook my head. "You barely even know her. *I* know her."

He yawned and rubbed his eyes. "Yeah, but that's the thing. You never really know anyone. You see what they want to show you, and if you're lucky, they show you most of the truth. My point is, there's only so much of this that you can blame on Davina. Millie made a lot of her own choices here."

"You're not making me feel better."

"I'm not trying to make you feel better," he said. "I'm trying to tell you the truth."

I flopped back into my pillow. "Yeah, *your* truth. And it's a stupid truth. It stinks."

He closed his eyes. "Fair enough."

"Little flies are zooming around it, it stinks so bad."

He opened one eye and looked at me. "You done yet?"

"Somewhere out there, there's a dead fish thinking, 'Well, at least I don't stink as bad as Tobias's truth.'"

He closed his eye again. "I'll take that as a no."

"Jack Nicholson called. He said even he can't handle the stink."

He laughed. "I must be really tired, because that one struck me as funny."

"It's not that you're tired. It's that I'm funny. I'm a woman of many talents."

"Yeah. You are."

I looked at him then, and our eyes locked for a while. Then he held out his arm, and I curled up into him, resting my head on his chest and letting the reassuring *ta-dum* of his heartbeat lull me back to sleep.

16

After a breakfast of Betty's incredible conjured blueberry muffins and my adequate coffee, Tobias left to get some things from his apartment, and Cain went into the living room to do something—he grumbled a few gruff words about research. Betty and I sat at my linoleum table and drank coffee and ate muffins until finally, she couldn't take it anymore.

"I saw Tobias coming out of your room this morning," she said.

I lowered my coffee mug. "Seriously? Everything that's going on? This is what we're going to focus on?"

Betty grinned. "You bet. The best cure for times of crisis is gossip. So, tell me . . . what's going on with you two?"

"Nothing." It was the truth. I'd woken up in his arms, and there was a moment of awkwardness, and then we got up and started the day. "He slept against the door. He's just being overprotective."

I must have looked really unhappy, because the hungry glint left her expression, and she simply nodded and sipped her coffee. "Oh. Well, that's good."

The doorbell rang while Betty and I were cleaning up. We exchanged a wary glance, and then we headed into the foyer, only to be cut off by Cain darting in front of me from the living room. He put his hands on my shoulders to stop me where I was, then touched his fingers to his lips. He grabbed a Clorox spray bottle from a collection of them that were sitting in a cardboard box by the door.

"What's he going to do?" Betty whispered in my ear as Cain stepped up to the door and looked through the peephole. "Disinfect her?"

I chuckled a little, and then Cain jerked his head toward the door, motioning for me to check out whoever it was. I walked up to the peephole and there was Stacy Easter, looking impatient on my porch.

I stepped back and nodded at him, feeling like I was in witness protection. "It's okay."

He pulled the door open, looking like a deranged Merry Maid with the Clorox bottle that, I realized now, Cain had likely spent the night emptying of antibacterial solution and replacing with magical pepper spray, or something like it. Stacy stepped inside, her eyes taking in a full drink of Cain.

"Hel-lo," she said, putting a sultry tone in her voice.

Cain grunted and stalked off into the kitchen. Stacy looked at me. "Where have you been hiding him?"

"He's . . ." I glanced toward the kitchen, unable to figure out a word for what Cain was. I gave up and looked back at Stacy. "Doesn't matter. What's up?"

She pulled a folded piece of paper out of her pocket and handed it to me. "Not much. Your father went missing ten years ago. His last known address was in Tennessee. There's been no sign of him since. Take that to a real detective, you might have more luck." She pointed to the paper as I unfolded it; it was a printout of a newspaper article, on which she'd scribbled an address in Avery, Tennessee, into the margin. "Sorry, that's all I got on him."

"Okay, so what's this?"

"An article from the *Avery Citizen-Times,*" she said carefully. "Is that your sister?"

I looked at it, and the first thing I saw was a picture of a smiling woman with long, wavy brown hair, and underneath her picture, the caption: *Avery Unified teacher Holly Monroe.*

I gasped and put my hand over my mouth, then absorbed the headline.

LOCAL TEACHER FOUND DEAD

My hand holding the printout started to shake, so I grabbed the other side with the other hand and tried to stabilize it enough to read. I absorbed it in bits, unable to take in the whole thing at once.

"Livvy?" Betty said, but I didn't look up.

Holly Monroe found . . . unidentified companion unconscious . . . while police won't give out details of the scene . . . possible satanic rites . . . thirty-one-year-old teacher was born in Avery, and taught at Avery Unified High School since . . . authorities still looking for anyone who can identify the companion, who has been unable to respond to medical staff . . . African-American woman in her late forties or early fifties . . . was calling the name,

"Gabriel," when she was first brought in, before slipping into unconsciousness . . .

"What's going on?"

When I looked up, Cain was standing in front of the kitchen door, looking grim. But to be fair, Cain always looked grim. He stalked over to me, and I handed him the printout. He glanced at it quickly; it was obvious he'd seen it before. He shot a sharp look at Stacy.

"Who the hell are you? What do you know about this?"

Betty stepped closer. "Cain, this is Stacy."

"Yeah?" He advanced on her, waving the printout. "Where'd you get this?"

Stacy widened her stance and met his eyes. "None of your fucking business."

I touched his arm, which was taut as a wire. "I asked her to find my father."

He shifted his focus to me. "What the hell did you do that for?"

"May I repeat?" Stacy said, stepping closer to him and drawing to her full height, which was still a foot shorter than his. "None. Of. Your. Fucking. Business."

"Cain." I touched his arm again. It took him a moment to look back at me, and when our eyes met, he softened a bit, but just a bit. There was still impotent fury in his expression, but he didn't seem quite as likely to act on it.

"You okay?" he asked.

I held my hand out for the article, and he gave it back to me. I looked at the picture, trying to find something in there that said *sister* to me. But it was just a black-and-white shot, taken probably for a school yearbook somewhere along the line. She was beautiful; a wide smile, dark eyes, and she seemed . . . I don't know. Smart. If you can tell that from a picture.

I looked back up at Cain. "This is what happened?"

Angry eyes met mine, but I could tell they weren't angry with me. "Yeah. I went to the hospital to get Davina, but she was gone by the time I got there. Been tracking her ever since. And now, you're up to date."

Every muscle in my body felt suddenly weak. I had known the story, known I had a sister who had died, known that Davina had killed her. But there was something so . . . visceral about seeing her, about seeing what could have been my fate. What could *still* be my fate.

"Liv," Betty said, putting her arm around me, "you go sit down in the living room. Stacy, go sit with her. I'm going to make some tea. Cain—"

But before she could give him any instructions, the front door was slamming behind him. Betty exchanged a look with Stacy, and Stacy walked with me to the living room, where we sat down on the couch. A moment later, I heard the kitchen door swing behind Betty.

"So, I take it that article means something then?" she said, motioning toward the printout in my hand.

I nodded. "Yeah."

"You want my take on things?"

I smiled. "I asked you, didn't I?"

"Yep. But I'd tell you anyway." She leaned forward. "I think your father's alive."

I felt my heart skip, and I stared at her. "You think so?"

"Look. People go missing for ten years without a sign, ten-to-one, they're buried in the cement foundation of a high-rise. But whoever it was in that forest with your sister was asking for Gabriel, and why would she call the name of a man who's been dead ten years?"

"I don't know," I said. "But then, I don't understand a lot of it."

"You don't need to understand," Stacy said. "What does your gut tell you?"

I thought about that for a minute, then said, "I don't know."

"Jesus Christ, Liv. Sure you do. You asked me to find him. You think he's alive, too."

Hope surged within me, and I tamped it down; I had no room in my heart for hope at the moment. "Maybe. So, what do I do now?"

"Hire a real detective, for one thing," she said.

"I don't know, you did pretty well for an amateur." I looked at her. "You seen Peach?"

Her eyes darkened. "I just came from there. She's still a little out of it because of the painkillers. Nick's with her."

I nodded. "Can I ask you something?"

"Has permission ever stopped you?"

"Millie . . . do you think she was always a time bomb, just waiting to go off?"

Stacy leaned back, stretched one arm over the back of the couch, and looked thoughtful. "Yeah, probably."

"Do you think we can get her back from this?"

Stacy looked at me, then slowly shook her head.

"It's over, isn't it?" I said. "The four of us?"

She sighed. "It was always going to end eventually. Peach is getting married, Millie finally toppled over the edge, and you're going away. Me, I'll always be the townie slut. I'm the anchor that will keep us marginally connected, at least."

She grinned at me, but I didn't smile back. "You're more than just the townie slut."

"Oh, I'm not ashamed," she said. "And speaking of shameless, I hope you don't take this the wrong way, but I think I'm in love with that man."

I was so surprised by the comment that I almost laughed. "What?"

"Oh, don't worry, I'm not gonna piss in your flowerpot again but"—she waved her hand in front of her face, and then motioned to the front door where Cain had gone—"he is something else."

"Go ahead and piss on him," I said. "He's not my flowerpot."

Her eyes widened. "Really? Because you know, he's just my type."

I laughed. "The type that will screw you senseless, give you shit, and leave you stranded?"

She looked at me and shrugged. "What can I say? Daddy issues." She gently took the article from my hands, and said, "You know everything's gonna be okay, right?"

"Yeah? How would I know that?"

"Because, eventually," she said, leaning back, "it always is."

And then, the article in her hands burst into flames.

It was quick, less like burning and more like disintegrating. A red ridge of fire rimmed the edges and consumed the whole thing with a *zip* sound, until there was nothing but pieces of ash floating to the ground. Stacy didn't seem surprised at all. She shook out her hand, and as she did, I saw flickers of red light dancing around her fingertips.

"Wow," she said, swallowing. It was the first time in my life I had ever seen Stacy even remotely flustered. "That was weird, wasn't it?"

"Oh, crap," I said. "You, too?"

She looked at me for a moment, then said, "Me, too, what?"

I reached over to the coffee table, picked up a cork coaster, and held it in my hands. I closed my eyes and concentrated, surprising myself with how easy it was this time to draw the energy through myself, to focus it. When I put the coaster back down on the table, it was a turtle, slowly making its way across the surface.

Stacy blinked a few times, then looked at me. "What the fuck is going on here, Liv?"

"Stacy, I'm so sorry. I didn't do it on purpose, I swear—"

She gave me a pointed look. "*You* did this to me?"

"I think . . . maybe. I don't know how. Something happened at that last Confessional—"

And then I stopped. The *coffee*. That Saturday morning before the girls came over, when Davina had told me about my sister, she'd given me a cup of coffee.

And I drank it.

"Shit." I shot up from my chair. "What an *idiot!*"

I headed for the door, Stacy following closely behind, and pushed my way through. I glanced both ways down the street and didn't see Cain, so I started down the street.

"Liv," Stacy said, on my heels. "Wanna tell me what's going on here, babe?"

And then Cain darted out of the narrow space between my house and Dale Hibbert's, and grabbed me by the arm.

"Where the hell you think you're going?"

"I was looking for you."

"Well, you found me." He shot a suspicious look at Stacy, then said, "What's going on?"

"Davina, she—"

Cain stepped out toward the street, putting me behind him. "What? She here?"

"No, last week. *Listen.*" I stepped around him to face him again. "She gave me a cup of coffee, and I drank it."

Cain's expression got even more grim, if that was possible, and he said, "What happened?"

"It was right before the girls came over last week; she brought me coffee. Later that day, I touched Peach, and there was this static electricity shock between us. I didn't think it was a big deal, but then Peach has started making things . . . I don't know. Kind of dance around? And I saw this pink light on her fingers, like the yellow light that I get, and the blue light that Betty gets. And now Stacy . . . there was a moment when we had a static shock thing, too, right?"

I looked to Stacy, who nodded. "I thought that was weird."

Cain eyed her. "So, what's your power?"

"Intense heat, apparently." Stacy pulled her car keys out of her pocket. One of them was wavy, as though it had been thrown into the heart of a blazing fire and then shaped around someone's fingers. "I don't have a normal goddamned spoon left in my house." She tucked her useless keys back into her pocket.

I pulled on Cain's sleeve. "Is there something you can do? Can you reverse it?"

He grunted a curse, and said, "Hell if I know. I don't know what she gave you. What'd it taste like?"

I thought about that for a moment and shrugged. "Coffee?"

"Great," he breathed, annoyed, and started back toward the house, me following close behind. "Next time a conjurer gives you something to drink, pass."

"Davina said that normal people with magic . . . she said it hurts them. Should I be worried?"

He climbed up the steps to the front door. "No."

I grabbed his arm, and turned him to face me. "Cain, these are my friends. If they're going to be hurt because of me . . ."

His expression changed to something approaching sympathy, then he quickly shook his head. "The magic Davina stole hurts her because she took all of it. If your friends just got a little bit, they're probably gonna be fine. Might even wear off after a while. She probably did it to make you freak out, turn to her for help." He shot a quick look at Stacy, then looked back at me. "You'd need to deliberately dose someone before they'd be in serious trouble, and you're not there yet."

Then he went inside. I stood on the porch with Stacy for a moment, absorbing the information, and then she touched me on the arm and said, "Did he say *magic*?"

I opened the door for her and let her in first.

It was going to be a long afternoon.

* * *

An hour later, Stacy sat back on my couch, turning the coaster turtle around in her hand.

"Magic," she said finally, and set it back on the coffee table, where it slowly started moving. It tended to favor its right back leg, and moved in slow, aimless circles across the surface of the coffee table. "All right. I think my mind's wrapped around it now."

I couldn't help but laugh. "Then you're doing better than I am."

The front door opened and Cain—who'd been sitting guard on the porch, although I think that was as much about not having to listen to me and Stacy as it was about security—came in with Tobias behind him. Tobias had a large army-navy duffel bag over his shoulder, which he dumped on the floor by the stairwell, and they both walked over to us in silence.

"Hey, Tobias," Stacy said casually, putting her feet up on the coffee table.

Tobias looked at Stacy, then at me.

"Stacy's lighting things on fire," I said awkwardly.

"Again?" Tobias asked.

Stacy waved one hand at him in a dramatic flourish. "Without matches this time." She angled her head at me. "Courtesy of magical Typhoid Mary over here." She stood up. "Anyone want a Diet Coke?"

Both Tobias and Cain just looked at her, then I said, "No, thanks, we're fine." Stacy shrugged and went into the kitchen.

"Get rid of her," Cain said, stepping into the living room. "We've got stuff to do."

"I think she's part of the team," I said.

"Yeah?" Cain narrowed his eyes at me. "And who decided that?"

I sat back in my chair. "She did."

"Well, tell her she's wrong and kick her out."

I shared an amused look with Tobias. "Spoken like a man who's never tried to tell Stacy Easter what to do."

Cain gave me an annoyed stare for a minute, and then cursed, and stalked off to the kitchen. Tobias, a small smile on his face, settled down across from me on the couch.

"How are you feeling?" he asked.

"Good," I said. "You know, considering."

We held eye contact for a little longer than absolutely necessary, but didn't speak again. From the kitchen I could hear Stacy's defiant tones overwhelming Cain's annoyed ones, and Tobias and I shared a grin. A few moments later, both Stacy and Cain came back into the living room. Stacy settled on the couch next to Tobias, sipping her Diet Coke.

"So," she said, "I guess we're having a meeting?" She looked from me to Tobias to Cain. "About how to take down the magical bitch?"

Cain ignored her, focusing on me. "Where's Betty?"

"Taking a nap," I said. "Want me to get her?"

"I'll do it." Stacy hopped up and headed up the stairs.

After she was out of earshot, I raised an inquisitive eyebrow at Cain. He shot me an annoyed look and grumbled, "Fire could come in handy."

"I didn't say anything." I got up to go sit on the couch, and Tobias put his arm around me when I settled down next to him.

A minute later, Betty and Stacy walked into the living room. Stacy seemed surprised for a moment at the sight of me and Tobias together, then shrugged and sat down on the other side of me.

"All right," Cain said once everyone was settled. "Here's the plan. Davina's gonna be weakened for a while, but I say she makes a move tomorrow night, Friday at the latest. She's angry, she's desperate, and she's running out of cards to play, so the play's gonna get dirty."

I tensed up. "The play hasn't *been* dirty?"

Cain looked at me, but didn't answer. "She's strong at night, so during the day, we won't find her if she doesn't want to be found. The only way to end this thing is to draw her out when she's feeling secure." Cain looked at me. "That means, at night."

My heart clutched in my chest. "But I don't have any power at night."

"Do what I tell you, you won't need it. She needs to come after you when she thinks you're weak. That's at night. We send you out on your own to someplace, she follows you, tries to make her move and then . . ." He looked grimly around the group. "Then you let me take care of it."

I felt a chill at the coldness in his voice. "What do you mean, take care of it?"

He met my eye. "That's my concern. Your job is getting her to me."

"So you can do what?"

Cain stayed quiet, and Stacy said, "You're going to kill

her." Cain turned his icy look on Stacy and she held it for a moment, then looked at me. "Yeah, he's definitely going to kill her."

"You can't," I said automatically. "No."

Cain looked at me, annoyed. "She'd break your neck without a second thought if it'd get her what she wanted. What are you protecting her for?"

"I'm not protecting her. But I'm not a killer, either."

"You don't have to be," he said. "This is my thing, and I'm gonna get her with or without you. Be easier with you, but either way, that woman is getting put down."

The hardness in his eyes scared me. Cain had never been exactly fluffy, but all the rage simmering underneath was coming to the surface now, and I felt like things were getting quickly out of control. I looked at Betty.

"Is it just me who thinks talking about killing people is insane?"

Betty took in a deep breath and shook her head carefully. "It's not just you."

Stacy shrugged. "I say the bitch started it, but then, I wanna kill someone at least twice a day, so . . ."

Betty looked at Cain. "I know Holly was important to you, and I'm sorry about what happened, but isn't there a way to protect Liv without killing anyone?"

Cain's cold eyes met hers. "No."

"I don't believe that," I said. "If she could steal Holly's magic, maybe we can just . . . I don't know. Steal it back. Then she'd be relatively harmless."

"She'd still be a conjurer, and a damn powerful one at that,"

Cain said. "Soon as she healed up, she'd be back for you. You wanna spend the rest of your life with her on your tail?"

"No, but—"

Cain slammed his hand down on the coffee table, sending a sharp report throughout the room.

"She killed Holly!" His voice was full of rage and heartbreak, and while he pulled the emotion back in quickly, it was clear what his dog in this fight was, and it had nothing to do with protecting me. The room went quiet, and I had no idea what to say, but Tobias did.

"Have you ever killed anyone, Cain?"

"No," Cain said, a sharp bite in his tone as he turned angry eyes on Tobias. "You?"

"Yes," Tobias said, and the room went silent.

17

I felt the breath cut out of me as I watched Tobias, but his eyes were fixed on Cain, who stared back at him.

"You don't come back from it," Tobias said. "Circumstances change, and sometimes, killing someone is even justified, but once you've taken a life, it changes who you are. It doesn't matter why you did it; you'll never be the same person again."

There was a moment of tense silence. Tobias walked over to Cain, stopping next to him by the fireplace. Betty, Stacy, and I stayed quiet, just watching.

"Look, if the only way to protect Liv is to kill Davina, I'll do it. I don't have as much to lose as you do. But I'll only do it if there's no other way."

"Tobias," I began, but he was focused on Cain, whose eyes were in turn locked on Tobias. There was some kind of manly communication going on between them, and neither one was paying attention to me, or anything else, at the moment.

"You kill that woman out of vengeance," Tobias went on, "and you'll stop being the guy that Holly knew."

"What the hell do you know about Holly?" Cain said through his teeth, his voice a low, angry growl.

"Nothing," Tobias said. "I know you loved her, that's obvious. And I know, better than you, the price you pay when you kill someone. That's all I'm saying, Cain. You pay a price, and it's a steep one."

Cain's eyes narrowed and he glared at Tobias. "I've already paid." And then he stalked out the front door. We all stayed where we were, frozen in silence, and then, finally, Stacy pushed herself up from the couch.

"Well, I haven't been in a room with this much tension since I tried to give my stepfather a tonsillectomy with a spork." She stretched. "Time for a break." And with that, she headed into the kitchen. A moment later, Betty stood up and silently followed her, leaving me and Tobias alone.

"So," I said. "Wow."

He raised his eyes to mine. I felt an involuntary shaking in my legs, and I put my hands on my thighs to stop it.

"You said . . ." I began, then hesitated. I had promised I would trust him, but even as I tried to stop myself, I knew I wouldn't be able to let this go. "You said you'd never killed anyone."

He lowered his head. "I said the firm never asked me to."

"Ah, semantics." I took a deep breath, trying to calm my racing heart. "How many people have you killed?"

He gave me a dull stare. "I lost count at twelve."

"Don't joke about this," I said. "Please."

He sat down on the couch, let out a long breath, and spoke.

"I was thirteen. My powers came in right as a school bully was beating my brother to a pulp. I stopped his heart. I didn't know it at the time. All I knew was that I had imagined something, and then . . . it had happened. I haven't used my power outside of a controlled setting since." He stood up, walked to-ward the wall, then took a few steps toward me. "My parents were both Magicals, so they knew the deal. They called ASF as soon as I told them what happened."

"Oh my god," I said. "They turned you in to the feds?"

He shrugged. "They thought it was the right thing to do. When kids show signs of extraordinary ability, the potential to really hurt someone, it's what people are told to do."

"Still." I reached out and touched his hand. "That sucks."

He let out a small laugh. "Yeah. Anyway, the firm came and got me, gave me a new name, and raised me in a special board-ing school until I was old enough to work for them. I haven't seen my family since."

"You can't visit, or write at least?"

His eyes looked sad and tired as he shook his head. "There was a kid in my boarding school who got a letter out to his mom. The entire family disappeared two weeks later."

"Disappeared? Like witness protection disappeared, or Jimmy Hoffa disappeared?"

He looked at me. "I don't know. But it's not a chance I'm willing to take."

I sat back, feeling dizzy. "God, Tobias, I'm so sorry."

He nodded. "Yeah. Me, too." He sat there for a while, his eyes on me, and finally said, "Do you understand now?"

"Of course," I said. "But you were a kid. It was an accident. You can't blame yourself for that."

"That's not what I'm talking about." He leaned forward, resting his elbows on his knees. "I'm going to help you finish this thing with Davina. I'm going to see you safely through to the end. Then you'll go to Europe, or stay here. Whatever you want to do. But when it's done, I'm leaving."

I felt a stab of panic run through me. "Why? Have they contacted you?"

"No. I'm gonna contact them."

"Are you going to say good-bye first?"

"Does that matter?"

"Did you get to say good-bye to your family?"

He watched me for a long moment, and then shook his head.

"Then you should know it matters."

He sighed. "Yeah. I'll say good-bye first."

With that, he grabbed his duffel bag and went upstairs. I watched him until he was gone, and then stared at the space where he had been for a while, my mind drifting over a million things, but never able to focus entirely on one.

Then, quietly and without the slightest question as to what the hell I thought I was doing, I snuck down to the basement, walked over to the cement steps that led out the exterior bulkhead doors, and walked into town.

Alone.

I barely noticed where I was on the three blocks into town. I was on autopilot, my body moving while my mind wandered around elsewhere, thinking about Tobias, Millie, Peach. It was as though my brain was in a jumble, too distracted to recognize what the body it was attached to was doing. I didn't regain consciousness of my surroundings until I made it to the town square, and saw her, sitting on one of the benches, just . . . watching. She looked so harmless sitting there, like a benevolent matron, surveying the activity at Grace and Addie's antique shop, the opposite corner where a crew was working to fix the damage done by Frankie Biggs . . . and she was watching CCB's.

She didn't look up, but I knew she knew I was there. My mind seemed to snap back into place, and I had an instinct to run but what good would it have done? There she was, maybe ten yards from me, just a few blocks from my house. In daylight, the time when I was supposedly strong, and she was supposedly weak. I realized then that it didn't matter what I did; this woman was in charge, and we both knew it.

So, I went and sat down next to her.

"I see you're recovering nicely," she said after a few moments, still not looking at me.

"What do you want?"

"Well, I think you know what I want," she said. "Now we got all our cards on the table, what are we going to do about it?"

I sighed. "I don't know."

She nodded. "Well, I have an idea about what we might do." And finally, she looked at me. "You want to hear it?"

"I'm all ears."

She leaned a little bit closer. "I have played this game before, and I have won. And the secret to winning is really pretty simple. I find out what it is you love more than anything, and I use that to get your compliance."

Tobias, I thought, with a catch in my breath, but then, as though reading my mind, she shook her head a bit and said, "Bigger than just a man, baby. I'm talking about this whole stinking, fetid town, and every sad soul in it."

She met my eye and I blinked, trying to wrap my mind around what she was saying, exactly.

"Don't worry. I'm not ready for any serious destruction yet. It's going to be a few days. But once I get my full strength back, I'm going to call for you, as I did just now. And if, somehow, you work up the strength to defy me, I'm going to take something in this town." She shrugged. "Or someone. Depends on my mood." She pointed to Grace and Addie's antique store. "I'll burn that place to the ground." Her finger moved in time with a busload of kids from the local elementary school. "I'll send that bus plummeting off an overpass." Then she looked at me. "I'll sneak into your precious Betty's apartment and choke the life out of her with her own apron strings." A cold smile broke over Davina's face. "And I can do it all without leaving the comfort of my bedroom. Isn't that amazing? No one will know what's happening to this town. Well, no one except you, and no one except me."

My heart clunked around in my chest, in response to the chunk of ice that had settled inside me. "So what is it you want from me?"

"You know what I want," she said, her voice going light. "Your magic."

"I'm not going to give you that. I'll die."

"Well, probably, but better you than a busload of kids, right? Honestly, baby, I never had you pegged for such a selfish type." She *tsked* and shook her head. "Very unattractive quality, that."

I sat in silence for a while, and then I said, "Cain's going to kill you."

She chuckled. "Cain's going to try. But here's the raw truth, just between us girls. He doesn't have it in him. If he did, he would have done it the night I killed your sister."

I gripped the edge of the bench in my hands, wanting to do something, anything . . . but what? Turn an acorn into a snail? With all my power at my disposal, and her weakened and only able to rely on whatever premixed potions she might have in her bag, she was still more powerful than me.

"See," she went on, "Cain had his chance, and he lost it, because the man—for all his wonderful qualities—is not a person who can seal that particular deal." She reached out and put her hand over mine, her skin feeling cold and alien. "And neither are you. And since the only way you're going to stop me is to kill me, then we're going to have to find another way to settle this little problem we have."

I pulled my hand out from under her grip. "If I give you my magic, who's to say you won't just go ahead and kill everyone anyway?"

She looked at me, her face shocked and almost hurt. "Oh, come on. You know why I'm doing this, don't you?"

"Ummm . . . because you're insane?"

She turned her body toward mine, leaning forward as if we were still friends. "Do you have any idea what this would mean to the Magical community? I'd be able to protect people. I'd have the power to keep them all safe from police, scientists, politicians. You think witch hunts are a thing of the past? Just look at Don't Ask, Don't Tell; they paint it over with nice little slogans, but bigotry and fear are real, and they are deadly.

If I had this power, no one would be able to harm another Magical again. We'd be on top, for once."

"And that was worth killing the man you loved?"

Her eyes flashed with emotion, and my heart sank. It had just been a hunch, both that Davina had loved my father, and that she had killed him, but her speed at regaining her composure didn't keep me from seeing what I was looking for.

"That's none of your business," she said, but I could see that I'd gotten a hit in on a tiny patch of soft underbelly, so I kept going.

"You loved my father," I said. "And he trusted you. That's how you knew who he was, what he was."

Her fists clenched, but she didn't say anything.

"You killed him when you tried to steal his magic," I went on. "You didn't mean to, but you killed him."

Her eyes met mine, cold. "Who told you this?"

"In the newspaper article, they mentioned that when they dragged you half-conscious from the woods after you killed Holly, you were calling for him in your delirium. There's only one reason I can think of why you would do that."

Her eyebrows raised. "Nice work, Sherlock."

She carefully smoothed her skirt over her legs, her eyes locked on her strong fingers, and then she turned a cold smile to me.

"I've already lost everything," she said, her voice quiet and oddly cold. "This is the only way to make it mean something."

"You're going to kill more people, including me, so you can get the power to save other people from being killed? To give my father's death, also at your hands, meaning? Your logic's missing a piece there."

"My logic is not your problem. Saving this town is your problem. The only choice you have to make is how many people die. Just you, or you and a whole bunch of others." With that, she stood up, tucked her purse over her shoulder, and landed cold eyes on me. "As you can see by this chance meeting, I can get to you whenever and however I choose. I will call you again, and when I do, you're going to want to heed that call. Because if you don't, I will rain such hell down on you and yours that you will wish you'd died the other night, the way you were supposed to."

She blew me a quick kiss, then turned and walked away. I sat on the bench, shaking, a potent cocktail of fear and rage running through my veins. After a few moments, it occurred to me that I should get up and go back home.

That's when I saw Tobias standing at the edge of the square, watching me with a stony look on his face.

18

I waited for Tobias as he walked toward me, knowing I should get up but unable to move yet. He got to me, his eyes never leaving mine as he flipped out his cell phone and hit speed-dial. A moment later, he said simply, "I got her," and flipped it shut again.

"Let's go," he said, his voice gruff and angry.

I tried to get up, then said, "I can't yet."

His expression morphed into concern. "What happened?"

I stared up at him. "I don't know. I just walked out of the house without thinking, and the next thing I knew, I was here." I swallowed. "I think she put the whammy on me."

Tobias sat down next to me on the bench and ran his hands over my arms and legs.

"I'm not injured," I said, my voice quivering. "I just can't move. I keep thinking, 'get up,' but I can't."

"It's okay." He pulled me into his arms and held me against him. "It'll pass. Just give it a minute. Calm down, and breathe. It's just a head game."

I rested my head against his chest. "She did the same thing with Nick the other night, when Millie attacked Peach. At least,

I think it's the same thing." I sighed. "I don't know. I just . . . I swear, I didn't mean to do this."

"I believe you," he said quietly. "We'll just make sure you're not alone again."

I shuddered, even in the heat, and pulled back to look up at him. "If she wants me, she'll get me, Tobias. I think she's just proven she can do that."

"No," he said, determination in his voice. "She can't. We won't let her."

We stared at each other for a while, and then I lowered my eyes, unable to deal with it all anymore. "Can we just go home?"

"Yeah. Sure." He got up and held out his hand to me, and I took it. I rose from the bench easily, naturally, the residual effects of Davina's power over me fully dissipated. Tobias released my hand and stepped aside for me to go ahead of him. We made our way back in silence, walking side by side.

Cain was on the porch when we got there, and he darted down to meet us on the sidewalk.

"What the hell do you think you're—?" he began, but Tobias said, "Leave her alone," and I was allowed to walk into my own home on my own power.

I went inside to see Betty and Stacy in the foyer, looking tense.

"I'm sorry," I said. "I just . . ." I shot a look at Tobias. "I needed some air."

"That's okay, honey," Betty said, but her eyes were tight with worry.

Stacy shook her head. "If you need air, you get air, Liv. Fuck 'em if they can't take a joke."

"Davina was there," Tobias said, and I shot him a look.

Cain stepped closer, looming over me. "Where is she?"

"She's gone," I said, then shot guilty eyes at Betty. "I don't know what happened. I just suddenly wanted to go outside. I didn't think about it, I just . . . went. And there she was."

Betty made a grim face. "Well, I guess that confirms our suspicions about Nick. She's exerting some kind of mind control."

"The coffee," Cain said, and I looked at him.

"You think she slipped me something *else* in that coffee?"

He gave me a dark look and nodded. "Tell me what happened."

I took a deep breath. "She said it would be a few days, and then, if I didn't come to her and let her take my magic, she'd systematically start destroying the town."

"That's it?"

"Well, she was more flowery about it but . . . yeah. Them's the CliffsNotes."

He was quiet for a moment, then said, "We're out of time. We move tonight."

"Wait," I said. "She told me it would be a few days, that she wasn't strong enough yet—"

"If she's exerting her will over you in the daytime, she's past strong enough," he said. "She's waiting for you to get your strength back, and then she's going to strike. I say we don't give her the chance."

I shivered and rubbed my hands over my arms. "Well . . . what are we going to do?"

Cain took in a breath, thought for a moment, and said, "You said she had someone under her control? Who was it?"

I glanced at Stacy. "Well, there's Millie."

"Can we get to her?" Cain asked.

Stacy tensed up. "What do you mean 'get to'?"

"If Davina's got a conduit," Cain said, "we can use that against her."

"Use Millie? How?"

Cain sighed, as though he was annoyed at having to explain everything. "Running a conduit gives power. She feeds off the extra life force. But it also takes power; we cut that off, it siphons that power away from Davina. It'll weaken her, buy us some more time."

"Cut off? How?"

Cain thought for a moment. "You could take her as a conduit, too. Feed her some potion, take control, maybe siphon off some of Davina's power through her."

"Maybe? You're not sure?"

"It's magic," Tobias said. "You can't ever be sure."

"And would this *maybe* include hurting Millie?" I asked.

Cain huffed. "It's not like we've been testing this stuff in a lab. It's all maybe."

I looked at Betty. "What about Amber Dorsey? That thing with Frankie Biggs was exactly what Amber would do if she was under Davina's control. I can spare Amber Dorsey. She stuck gum in Millie's hair in the eighth grade."

Betty shook her head. "She went to stay with her sister in Syracuse."

"Then it's gotta be Millie," Cain said.

"No, it doesn't," I said. "Besides, it's not like I could get her to take potion anyway. She's under Davina's control at night. She'd never say yes."

Cain looked at me like I was an idiot. "She doesn't have to say anything. You drop it in her drink when she's not looking, the way Davina did."

"No. Millie's my friend. I'm not dosing her with anything without her knowledge. Jesus. What the hell's wrong with you?"

Cain advanced on me. "Look, you can play nice or you can win. You think Davina had even a second thought about dosing your little friend?"

I took a step forward, getting in his face. "I'm not Davina. I don't work like that."

"You don't have a choice."

Tobias took me gently by the shoulders, pulled me back, and stepped in between me and Cain.

"What other ideas do you have?"

"None that involves getting permission first," Cain spat, eyeing me with disdain.

"Oh, screw you, Dr. Doom," I muttered.

"Enough." Tobias looked at me, and his expression told me he meant business, so I backed off a bit. He turned to Cain. "Is there anything less risky that you can think of?"

Cain eyed him for a moment, then shrugged. "Less powerful."

"What is it?"

"I can put something together that will impede all magical influence," he said. "That'd take a chunk out of Davina, for a little while."

"But she'd still have to sneak it to Millie?" Stacy asked.

I sighed. "If it's returning her free will to her . . ." My stomach turned at the thought, but then I relented. "I could sneak something like that. I guess. You sure it won't hurt her?"

He met my eyes. "Sure as I can be." Cain looked at the clock. "Okay. We got five hours till sunset. I got work to do."

"Wait, *sunset?*" I said. "We're going at night?"

He nodded. "The connection to the conduit is only open when she's got power. That's night."

"But won't Davina . . . I don't know . . . kill us all?"

"Not if you leave me alone, let me get some work done." And with that, he grabbed his backpack off the floor, and headed toward the basement.

Betty, Stacy, Tobias, and I stood in silence, just looking at each other for a while, and then Stacy nudged me and said, "I'm sorry, how can you not think that's totally hot?"

We went to CCB's a little after closing. The plan was fairly simple. I had called Millie and asked her to meet me there for coffee, and to talk. When Millie wasn't looking, I was supposed to dose her coffee from the small vial Cain had tucked into my pocket.

Simple, as long as I didn't let the idea of dosing my best friend without her consent bother me.

I waited at the counter for Millie, while Cain hid out in the kitchen, and Betty, Tobias, and Stacy sat outside in Stacy's car, ready to charge should it all go to hell. I waited for nearly twenty minutes after our designated time, but finally, the bells on the door jingled, and Millie stepped into CCB's. This time, her dress was black, creating a dramatic contrast with the red shoes, lipstick, and fingernails.

"Hey, there, Elvira," I said.

Millie smirked and headed for the counter. She dumped her purse beside her, and leaned on her elbows, exposing cleavage, which, in the twenty-odd years we'd been friends, I had never seen. Even her bathing suits had been modest.

"Thanks for coming." I went to the carafe of coffee I'd made on the mini-coffeemaker and poured us each a mug. Millie watched me carefully. She was suspicious, which made me feel even worse about dosing her, but I was already here, and it would help her.

Maybe.

I set the cream and sugar on the counter and mixed them into my mug, took a sip, then set the coffee down.

"I really don't see what we have to talk about," Millie said. "But for old time's sake, I guess it made sense to come." She left her coffee black and sipped it.

"We need to talk about Peach," I said. "And Nick. And what the hell's been going on with you."

She gave me a flat look. "Oh, please. Like you don't know. Davina told me all about you, you know."

I couldn't help my surprise. "What do you mean?"

"She told me that you and Stacy and Peach had been laughing behind my back about Nick, all these years. Saying I didn't stand a chance with him. Calling me *pathetic!*" Rage flashed on her face, and then she calmed down. "Who's pathetic now, Liv?"

I shook my head. "That never happened."

"Right," Millie huffed. "I've always been the laughing-stock. It's always been the three of you against me."

"Millie, that's not true. I swear."

"Like your word means anything."

"Look," I said, slowly, "I know how convincing Davina can be. I believed her, too, but Mill—"

"Just stop it, okay? I'm not interested in hearing more lies. I've got what I want."

"And just what is that, Mill? Nick wants Peach. Once Davina stops needing you, you won't have her mind-control trick anymore. What are you going to do then?"

Millie shook her head at me. "You know, I would have thought at least you'd be on my side. Stacy and Peach, they think that because they're beautiful, they can have whatever they want. They just step over the bodies of girls like us. How can you side with them after the way Stacy treated you?"

"Stacy never stepped over me," I said.

Millie slapped her hand down on the counter, making me jump back a bit. "She *slept* with *Tobias*! He was yours, and she *slept* with him! Doesn't that make you mad?"

"He wasn't mine, Mill. And Nick wasn't yours."

"Yes, he was. I was there for him, every day. I made him coffee, I laughed at his jokes, *I* loved him. And Peach just swoops in with her perfect face and her perfect ass and just—*agh!*" She flashed her fingers out in frustration. "She had no right! He was *mine.*"

"No, he wasn't."

And it was then that I saw it, a hint of uncertainty, the old

Millie inside this new, awful thing. I leaned forward and took her hand in mine.

"Millie, you can't let Davina do this to you. This isn't you. I know you, and you're not like this. You're kind and you're sweet and you love us. Peach, Stacy, and you and me, we're family." I sighed as I let out a sharp breath, my eyes filling with tears. "I miss you, Mill."

She lowered her eyes, looking down at her hand in mine, but she didn't pull away, so I went for it.

"I can help you," I said. "I just need you to trust me."

She raised her eyes, and they were full with tears, her lower lip quivering. "Trust you?"

"Yeah." I reached into my pocket and pulled out the vial Cain had given me. "I can mix this in your coffee. It'll cut off your connection to Davina, and cut off some of her power. It'll make it easier for me to take her down. She's trying to kill me, Mill."

Millie shook her head. "No. No, she wouldn't do that. She's been really nice to me. She helped me."

"Here." I put the vial in her hand. "I won't dose you against your will, but I'm going to ask you to take it."

Millie examined the vial. "What is it?"

"It's a potion. My friend Cain made it. He's really good. When Davina got to me, he saved my life."

Millie stared at it for a while as a tear tracked down her cheek. I reached out and put one hand on her arm, but she pulled away from me violently, and when she looked at me, her eyes were glittering with hatred.

"Mill?"

"I told her you'd never betray me," she said, shaking the vial in her fist as she stepped away from the counter. "She told me you would, she told me you'd do exactly this, but I said no. *Liv* would never do that to me, I said. What an idiot!"

Behind her, gray smoke started to whirl, coming up from under the tables behind her. Within the smoke, sparks started to fly, at first small and then growing bigger, illuminating the smoke around them like lightning. Millie closed her eyes for a moment, and when she opened them, she was smiling.

I stepped out from behind the counter, and as I passed by the kitchen door, I smelled it.

Gas.

I turned around, looking at Millie, those sparks in the smoke whirling behind her even more ominous now. "Millie, I smell gas. We need to get out of here."

"Of course you smell gas," she said. "Who do you think turned it on?"

"Goddamnit, Millie!" I said, and headed toward the kitchen door, but I couldn't move it. Something was wedged up against it. I pushed against it with everything I had, and moved it an inch, just enough to see the blue of Cain's T-shirt as the dead weight of his unconscious body sagged against the door. I coughed as the gas that had saturated the kitchen swept in through the crack in the door, then twirled around to see Millie there, arms raised, smoke and sparks seeming to come from her fingers.

"Millie, stop it!" I yelled. "If this place goes up, it'll kill you, too."

"Yeah?" Millie rolled her eyes. "You think she'll let anything happen to me? *She's* my friend. She loves me."

"She's *not* your friend!" I ran for the front door. I pushed back the Venetian blinds and tried to open it, but the dead bolt was flipped, and the key we usually kept in there was gone. I coughed again as the smell of the gas scorched my lungs. There was a pounding on the glass and I looked up: Tobias. I motioned for him to go around the back. If he could get Cain out in time and open the kitchen door, we might be able to get out the back. He gave me a quick, frantic look, then ran off. Stacy and Betty, who'd been standing behind him, moved closer. I waved for them to go away, but Betty was motioning to Stacy, saying something I couldn't make out, and Stacy ran off. Betty stood on the other side of the plate glass, her hand flat on it.

"Go away!" I hollered, dizzy from the gas. I fell to my knees, frantically motioning for her to get back. All I could see was her head shaking back and forth, a simple *No*.

I experienced the explosion in phases, my mind unable to process it all together at once. The first thing I saw was Betty's face, illuminated in red as the flames flashed through the dining room. Then, she was gone, thrown back by the force as all the windows and doors blew out in a million screaming shards. I pushed myself down to the floor and covered my head as the oppressive heat consumed the air around me. Then there was the concussive boom of it, making my ears ring. I gasped for air, unable to hear anything aside from the ringing in my ears, unable to feel anything but the heat from the flames.

A moment later, I felt myself being dragged out, and after a few gasps of fresh air, I realized that Tobias had me. I clutched at him and yelled, "Betty! Where's Betty?" but if he answered me, I couldn't hear him. The street was a mass of emergency vehicles, blue and red flashing lights, and the first thing I was able to focus on was Cain, breathing through an oxygen mask, an EMT next to him inspecting a wet rag. She must have snuck up behind him with chloroform or something.

Someone was prodding at me, asking me questions, but I couldn't answer. There was a mask over my face, and the tanked oxygen felt stringent against my ruined breathing passages. I pulled the mask down and grabbed the EMT attending me by the arm. "Betty? Where's Betty?"

The EMT shook her head, then pointed across the street. I turned just in time to see Stacy crawling into the back of an ambulance and sitting next to a body strapped to a gurney.

Betty.

Then the doors shut to the ambulance and it started away, and I watched it go, my eyes filled with helpless tears. The sound around me started to come back, and when I heard my name being called, I turned to see Tobias moving toward me, covered in soot but seemingly okay. He sat next to me on the edge of the truck, hesitated for a moment, then pulled me into his arms. He put one hand on the back of my head and kissed my forehead, then my cheek, and then held me to him again. Every muscle in my body was shaking, I had no strength left, so I leaned against him and allowed his to seep into me until I had enough to pull back and look at him.

"Millie?" I said, pulling my oxygen mask down. "She's still in there?"

Tobias shook his head. "They pulled her out. She's on her way to the hospital in another ambulance."

My eyes filled with hot tears. "And Betty? Is she . . . ?"

"She's alive, but . . ." He let out a rough sigh. "Stacy said she'd call as soon as they knew anything." He pushed my hair back away from my face. "What the hell happened?"

I swallowed, trying to soothe the rawness in my throat. "I didn't want to trick her. I told her what was going on. I was so stupid, and now Betty . . ." I crumpled against him. "It's all my fault."

"She knocked Cain out and turned on the gas before that conversation ever started," he said. "It was going to end badly, no matter what you did."

I felt a hand on my shoulder, and a harried EMT stuck my oxygen mask back on my face. "Take that off again, and I'll put you in restraints," she warned, and then went to check on Cain.

I leaned my head against Tobias's shoulder, and watched as the EMT fussed over Cain. He looked up, and our eyes met for a long moment, and then we both looked away to watch the firemen as they hosed down the hollow, charred remains of Crazy Cousin Betty's.

19

Stacy came back from the hospital the next day, somewhere around 11 A.M. I had crawled onto the porch roof outside my bedroom window, and saw when she pulled up, but I didn't make a move to go down and talk to her. The news, whatever it was, would come and find me, I was sure. In the meantime, I stared out at the neighborhood where I had grown up, feeling disconnected from this place that had been a part of me as far back as I could remember. I remembered riding bikes into town with Peach and Millie and Stacy, remembered getting our prom pictures taken out front by my tree. It all seemed so far away from me, as if it had happened to someone else. I was just the observer, the one who came in to finish the story off. The rest of it had belonged to someone else, and somewhere, that Liv was still completely herself, serving waffles at a whole CCB's, living a mundane but reasonable life.

I wasn't that girl. I was the girl who, when she closed her eyes, could only see and feel fire. The roiling flames of the explosion, the oppressive, sickening heat of it as I was crumpled up, helpless on the floor. The hellish glow flashing over Betty's face before the explosion tossed her into the street. The dancing shadows on Millie's face as she made me realize what I should have known all along.

I was going to lose.

"Liv?"

I opened my eyes, but I didn't turn around. A few seconds later, Tobias was crawling out onto the roof through my bedroom window. Somehow, despite his size, he gracefully managed to settle down next to me.

"Stacy's here," he said.

I nodded, keeping my eyes on the neighborhood. "How's Betty?"

"The swelling in her brain seems to have gone down, and the doctors are really hopeful, but . . . she hasn't woken up yet."

"And Millie?"

He sighed. "Left the hospital this morning. No one knows where she went. She's not answering her cell phone."

I nodded. It didn't matter where Millie was, really. It would be over before she had a chance to do any more damage. I took a deep breath, and raised my eyes to meet his. I was still the Liv who loved Tobias; no matter how disconnected I felt from everything else, I hadn't lost that.

I found that interesting.

"People are starting to worry," he said. "Cain asked about you, and when Cain notices a person's emotional state, I think it's pretty bad."

I smiled at him. "I'm okay."

"You don't look okay."

I held his gaze for a bit, then motioned back toward the

room. I crawled inside and he followed me. I waited while he came in through the window, and then I placed the flat of my hands against his chest and looked up into his eyes.

At first, he seemed wary, but then the pull between us got the better of him, and he let his arms find their place around my waist. I moved closer to him, my hands traveling down his chest, around to his hips, and he had a sudden, sharp intake of breath that was so simple, raw, and real that it made me smile. It was all simple, really, and we'd spent so much time making it so much more complex than it ever needed to be.

I leaned into him, pushing up on my tiptoes to place a gentle kiss at the base of his jaw. He moaned and his hold on me tightened; I could feel him hard against me, and the sensation was accompanied by a rush of raw desire that would have knocked me over had he not been holding me up.

"I need you inside of me," I whispered. "Right now."

He groaned and took my mouth with his, hard, punishing kisses that spoke to the breaking of restraints we'd both held in place for far too long. Clothes peeled off easily as our need to touch and feel overwhelmed us, and when we fell back onto my bed, there was nothing in the world but the two of us, the one of him. His lips set off explosions under my skin, and I writhed under his touch as he tasted every part of me until my hands gripped his hair as his tongue made me forget everything but the feel of him. I closed my eyes and let it take me. I wasn't worried about anything, not the past, not the future, just this moment now when he was making explosions of color dance behind my eyelids as I moved beneath him. Moments later, we rolled together and he was underneath me and I was taking him inside of me, watching his face as I moved rhythmically, loving what I did to him, the power I had in that moment. He was mine, to do with as I pleased, and this was what I pleased, to see him helpless beneath me as I loved him with everything I had, until there was nothing left of me. Nothing to hold back, nothing to save for later, nothing to do but collapse upon him, my ear to his chest as we both gasped for air. His arms tightened around me and he kissed the top of my head, and I listened as his heartbeat drummed out the chant. *Mine-mine, mine-mine . . .*

Mine.

We shifted to lie side by side and fell into an exhausted sleep, the peaceful darkness of his naked embrace keeping me from having to deal with my pressing reality until about a half-hour later, when I opened my eyes to find him propped up on one elbow, watching me.

"Don't say it," I said.

"What?" He reached for my hand and kissed my fingertips.

"I can see the gears working in your brain." I snuggled up next to him, nuzzling his bare chest with my nose, loving the solid, manly scent of him, wanting to remember it forever, however long that was. "If you start thinking, we'll lose this, and I'm not ready for that."

He held me to him, running his fingers down my side, kissing my forehead, my face, my shoulder. I could feel him hardening next to me, but when I reached for him, he took my hand in his and pulled it to his chest.

"Stop," he said, his voice coarse and breathy. "I can't think when you do that."

"No thinking," I said. "Please. Not yet."

He opened his eyes and focused on me, and despite my pleas, I could see the pieces coming together for him, the worry creeping in.

"What's your plan?" he asked, and I sighed and pulled back from him. Quietly, I gathered our clothes from the floor, passing his to him. Once we were both dressed, I sat on the edge of the bed and said, "You should go now."

"Wow." He let out a sharp laugh, but there was nothing happy in his tone. "Give me a minute to process the whiplash."

"You know how I feel about you," I said softly. "You know that was all real. It's just that now . . . it's over. And you should go."

He got up off the bed and stood before me. "Yeah? Why?"

I looked at him, then pushed up off the bed and stepped away from him; the closer I was to him, the more it hurt, and I'd made up my mind. There was no point in making it any harder than it already was.

"You know why," I said.

"I want to hear it from you."

"It's my decision, Tobias. My life, my call. It's over."

He crossed the room to stand next to me, his hand gripping my arm. "No."

I pulled out of his grip and felt the first pang of fear and regret since I'd made the decision. "Stop it. You're only making this harder."

"Goddamn right," he said. "You're not committing suicide by Davina. We can still win this."

I laughed outright at that. "No, we can't. I'm done. Betty

almost died last night, so did Millie, and why? Because I thought I could take her on. I can't."

"They got hurt because they're part of this fight, because they chose to be. People get hurt, you can't prevent that. But if you go and give yourself to Davina now, then you make it all meaningless."

"And if I don't? People die. We got lucky last night. No one died." *Yet,* a black voice whispered in my head. "But if I keep up this ridiculous fight, they will. And who's next? Stacy? Cain? *You?*" I shook my head, my entire body recoiling at the thought. "No. I have the power to stop all this, and I'm doing what needs to be done. As soon as the sun sets, I'm going to her."

He gripped my shoulders and pulled me to him. "No."

"Go, Tobias."

"No."

"I can't do this if you're here."

"Good."

"Tobias . . . please." I felt a tear slip down my cheek, and I could see the response to my pain in his face, and suddenly, I knew.

"You love me," I said, my voice quiet with wonder.

He put his hands on my face. "Yes."

"I love you, too."

"Then stop talking like this," he said. "Let's think of something else."

I angled my head, kissed the inside of his palm, and pulled his hands into my own. "There is nothing else. I have to do this, and I need you to go." I reached up and touched his face, the sandpaper scruff tickling my palm. I breathed in the earthy scent of him, and remembered the taste of his skin. For the first time in my life, I understood why my mother had been the way she had been. I didn't need to imagine what it felt like to leave someone you loved and who loved you back. At least I wouldn't have to live with it for too long, the way she did.

Tobias, however, would. But there was nothing I could do about that.

"I'm asking you to go," I said. "I'm asking you, please. For me."

He didn't say anything, just kept his eyes on mine. I leaned into him, kissing him lightly on the lips, and he pulled me tighter against him. We stood together like that for a long time, and then, without a sound, he was gone, and I was alone in my room. At first, I felt like my heart was being ripped out of me, and it was too painful to even cry.

And then, slowly, all feeling receded, and I was back to the mild numbness I would need to hold onto if I was going to get through this. I exhaled a long, low breath, and turned to go toward my porch roof again.

I was halfway through the window when I noticed something flat, square, and a little charred at the edges laying on the edge of my desk. I reached for it, and it took me a moment to realize what it was.

The magic square.

I leaned against the desk, angling it in my hands to play with the sunlight streaming through my window. Tobias must have gone and gotten it for me while I'd been sleeping this morning. Of course, he would know the one thing that would mean more to me than anything else in that place; my magic square, my beautiful illusion.

I crawled out of the window and settled on the porch, then held it in my hands, allowing the energy to build up. I concentrated it, letting it flow into the square, which began to curl in on itself, the sparkly part forming the outside of the blue bird. By the time it was done, it looked and moved like an actual bluebird, its glittery wings flapping in the air as it flew in little loopy circles by my head. I laughed—a hollow, pained laugh, but still a laugh—as I noticed it sending little shards of light onto my skin like a disco ball.

And that's when it hit me, the spark of an idea. I dismissed it at first, but as I watched the glittery blue bird, other elements fell into place in my head, and I could see it, the beginnings of a plan forming as I watched the bird dance away from me, only to come back and sprinkle its captured sunshine on me.

I ran my hand over my face and took a deep breath. Somewhere in that cavern inside hid an emotion I needed to access. All I had to do was find it. I closed my eyes and breathed in, searching myself for it, ducking into dark corridors and running through long hallways of whistling cold.

And then, finally, there it was.

Hope.

I opened my eyes and smiled, then held out my index finger. The sparkly blue bird landed on it easily, and I cupped it between my hands, looking it in the eyes as I spoke.

"I wish that this plan will work," I whispered to it. The bird cocked its head to the side, and then, seemed to nod.

I took that as a sign.

* * *

"So," I said to Cain and Stacy as we sat at my kitchen table. "What do you think?"

I'd spent the last hour laying out the plan to them, refining certain points with Cain while Stacy pointed out holes in the logic that needed closing up. Tobias was gone, but I was trying to focus on the plan; if it worked, I could try to make it up to Tobias later, and if it didn't . . .

Well. If it didn't, it wouldn't matter.

Cain sat back in his chair, released a sigh, and gave a brief nod. "Worth a try."

I looked at Stacy. "What do you think?"

"I think you're crazy," she said. "But it's better than sitting around here waiting to get magically buggered."

I laughed. "Okay. Well, I need to head to Peach's. Stacy, can you make the phone calls?"

Her expression dulled. "Really? Can't I be in charge of the potions or something?"

Cain gave her a dull look, then turned and headed to his mini-lab in my basement.

Stacy looked at me. "You really don't think that whole angry, distant, and disinterested thing is hot?"

I took a moment to think about it, then slowly shook my head.

"Whew," she said, heading toward the kitchen door. "We live through this, I'm getting a therapist."

By the time everyone had gotten there, it was midafternoon. Cain had been working in the basement for hours, the result being an uninspiring line of various plastic cups filled with what we really, really hoped was the right concoction set up on the coffee table as everyone settled around.

"Thanks for coming, everyone," I said, looking around my living room at the group. Grace Higgins-Hooper and Addie Hooper-Higgins were sitting on my floral love seat, holding hands and smiling casually. Stacy sat on the leather easy chair, her arms crossed over her stomach. Peach and Nick took opposite ends of the couch. Nick hadn't left Peach's side since the incident with the walnuts. It was evident from Peach's body language—posture straight as she sat as far away from him as the shared space would allow—that she hadn't entirely forgiven him, but that didn't seem to bother him in the least. Nick Easter had never been the kind of guy who gave up, and this situation seemed to be no exception. Cain stood with his back against the wall in the corner, watching in his typical stark, detached silence.

"This is all going to sound a little crazy," I began, "so please just bear with me." I took a deep breath. "I've got magical powers."

Addie didn't blink. Grace allowed a skeptical, "Hmmm," and Peach said, "What do you mean, like . . . card tricks?"

I almost laughed, then looked to the two plastic bins full of cranes that I'd been working on all day: showtime. I concentrated on them for a moment, and the bin started to shake a bit, and then, like a bunch of released doves, the two hundred or so cranes I'd worked with that afternoon began to fly in a circle around us. As they flew around, I felt their power—*my* power—flowing around me, through me, into the air. It was like

I was no longer contained in just my body, I flowed outward. I communed with the world and everything in it. I couldn't help smiling; I controlled them so easily, the power thrumming in my veins, my own unknown second nature. For the first time since all of this started, I had a feeling of what I really was, and it was glorious.

Slowly, I commanded the cranes all back into the bins, and then pulled their magic back into me. I took in the rush of it, allowed the magic to resettle in me, and then looked around at the group.

"I know it's a lot to absorb," I said, "and I want you to know that what I'm about to ask you, you don't have to say yes. It's a big deal."

"Get to the good stuff, babe," Stacy said, leaning back with one arm resting on the arm of the easy chair.

And so . . . I got to the good stuff. I explained, as simply as I could, what was going on with Davina, what had been happening in the town, and what we were up against. I included a brief explanation of what happened with Millie, and about the mind-control effect. Nick lowered his eyes as I went through that part, and Peach glanced at him, then away. I didn't have time to try to convince either of them now, but at least, if something happened to me later, I had planted the seed.

"So, this Davina," Grace said. "She really wants to kill you?"

"Yeah," I said. "She really does. But I think, with your help, we can do this. What I need are . . ." I looked back at Cain, who gave a short nod: *keep going.* I turned back to them. "What I need are conduits."

I stood there for a long moment, waiting for the questions to come. What are conduits, how does it work, why should I do this for you, et cetera, to be followed by the immediate exodus of the lot of them.

"You got it," Addie said. "What do we do?"

"Well," I said, a little caught off guard, "let me explain first. This is a big deal. It basically involves giving over your free will to me for a while, and—"

Grace leaned forward. "Is that what the cups are for?" She lifted one and sniffed it. "Smells like Dr Pepper."

"Well, Cain has tried to make it as palatable as possible, but before you drink any—"

Grace downed the contents of her cup. "Oh, yum."

"Grace!" I said. "Wait, I need to explain—"

Addie grabbed hers and took a sip, then gave a little shudder. "Oooh. It's got a bit of a kick there."

"Guys, *wait* you have to let me tell you what this is going to do to you."

Stacy grabbed her cup and threw it back like a shot of vodka. "The trick is, open your throat and just pour."

I started to feel a little dizzy; the power coming from them already was making my limbs tingle. I had known that Stacy was in, and I'd planned on working with just her if necessary. I hadn't thought I'd have more than two at the most, but as they all reached for the cups and downed them, I found myself reeling with the heady effects of it.

"Okay, wait!" I said, putting my hand on my forehead as I tried to remember all the stuff I'd intended to tell them before they made their decision. "It's a small dose, gonna last twenty-four, maybe forty-eight hours. It also . . . it could hurt a little, although we're not sure because this is a new thing for us. You might lose time, not remember everything. And . . . shit. Guys, hold on a minute."

"Calm down, sweetheart," Addie said. "I went to college in the sixties. You think this scares me?" She looked at Stacy. "Open the throat, you say?"

Stacy nodded, and Addie threw the rest of her drink back, slamming her cup on the table and belching afterward.

I blinked hard, trying to wrap my mind around what was happening. Finally, when I could speak again, I could only say, "Thank you."

Grace winked at me, then looked at her hands. "I'm feeling a little tingly. Is that right?"

I glanced back at Cain, and he moved forward. "Yeah, that's about right. Now you guys need to spread out. Go home, and come back here at sunset. If you're too close, y'all are going to exhaust Liv and we won't be able to get this off the ground."

Grace and Addie filed out, murmuring to themselves about the power they were feeling flowing through them.

"Hey," Nick said, rummaging through the empty cups. "Where's mine?"

"Oh." I shook my head, working to keep my equilibrium with all the heightened power running through me. Even with just Stacy and Peach in the room, I was starting to feel a little lightheaded. "No, Nick, it's okay. You don't have to. I've got enough."

He shook his head and stood up. "If Peach is part of this, I'm a part of it."

"I got a little more downstairs," Cain said. He walked up to me, touched my arm, and said, "How you feeling?"

"I'm okay," I said.

He nodded, then led Nick downstairs. I sat on the couch next to Peach and took her hand in mine.

"I need something from you, too. You know all those solar walkway lights you were telling me about? I need you and Nick to open them up, and set them out in the sun. You can stake them in my backyard if you want. I'll pay for them."

"Don't worry about it." She smiled at me. "It's Nick's treat."

A wave of dizziness hit me, and I had trouble focusing on her; I could see the power shimmering around her, like heat coming off asphalt on a hot day.

"Oh, honey," she said, "you're looking really flushed. You need me to go now?"

I took in a breath, then nodded. My arms and legs were beginning to vibrate with the power and Cain had been right; it was exhausting. Peach squeezed my hand, then quietly got up and left. I looked at Stacy and smiled.

"Are you ready?"

Stacy nodded. "Always."

I closed my eyes, took a deep breath, and tried to concentrate. I felt strings of power connecting me to her, and soon, she was walking in a circle around the room, just the way I commanded. Slowly, I released my grip on her, and she stumbled a bit but regained her footing before she fell.

"Sorry," I said. "I've never done this before."

When no quippy retort came, I got up from the couch and walked over to her, taking her arm.

"You okay?"

Slowly she nodded, and then patted my hand. "He'll come back. Don't worry."

"What . . . ?" I began, but then let it go; there was no point in pretending that I wasn't aching from Tobias's absence.

Stacy managed a shaky grin, then said, "Remind me to play poker with you once we're done with all this. I need a new TV."

"Right." I sighed heavily again, trying to shoot that emotion away from me. I had five hours to learn how to get all this under control, and Tobias was too much of a distraction.

"Okay," I said. "You ready to try again?"

Stacy looked at me, the tiniest glint of fear in her eyes, but then she squelched it and the badass was back.

"Rock it, puppet master," she said.

20

By an hour before sunset, Stacy and I were both exhausted, and while my control wasn't perfect, it was as good as it was realistically going to get. We both decided we needed a little nap, and while Cain finished up the last of his preparations for the night, Stacy retreated to a guest room, and I went into my room. I tried to close my eyes, tried to sleep, but even with the conduits spread over town, my body was still vibrating with power, and I knew I wouldn't get any sleep. The best I could hope for was a little rest. I curled up on my bed, Gibson next to me, his little nose twitching as I pet him and stared off into space.

Despite the direness of the situation, despite the fact that I didn't know if it would even work once the sun had set, I felt oddly exhilarated. For the first time, I could understand Davina's hunger for this feeling, this power, this sense that anything and everything was possible simply for the wishing of it. I sat on the porch roof, staring at the sky as it grew ever pinker, and tried not to think about the two possible outcomes for the night. Both of them were frightening in their own way.

Occasionally, I would see a form appearing at the corner, and for a moment, my heart would catch, thinking that it might be Tobias, but he didn't show up. Not that I expected him to. I had asked him to leave, and he'd done what I'd asked. I could only hope that he was already on his way out of town, that any danger that might erupt from what would turn out to be either my genius or my extreme foolishness wouldn't touch him. If I got nothing else out of tonight, Tobias's safety would be something. It would be enough.

It would have to be.

The sky grew darker, and as the last bits of pink dimmed on the horizon, I reached into the cardboard box I'd set next to me, where Niles and Gibson curled up together. I picked up Niles and slowly pulled him out, his wings flapping roughly as I moved him away from his companion. For his part, deaf and blind, Gibson felt Niles's absence and shuffled from the place where he'd been napping, ramming his head against the cardboard edges of the box. I picked up the pencil I'd also stored in the box, and lifted Niles's little wing.

"Sorry, this might tickle a bit." I wrote, "Tonight," on the underside of one wing, then held him up and said, "Go find her," and released him into the night. He circled Gibson's box a couple of times, then flew on his way.

I took the box back inside and set it down by the open window, which I left open so that, when Niles was done with his journey, he could find his way back to his best friend, and they would be together.

If you can't get the happy endings you want, sometimes you have to settle for the ones you can have.

Cain and Stacy had been at work for a while, gathering up supplies and conduits, transporting them as close to the site as they could using Grace and Addie's B&B van. I walked; although it was well past sunset, I knew Davina wouldn't show up until closer to midnight, and the idea of being so close to the conduits, so rushed with all that power made me feel a little dizzy and sick. I enjoyed the walk, noticing each step, feeling gratitude for each breath. In the afternoon, when the sun was out and this moment was beyond my comprehension, it had all seemed like a really good idea. Now, it felt a bit like walking the plank. No way to go but forward, and no idea what would be waiting for me after the initial splash.

I got to the clearing faster than I had expected; it seemed like I was on my road, and then a moment later, at my destination. Cain had done his work; the white sand circle close to the moving water practically glowed in the light of the full moon. Everything and everyone else was well out of sight; close enough to be called upon when I needed them, far enough away that hopefully, Davina's spidey sense wouldn't go off.

I was alone there for a while, the summer air sticky and warm on my skin. I tried to feel for the power from the conduits, but there was nothing. Had it been daytime, I would have been overwhelmed with it, but now . . . nothing. No tingling in my hands; it was all gone. Nighttime had brought its shade of normalcy; no magic, no power, just my wits and hopes to keep me going until morning.

If I made it until morning.

I tried not to think about that, though.

"Well, hello, baby."

I looked up and there was Davina, her heavy backpack slung over her shoulder, her bright yellow dress making her look beautiful in the moonlight. Niles fluttered in a circle around her head for a bit, then flew over to me, buzzed my shoulder, and flew off to find Gibson, I presumed. If I'd had the choice, I would have done the same thing. As it was, I turned my focus back to Davina and the task at hand.

I had expected my heart to clutch in terror at the sight of her, but instead, what I felt was so conflicted. I had liked her, a lot. She had been a friend, some part of her had wormed its way into my heart, and despite all reason, that was still there.

"Glad to see you came to your senses." She poured the white sand into a circle around us, her voice casual, as if we were girl-friends out for a night's friendly witchcraft. "I know it feels awful, but you really are doing the right thing. You're a damn hero."

"Right." I stepped inside the circle, and she did the same. "Give me the potion. Let's get it over with."

"You're a down-to-business kind of girl, I can respect that." She reached into her backpack, pulled out a blue water bottle this time, and handed it to me.

"I need a minute," I said. "This stuff smells awful, and I just have to get my courage up."

"Fair enough," Davina said, then grinned a very cold grin. "I got all night."

"There's no way you can make it easier to get down?" I asked. "I mean, what's in this stuff?"

"Eye of newt. Little turpentine." She rolled her eyes. "It's a potion, baby, not a nightcap."

"Let me drink some water first," I said, and bent down to my bag, pulling out what would appear to be a normal bottle of Aquafina. Davina's eyes narrowed as I slowly undid the cap.

"What are you—"

And then, while her mouth was open, I jerked the bottle, splashing Cain's conduit potion in her face.

"What the . . . ?" She sputtered a bit, and I could see that some—not much, but some—had gotten into her mouth. Cain had made the potion strong enough that it just seeping through her skin might work, but getting it into her mouth was the holy grail. For every drop she swallowed, I got a little more control, and I was going to need that control to get this ball rolling. I recapped the bottle quickly and dropped it to the ground at my feet; it bounced outside of the circle, out of my reach. *Damn.* I doubted I'd get an unguarded shot at her twice, but I'd wanted to have it handy, just in case.

Davina stared at me, her eyes wide with rage, and for a moment, I felt nothing. My terror began to grow—*it's not going to work, oh hell, I'm going to die*—and then, I felt it. Her power, her night magic, flowing into me. Just a little, just a bit, but it was enough to get me started.

"You little bitch," Davina said. I could feel her trying to fight me, her power pulsating within her, but I had enough control to hold her back . . . just barely, and only for a little while longer. I needed to move fast.

I closed my eyes and called to the solar walkway lights I'd spent much of the day preparing, sending them in bunches to their assigned spots throughout the wooded perimeter around us, where my conduits waited. The lights sounded like a plague of manufactured locusts, their plastic wings clattering as they were finally released to do the job I'd commanded of them in the day. Slowly, the flying lights came into view, hundreds of them, in their new form of fireflies, assembling in clusters over myself and every conduit, shooting stored sunlight out of their asses and down onto us.

Davina turned in a circle, slowly, watching as the conduits stood up in their little pools of light, as the solar-light fireflies danced frenetically above them. My control over Davina was fading, rapidly, and the captured sun in the solar lights was not paying off as well as I had hoped it would. I couldn't feel my power, or the power of the conduits. What little charge I'd been able to get off Davina was fading, and my nerves began to rise. The idea of stored sunlight had been a long shot, and I'd known it, but . . . *shit.*

"Baby, what kind of woman do you think I am?" Davina said, her voice cold and dangerous. What little control I'd had over her was gone.

"I don't know, Davina," I said, trying to concentrate on the fireflies, slowly pulling them closer, away from the conduits. Plan B would have to do. "What kind of woman are you?"

Davina walked closer to me, her eyes almost sad, like she felt a little sorry for me. Once, I would have believed that expression, but now . . . I saw something else behind the false emotion in her eyes.

It was the certainty of an easy victory.

"I'm the kind of woman who always has insurance," she said.

I couldn't guess what she meant by that, so I had to just stick to the plan. I closed my eyes, breathed in deep, and pulled the stored magic in from the fireflies. With a thunderous crash, they fell in the forest, leaving the conduits in the dark. I felt the power from the fireflies gather within me; looking down, I could see little wisps of yellow light dancing around my fingers. It wasn't much, but if I thought fast, I might be able to do something . . .

"Liv?"

A quiet, trembling voice came from behind me, and I turned around. In the moonlight, I could see a stocky form coming toward me, walking in jumpy steps, as if being forced to do every move. When she got close enough, I could see Millie, her hair wild, her face streaked with tears, still wearing the hospital gown she'd probably been in when Davina had taken her. She looked haggard and tired and terrified.

"Millie."

"You were right, Liv," she said. "She's not my friend."

"It's okay," I said. "Millie, just . . . fight her."

"I can't." She sniffled. "Tell Peach and Nick that I'm so sorry."

And with that, she lifted one hand, and I saw the moonlight glinting off of it before I could fully process what it was: a chef's knife, industrial grade and sharp.

I turned around to face Davina. "What the hell are you doing? Let her go!"

Davina rolled her eyes. "I'm doing what I have to do, baby. That's what I always do." She motioned to Millie, and when I turned, Millie had the chef's knife in both hands, not pointed at me, but at herself. At her heart.

"Liv, please . . ." Millie said, tears rolling down her face. *"Help."*

"Do what I tell you to do," Davina said, "or Millie here commits hari-kari right in front of you."

I twirled around to face Davina. "Stop it!"

"Call off your conduits. Send everyone home, and give me my fucking power," Davina said, "or this gets real ugly, real fast."

I turned back to Millie, whose eyes were big, focused on the knife poised at her heart. I closed my eyes, concentrated what power I'd borrowed from Davina, and shot it out toward the knife, as well as I could. It morphed into something sort of lizardish, wriggling in Millie's hand until she couldn't keep hold of it anymore. It fell to the ground and skittered away toward the water, which was good, but I'd just spent everything I had.

Which was very, very bad.

"Oh, gee, that's a damn shame," Davina said. "Whatever will I do now?"

She reached out her hand, curling her fingers into an eerie grip, and behind me, I heard Millie gasp and choke. I turned to see her, feet dangling and kicking beneath her, clawing at her neck.

"Stop!" I screamed, and started toward Davina, but she held up her free hand, ticking her index finger in warning.

"Ah, ah, ah," she said, and Millie gurgled behind me. "Call off your dogs. Send them home, or your friend here dies a wretched death."

"Okay!" I held out my hands, and while I could hear Millie struggling behind me, Davina's eyes were on me; she wasn't releasing Millie, but neither was she tightening her grip.

"All right, guys. You heard her. Go."

There was silence in the darkness, but around me Peach,

Nick, Stacy, Grace, and Addie moved in closer, preparing to fight; I could feel them like little points of psychic light. I could feel my power flowing through them, and theirs flowing back to me, like daylight. We could take Davina. Maybe. But we definitely couldn't do it before she killed Millie, and I couldn't take that chance.

"Go!" I hollered, my voice bouncing off the trees. I felt their resistance, but they were mine, and I controlled them; one by one, they backed off, disappearing into the forest, taking my power with them. One by one, bit by bit, I lost the only advantage I had.

"They're gone," I said finally. "I held up my end of the bargain." I glanced back at Millie. She was alive, still clutching fruitlessly at her neck, but she was weakening. She wouldn't make it much longer.

"Goddamnit, Davina. Let her go!"

Behind me, Millie cried out, and I could see Davina's fingers clutching deeper into the air as her magical grip on Millie's throat tightened.

"Stop! We had a deal!"

"You're right. We did. But you know what, baby?" Davina's eyes glinted with malice and insanity, and I felt the coldness in her expression sink into me. "You shouldn't have pissed me off."

Behind me, I heard a cracking sound, like thick branches snapping, but by the time I turned around, it was already over. Millie's head was lolling on her shoulders at an unnatural angle, her dead eyes blank in the moonlight as her body fell to the ground, lifeless.

"Millie!" I screamed, but it was already too late. I fell to the ground trying to reach for her, but the white sand on the outside of the circle started to rise up and move around the barrier, like a cyclone. I pulled my knees in and skittered as far to the edge of the circle, only stopping when my hand touched the wall of flying sand. I shrieked at the pain and pulled it back in to me, the knuckles sanded raw and bleeding. I swiped at the tears on my face, trying not to give her the satisfaction of my terror, but since my entire body was shaking with it, it was a pretty moot point.

"Baby," she said, a little breathless, but still in control, "you tried to beat me, and I applaud you for it. Shows a lot of guts, more than I would have given you credit for. But you've lost. It's done. Give me my magic now, and no one else gets hurt."

"No," I said.

She had the nerve to look surprised. "Did you just say *no*?"

I got onto my hands and knees, my muscles weak from the influx and subsequent withdrawal of power, but I managed to push myself up to standing and take a step toward her.

"Yeah, I said *no*. You don't get my magic unless I willingly give it to you. You can go ahead and do what you want with me, but you're not getting the magic. It's over."

"We'll see about that." She moved toward me, her skirt and hair shifting around her in the wind from the cyclone that surrounded us. I was too scared and tired to move away from her, afraid I would fall if I tried, so when she put her hand on the back of my neck and leaned in to whisper in my ear, I could do nothing but stand there and let her.

"You seem to be under the impression," she said as the cyclone around us died down, the sand falling neatly back into its original circle, "that I've played all my cards."

With that, she spun me around. I felt dizzy from the movement, and it took me a moment to be able to focus my eyes, even with the full moonlight, but once I did, my heart jolted painfully in my chest.

Tobias. He stood not ten feet away, just outside the edge of the circle, his head hanging as though he was only standing due to some force other than his own will. His face was bloodied, his clothes ripped. I let out a cry, and Davina dug her fingers into my shoulder.

"Now," she said, "you're going to need to be quicker on your feet this time. He's so close to dead anyway that it won't take much more than a push of my finger to knock him over and finish the job. So you tell me, right now, baby . . . is it yes or no? Give me your magic now, without any more of this foolishness, and he lives. Hesitate even for a second, and you will watch him die, just like you watched Millie. What's your answer?"

I opened my mouth to squeak out a helpless, "Yes," but the dizziness overtook me, and I stumbled to my knees. Something was weird, and it took me a moment to realize what it was that I was feeling; it was both familiar and unfamiliar, stronger than I had felt it earlier, and coming from only one source rather than five. I almost thought it was my imagination until I saw the Aquafina bottle lying at Tobias's feet, uncapped and empty. I raised my eyes to his face and saw that his eyes were closed, but there was the tiniest trace of a smile on his lips.

He'd finished off my concentrated conduit potion.

He was *mine.*

I rose to my feet, pooling the borrowed power from Tobias, and I curled up my fist and hit Davina square in the face, sending her sprawling. The pure shock of the non-Magical attack did what I had hoped it would: her concentration faltered, and what grip she'd had on Tobias ebbed away. He was open now, a true conduit of power, only instead his life force flowing back into Davina, he now served as a connection between her and me.

"What the . . . ?" Davina got to her knees and touched her face, smearing the blood on her lip where I'd struck her. She looked at me, her eyes wide and shocked, and I could tell she still didn't know what was happening. She probably thought the drain on her power was from holding Tobias up; she hadn't yet noticed that he was standing just fine on his own, his head raised as he watched us, holding his place, keeping the connection open.

God, I loved that man.

"Oh, wow." I took a step toward Davina and crouched in front of her. "My sister's power doesn't want you, does it?"

I moved my fingers, feeling the power within me, taking root, finding home.

"That's how you found me, isn't it? It wants me; it drew you to me. But when I have conduits, the pull is too strong. It wants me too much, and you can't hold onto it."

I tested this theory, pulling Davina to her feet, making her step closer to me even as her ankles buckled under her. Her eyes glittered with fury as she did it, but she stepped exactly where I commanded her to.

"All right, then," I said. "As long as we know who's in charge here."

Sweat broke out on Davina's upper lip as her eyes widened in fear.

"You can't do this," she said, gasping as she struggled to fight me. "You need my permission to take it . . . my will . . ."

"Hmmm, that is a sticky point. Let's test it, shall we?" I concentrated on her and began to pull. At first, it was slow going, a lot of effort for very little return, but eventually, I could see the gray smoke that was seeping out of her. My yellow light curled around it, pulling it back to me through Tobias, the portal between us, and with every breath, I felt it settle home inside of me—a power unlike mine, darkened and brittle, but there was also a hint of familiarity in it. Davina had corrupted my sister's power, but my sister was still in there, her power different from mine, but ultimately complementary. I took it in, as much as I could, not everything, not quite all of it, but most of it. If Davina could manage someday to light a candle without a match, I'd have been surprised.

"I think maybe you're wrong about that," I said, slowly lowering Davina to her knees as I released my hold on her. "I think it's not your will, it's Holly's. After all, it was her magic. And I think she wants her magic with me."

Davina groaned and writhed on the ground, fighting me as much as she could, but she was weak. Eventually, she stopped moving except for the short, shallow breaths she was taking, and only then did I disconnect from her entirely, releasing both her and Tobias in a rush of relief.

When it was done, and Davina was passed out on the ground, I stumbled outside the circle and managed to get myself to the flat rock by the brook. The power made me shaky and, ironically, weak. I didn't have the strength to wield it all, not at the moment. Someday, I would, but for now, it was all I could do to maintain consciousness.

"Liv!" Tobias was beside me on the rock, pulling me into his arms, and the relief of it was enough to make me cry out. He pulled back and looked at me. "You all right?"

"I'm okay," I said. "How are you?"

I looked at his sweet face, bloodied and beaten, but still, my own Tobias. I put my hand over his chest and felt the heartbeat under my fingers.

Mine.

"Don't leave me," I said, too tired to keep from expressing the thought out loud.

He wrapped his arms around me, holding me close. "I'm not going anywhere."

I pushed him back so I could look in his eyes. "No, I mean, *ever.* Don't you ever, ever leave me again. *Ever.*"

He smiled. "Never."

"I mean it," I said. "None of this 'when they come to take me away' bullshit. If they come for you, we run. We go rogue. Whatever. I don't care, so long as we do it together."

He took my hand in his and kissed the tips of my fingers. "Deal."

"Really?"

He nodded, and brushed some hair away from my face. "Yeah. I'm in."

He smiled at me, and I smiled back, and then I heard twigs crunching as footsteps approached. Instinctively, I flinched, and

Tobias tightened his grip around me until we saw the shadowy figures of Cain and Stacy emerge into the clearing.

"For fuck's sake, Liv," Stacy began, "we've been waiting for you. What the hell happened?"

I didn't say anything, just watched as Stacy caught a glimpse of Davina lying helpless on the ground, and she whooped.

"Yeah, that's right, baby!" Stacy said. "The bitch is—"

And then she stopped, frozen, and her eyes landed, as I knew they inevitably would, on Millie. Cain, a second too late, stepped between Stacy and Millie's body, putting his hands on her shoulders and angling her away.

"You don't wanna see that," he said, his voice as soft and kind as I'd ever heard it.

"Millie?" Stacy's voice cracked as she said the name, and I could see the moonlight glittering in the wetness in her eyes as she looked at me. "Liv?"

I was too tired to say anything, so I just squeezed Tobias's hand. "Take Stacy back to the van. Can you find it?"

Tobias nodded. "Yeah, I passed it on the way in, but—"

"I'll be okay," I said. "You can come back for me. I'm not going anywhere. Please, take care of Stacy. I need to deal with Cain for a bit."

Tobias kissed me gently, then walked over to Stacy, put his arm around her, and gently guided her out. When I looked back at Cain, I saw him standing over Davina, his hands at his sides, the glint of the gun he'd just pulled out of the back of his jeans barely visible in the moonlight.

"Please, Cain," I said. "Don't."

He didn't look at me, just kept staring at Davina. "Have to."

"I took the power," I said. "All of it. She may not survive the night as it is. But you have to make a choice now and I'm asking you, for Holly. Please don't."

He raised his head at Holly's name.

"I'm so tired," I said, not to him, but to her. I could feel her, with me, her desperation growing stronger as her power found home with mine.

Please. There isn't much time.

"Please," I repeated. "There isn't much time."

His entire body froze as I said the words, and I felt the memory; the darkness Holly had felt, the coldness even as he held her to him. *There isn't much time. I love you.*

"She loved you," I said.

He has to move on.

"She wants you to move on, but you never will. Not unless you drop the gun."

Please.

There was a protracted silence as Cain stared down at Davina, the gun still in his hand. Finally, I heard a clatter as he dropped it to the ground. When he spoke, his voice was thick with emotion.

"Tell her . . ." He cleared his throat. "Tell her . . ."

"She knows," I said. She was gone by then, but I knew it was the truth. She loved him so much that I could feel that love for him within myself, solid and unconditional and more real than anything else in the world. Most of that love was hers, but some of it was my own to keep. In a weird way, he was the only family I had left. A brother, of sorts; the man who had loved the sister I'd never known.

I'd take it.

He looked at me for a long moment, then quietly took off his flannel shirt, revealing a white T-shirt that glowed an ethereal blue in the moonlight. He draped the shirt over Millie's head and shoulders, then picked her up and disappeared into the forest, leaving me alone with Davina. I took a few deep breaths, and drew what strength I could for the last thing I had to do.

I got up, stumbled past Davina and the circle, and found her backpack. It was impossibly heavy, but I managed to drag it back to the brook. One by one, I emptied her vials and potions and herbs into the running water; she may be able to build herself back up as a conjurer one day, but at least she wouldn't have a head start.

Once I was done, I went into my bag and pulled out the second bottle I'd had tucked in there, one I'd taken from Cain's stores. I walked over to Davina, tilted her head, and poured it into her mouth. She sputtered and coughed, then swallowed. I left her there to vomit by herself; I'd done my part. She could recover and get back to town on her own. If she died in the process, it wouldn't be on my head. I sat on the rock by the brook again, gathered up what strength I could, and finally stood up. As I took my wearied and wobbly steps past Davina, I said, "Set foot in this town again, and no force in the world will save you."

A powerful, rage-filled scream reverberated off the trees, and a strong grip pulled on my ankles. I went down, face-first, into the dirt. Before I could get my bearings to turn myself over, something hard hit me on the back of the head, and I saw stars. I scraped and pulled at the ground, managing to flip around just in time to see Davina, up on her knees, a huge rock in her hands. Her eyes were wild and glassy, her hair matted with dirt and leaves. Guttural, primal sounds came from her as she threw her body onto mine, sending sharp shards of pain through me. I screamed as she regained her balance, pulling herself back and lifting the rock, preparing to brain me. I was trapped under her bulk, unable to access my magic through the haze of my exhaustion, and unable to physically move or scramble out of the way.

Never underestimate the power of crazy, I thought, and waited for the blow that would certainly kill me.

But no blow came. I saw a small flash of light, and heard a strangely innocuous-sounding *pop.* It took me a moment to place the sound, as I'd only heard one like it once before, when Stacy's mom had taken all of us to the shooting range.

Davina jerked back and fell away from me. With her weight off of me, I scrambled away as best I could, getting a few feet between us, and the pop happened again. The world started to spin around me, and there it was again. *Pop. Pop.*

"Cain!" I called out into the dark, not sure where he was, but sure he could hear me. "Stop!"

I tried to focus, but all I could see was a dark form, one hand extended, and the final blast of light from the end of a gun.

Pop.

"Cain," I said. "No."

Pop. Davina's body jerked again, but there was no life left in her. She was gone. He'd killed her.

I fell back onto the ground, barely able to move. A second later, arms were around me, pulling me up, and carrying me away.

"Liv." Tobias's voice, quiet, shaky. "Are you okay?"

"Tobias?" I was dizzy, and confused. "Where's Cain?"

"Back in the van," he said. "It's okay. I've got you."

And then, everything went dark.

21

A week later, Betty moved in.

"Stop treating me like a damn invalid," she said when I carried the last of her things to her room, where I'd made her sit on the bed while I puttered around her. "I'm *fine*."

"The doctor said you needed to rest for your first few days back." I set the suitcase of clothes Grace and Addie had rescued from her apartment down next to the bed. "You rest, or so help me, I'll duct tape you to that bed. What do you want for lunch?"

"I don't want lunch," she said. "I want you to sit down for five minutes and talk to me."

I hesitated for a moment. I'd spent the last week keeping busy, managing Millie's funeral, visiting Betty in the hospital, preparing the house for her to move in. Ordinary, mundane tasks had been my lifeline, and the idea of sitting and talking didn't necessarily appeal. But, since I'd never actually won an argument with Betty, I sat down at the desk chair and said, "What do you want to talk about?"

"I want to talk about you," she said. "How are you doing?"

I smiled. "I'm fine."

She stared at me, and I relented.

"I'm okay. I'm . . . managing. The night magic takes a little getting used to, it's like it never turns off, you know?"

"Have you slept?"

"Sure." Not a full night, not more than a couple hours at a time, but I had slept. The nightmares were getting less and less frequent, so progress was being made. "I'm sleeping fine."

She nodded, but I could tell she didn't believe me. We fell into a silence, and then she said, "You know it's not your fault, right?" Her expression tightened a bit, and she added, "Everything that happened with Millie."

"I know." There was a noise down by my ankle, and I looked down to see Gibson bumping into the side of the bed. I glanced up to see Niles floating in circles above Gib, and I smiled as I picked Gibson up.

"Well, that's weird," Betty commented.

"They're inseparable," I said. "I think it's sweet."

"It is sweet," she said. "But your piece of paper's in love with your mug. It's also weird."

I gave her a small nod. "I concede the point." I got up, opened the empty bottom dresser drawer, and set Gibson into it to keep him safe for the time being. Niles floated down next to him and settled into the drawer as well.

"Weird." She sighed. "Still no word from Cain?"

"Nope, and I don't think we'll get any." By the morning after the showdown with Davina, Cain had disappeared. Stacy had talked about tracking him down, but I figured we wouldn't see him again until he wanted to be seen. I hoped that would happen someday, but who knew? Cain wasn't a terribly predictable kind of guy.

"So, what did you do with the body? Are we worried about Tobias going to jail? Do we need to find a good lawyer?"

I sat back down on the edge of the bed. "You know, Betty, we don't have to discuss—"

"I. Am. Not. An. Invalid," she said. "You've danced around this when I was in the hospital and I couldn't come after you because they had tubes in me. Now, however, I will hurt you."

I sighed. "It's possible that people might come around asking about Davina, but Cain said she didn't have any family, or friends, or any kind of employment that he was aware of, so if no one reports her missing, we're probably okay just not saying anything about it. But, just in case, Stacy took care of it."

Betty's brows knit for a second. "Stacy?" And then her face cleared. "Right. Fire. So she . . . ?"

"Cremated her. Right there in the forest, and didn't catch anything else on fire. The girl had talent."

Betty raised her brow. "Had?"

"It was borrowed power, both her and Peach. Yesterday, Stacy had trouble lighting a match head." I remembered the disappointment on Stacy's face, and how she'd stalked away after the failure. "Possibly, that's a good thing."

"I think maybe," Betty said. "And what about Millie?"

I sighed. Millie's death had been harder to explain. We brought her in, told the hospital that we'd found her in the forest, and for lack of a better explanation for her injuries, they had deduced suicide by hanging. The note found at her apartment, written in Millie's careful hand, confirmed this, and we didn't say any different to anyone. I tried not to think about

Millie, sitting alone at her desk, being forced to write the note against her will as Davina controlled her every move, but I couldn't get the image out of my head anyway. It was a small comfort that her fate had been sealed before we'd ever walked into that forest; Davina was never not going to end Millie that night, no matter what I did.

"I don't think anyone's going to question the suicide," I said. "It's not like Millie was the most balanced person in the world, even before Davina got here."

Betty nodded. "When's the memorial service?"

I looked down at my hands. "Tomorrow."

She reached over and took my hand, and we sat in silence for a little while, then I worked up a smile and said, "I have some gossip for you."

Betty's face lit up. "Oh, thank god. I was starting to get the shakes."

"Peach and Nick are back together. I'm not sure if they're re-engaged or not, but he's moving in next weekend."

Her expression flattened. "Oh, hell. Addie told me about that two days ago."

"Sorry. You'll get better gossip once we get CCB's back up and running. Speaking of which, work is coming along. Did Ray talk to you? He was supposed to tell you when he thinks it might be done."

"He swears by late August," Betty said. "Which in contractor speak means January at the earliest."

"Well, you can stay here as long as you need to," I said.

"Of course I can. You blew up my home and business." We shared a smile, and then she said, "And how's Tobias?"

I sighed. "I don't know. We haven't talked much since . . ." I lowered my eyes. "You know."

She nodded. "Yeah."

"I think he's worried that I'll never see him the same way again," I said. "And I'm worried that he'll never forgive me."

"Forgive you? For what?"

I thought back to that moment when I'd told him to leave, and I cringed once again at my own hubris and stupidity. "I was the reason Davina got him. He tried to take her down on his own because I'd sent him away. Then he killed her to save me."

Betty reached out and patted my hand. "Oh. Idiots in love. So heartwarming. And annoying." She reached up and gave me a light, playful slap on the face. "Talk to him."

"I know," I said. "I will. I just wanted to give him a little time." I didn't mention that I needed time, too. It would be a little while before I could gracefully handle bad news from that sector of my life.

At that moment, through the open window, the sparkly magic-square bluebird flew in through the window and landed on my shoulder. I smiled at it.

"Told you that square was magic," I said.

Betty laughed. "I'll never doubt you again."

"Damn straight." I took him off my shoulder and put him into the decorative cage that I'd brought into Betty's room. "I thought maybe you might like to keep him."

She got up and walked over to me, looking at the bird in the cage. I put my arm around her shoulders and hugged her to me.

There were moments, more frequent with every day, in which the darkness from that night got chased away. When Tobias smiled at me, when Stacy and Peach came over with another crazy martini recipe to drink over rented movies; and now, with Betty next to me, healed and marveling at the magic-square bluebird.

"What are you going to name him?" I asked as she straightened up.

"I don't know. Linoleum?"

I laughed. "How about Linus?"

"Yeah," she said, angling her head at the bird. "Linus sounds good."

That Saturday, Peach and Stacy and I gathered on my patio after Millie's memorial service, a tray of margaritas sitting untouched on the table as we stood by my mother's garden of wildflowers. I held the urn containing Millie's ashes tightly against my stomach, then placed it in the middle of the garden, next to a similar urn that held my mother's ashes.

We didn't say anything for a long time, just stood there, the three of us holding hands. Tears dropped from Peach's face and she swiped at them periodically. Stacy's eyes were dry, but her hand clutched mine tight, and I could feel her pain reflecting my own as we stared down at the earthly remains of the woman we had all loved as a sister.

"I wish I'd gotten the chance to tell her I forgive her," Peach said finally, sniffling. She looked at me, her eyes red-rimmed and overflowing. "You know, for all that with Nick."

I nodded toward the urn. "Tell her now."

Peach's lower lip trembled, and she released my hand, then stepped forward. She lowered her head and said, "It's okay. I forgive you, Millie. And I love you." Her voice cracked on this last part. She blew a kiss to the urn, stepped back, and joined the three of us again.

I turned to Stacy. "Is there anything you want to say to her?"

Stacy shook her head. "I don't forgive so easily."

"Then tell her," I said.

Stacy watched me for a minute, her expression hard but contemplative, and then she stepped forward.

"You were stupid," she said. "You had friends. We would have helped you. You didn't need to do what you did, and you didn't need to die, you dumbass." She stood there, her back to us, for a while, and I saw her swipe at her eyes before turning back to face us.

"Your turn," she said to me.

I stepped forward, staring down into the wildflowers my mother had cultivated so absently for all those years, simply so she'd have something to stare at while she thought about my father. And now here they were, together, my mother who had replaced Millie's missing one, and Millie, who had given my mother the second daughter she'd lost. It was a tragic end to a tragic tale, and there was only one thing I could think of to say.

"I'm sorry," I said.

I turned to Peach and Stacy, and we nodded at each other, then walked to the patio table where our margaritas had been waiting. At the base of Millie's urn, one by one, we poured our drinks into the ground, and then went inside.

"Step away from the square, Kiskey."

I looked up from my feet. In the two weeks since reconstruction had started, our first major hurdle—CCB's dining-room floor—was finally done, complete with one blue sparkly square, just a few feet from where Booth 9 would someday be, and right next to where I was futilely attempting to sweep up the endless construction dust at the moment.

"Hey, stranger," I said as Tobias crossed the sunny dining room to where I was standing.

He stopped a few feet away, and tucked his hands in his jean pockets, his hunched posture reminding me vaguely of a little boy about to get scolded. This was only the third time I'd seen him since that night, and the first time since Millie's memorial service, where he'd disappeared before we got the chance to talk to each other, so I could see why he was a little worried about how I'd respond to seeing him again. I was a little worried, myself.

"I'm sorry I haven't been around," he said after a while.

"It's okay. I understand." I gripped the broom handle tightly in my hand, curling it in to me.

"I knew things were busy for you," he said, "with putting this place back together, and the memorial service and everything."

"Yeah," I said. "Thank you for coming, by the way."

"Of course." He hesitated a moment, then said, "So, how are you doing? You okay?"

I nodded, and looked up at him. "You?"

He shook his head, but kept his eyes on mine. "No. Not really."

I took in a breath and lowered my eyes as my heart beat raggedly in my chest. "Oh."

"I miss you."

I looked up at him. "You do?"

"I know you probably don't want to see me—"

"Don't want to see you?"

"—after everything that happened—"

"Are you insane?"

He blinked, his eyes uncomprehending. "You watched me kill someone."

"Yeah, while saving my life. I thought you didn't want to see me, because it was all my fault."

He took a step toward me. "No. You just seemed so upset whenever you looked at me. I thought I upset you."

"I was upset because my best friend died," I said. "And because it's a little traumatizing when a magical wingnut tries to kill you. Mostly, I was upset because I missed you, but I didn't want to push because I thought . . ." I trailed off, and then we both laughed, and I said without thinking, "Idiots in love."

His smile faded a bit, and I cringed.

"I'm sorry . . . I didn't mean . . . it's just something Betty said."

"No, we're definitely idiots in love," he said, his expression serious. "At least, one of us is."

"An idiot or in love?" I said. "And are you talking about you or me?"

"Are you still going to Europe?" he asked, ignoring my question.

I took a breath. "Yeah. Two weeks from Friday."

"Oh." He nodded, swallowed, and pulled on a smile. "It'll be good for you to get away."

"It's just . . . I already bought the ticket and got my passport . . ."

"No, no. That's good." He forced a full smile. "That'll be good for you."

"I'm coming back," I said.

His brow, which had furrowed a bit, smoothed out in surprise. "You are?"

I nodded. "I changed my ticket to return after two weeks."

"Oh. Good."

He smiled and we stood there in awkward silence for a long moment. Then I let the broom clatter to the floor, took his face in my hands, and kissed him. He kissed me back, his arms wrapping naturally around my waist. We indulged in each other for a while, and then I pulled back to look at him.

"I love you," I said. "I will always love you, and nothing in the world is ever going to change that, so I'm accepting it now, and I'm telling you. No more idiots in love."

He smiled. "No more idiots in love." He leaned in and kissed me again, then hugged me tight.

"I love you," he whispered into my ear. "I've been miserable these past few weeks."

"Me, too. Let's not do that again."

"Deal." He released me, and I reached up and touched his

face, my smile widening as the tension drained from me. "Come to Europe with me."

His expression darkened a bit. "I can't."

"Oh." I lowered my hand. "Okay."

"I want to, but if I leave the country without telling the company . . ."

"Hell. You have to get permission? Really?"

He nodded. "And if they think I'm a flight risk, they could come take me."

"A flight risk? Jesus, what are you? A prisoner?"

He nodded. "Yeah. Kinda. But . . . go. Have your fun in Europe. Get away, and have a good time. You've earned it." He took a step forward, put his warm palm against my cheek, and looked deep into my eyes. "Then come back to me."

"I will." I put my arms around his neck and hugged him to me.

"And take a picture with every goat," he said. "I want you to be reminded how much I love you every time you see one."

I stepped back and looked up at him. "Oh, hell."

"What?"

"Goats are gonna be a thing with us now," I said. "Every anniversary for the rest of my life, I'm gonna get goats. I can see it now. Goat stationery, goat slippers, stuffed goats."

He smiled. "Or real ones."

I laughed. "I'm gonna be lousy with goats, just like Europe."

"No," he said. "*We're* going to be lousy with goats."

I smiled up at him. "Damn right, we are," I said, and then he took me into his arms, and we stopped talking.

Acknowledgments

I don't know if every author eventually comes to a book that actively tries to kill her, but for me, this was it. Writing it as I went through a devastating divorce and a simultaneously terrifying and euphorious life-reboot, I found it to be both trial and triumph, and now what's left is this, a story about a woman whose life turned her upside down and shook her until her courage came out. Probably not a coincidence that this is the book I was supposed to write during this time.

After such an extended period of alternately collapsing and forcing myself to get back up, merely thanking the people who gave me the strength to keep moving—through my life and through the book—seems too anemic an act considering the miracle they wrought through their support and patience. I am now sitting safely on the other side of that treacherous cavern, book in hand and the sunny road to a new life stretched out before me, and "thank you" just doesn't cut it.

Still, thanks are what I have to give, so here we go:

To my agent, Stephanie Rostan, who held my hand when I quit this insane business forever, and then held it again when I changed my mind a week later . . . thank you.

To my editor, Jennifer Enderlin, whose patience and genius

inspired me to make this book as good as I had the skill to make it . . . thank you.

To Jennifer Crusie, Anne Stuart, CJ Barry, Toni McGee Causey, Molly Haselhorst, Ellen Henderson, Catherine Wade, Rebecca Michaels, R. L. LaFevers, and the Glindas, who trudged through endless versions of this dragon, then comforted and soothed me through the process of slaying it . . . thank you.

To the Betties, who kept me sane by indulging my insanity . . . thank you.

And to Alastair Stephens, who found me at my lowest moment, picked me up, dusted me off, and loved me anyway . . . thank you.